MARKUS

DAVID ODLE

Black Rose Writing | Texas

ISBN: 978-1-68433-308-0
PUBLISHED BY BLACK ROSE WRITING
www.blackrosewriting.com

Printed in the United States of America
Suggested Retail Price (SRP) $18.95

Markus is printed in Calluna

For my Aunt Joy.
Who always believed. Even before I did.

MARKUS

PART 1
THE SOCIETY

CHAPTER 1

Phillip drove down the long lane to the Taylor County Nursing Home. As he parked and shut off his car, he gazed at a structure towering like a medieval castle above the trees. The building leaned toward him as if warning him to stay away.

Markus Blue was inside. The man he was here to meet.

His palms sweat as he drummed his fingers on the steering wheel. *I've got nothing to be afraid of.* Damn right, he didn't. It was his job to be here. He muttered to himself, "yep, let's do this," then stepped out and sauntered across the driveway. Gravel crunched under his shoes like brittle bones, and he wondered, not for the first time, what Markus Blue actually looked like. Old, he knew that. Going off the stories he'd heard, the man would be ten-foot-tall, and maybe wearing a cape with a big "S" on it.

He reached the sidewalk and continued his stride. His steps clicked on weathered concrete, and an earthy smell festered the air, like what freshly churned dirt might smell like. As he neared, he noticed a group of children seated on a massive porch that jutted from the side of the building. The youngsters focused on an elderly man with Sesame Street puppets perched on his hands, imitating Burt and Ernie. Behind them, a young woman sat in a chair, her eyes darting from child to child, watching them closely.

"Do you know what to do if a stranger comes up to you Burt?" The old man gestured with the Ernie puppet, forcing his voice a little higher, but unable to remove the scratchiness of aged vocal chords.

The old man glanced up at him, his gaze cold and piercing, with crystalline blue eyes that bestowed something dark, something powerful.

Markus.

Phillip's pace slowed, and he kept his expression stoic. He swallowed dryly. This was supposed to be one of the most feared men in the world. A

Sesame Street puppet show blew that image like finding Conan the Barbarian baking a fruit cake.

"Yes, Ernie... I know." The old man shifted his gaze back to the children and raised the Burt puppet on the other hand. The children smiled. A little boy temporarily looked away and picked his nose. The young woman seated behind him reached down and tapped the boy's hand in a *quit-that* gesture.

Phillip climbed the steps to the porch, making no effort to quiet his shoes clonking on the hollow wood. At the top, he stopped, then moved to a wooden rocking chair and plopped down, resting his hands on the chair arms. The sun cast its radiance beneath the cover of the enormous overhang and Phillip noticed a bright, orange patch of light on his feet. In a few more hours, long after he was finished talking with Markus and back on the road to Indianapolis to catch his plane home to Houston, the sun would be low enough to shine in his face while sitting in this chair.

He tapped his thumb lightly as he waited. He didn't want to be here, and he thought to himself as he sat *I've got better things to do.* But the truth was, he didn't. This was all he had to do. This was his job. Perhaps it was admitting he was afraid that he hated.

Within a few minutes, the puppet show ended, and the kiddos milled about; the young woman fought gallantly to organize the impatient bunch into something resembling a line.

"Quit pushing!" One boy whined.

A little girl wandered off toward a flower pot full of tulips, her eyes blazing with wonder. The young woman, slender with dark hair pulled back from her pretty face in a loose ponytail, somehow got all of them in a single file and marched them down the steps. She led the kids around the corner of the building and out of sight. Phillip hoped for one more glimpse of her.

"From the first-grade class at the elementary school, out by Grant." The old man's voice drifted from behind him.

Phillip swallowed hard, his pulse quickening, but kept his gaze in the direction that the children had gone, hearing their voices fade as they got farther away. He didn't want Markus to know he was afraid, though he wasn't so sure he was pulling it off.

"Christopher didn't mention that you gave puppet shows," he said and could sense Markus's mouth curl into a smile. He shifted his gaze to the old man and confirmed that he was right.

"Yes... I'm giving puppet shows. They asked me to come down to the school, but I don't like leaving the home here," Markus remained seated in the porch-swing.

"Why?" Phillip stood, stretched, and walked to the edge of the patio.

Markus placed his puppets of Burt and Ernie into a small, leather bag. "As I'm sure you know, I was born here in Taylor County." Phillip didn't know but kept silent. "Daisy Howard, the caretaker here, asked if I'd like to do a little puppet show. I told her sure, as long as they come here. And so they did."

Phillip shrugged, not sure if Markus answered his question, then turned to gaze across the open pastures that led to the horizon. No way would he stay in this creepy old place in the middle of nowhere. The chipped paint, topped with a roof that needed new shingles, only added to the feeling of isolation. He never understood why anyone would want to live in a place like this, not when you had the city where everything was close and convenient. But there were plenty of things to worry about; plenty of bad things in the world and neither the middle of nowhere nor the city was safe from them, which was why he was sent here to talk to Markus.

"So why are you here?" Markus asked.

"You don't know?" Phillip didn't face the old man. He didn't want to face him, not yet.

"I'm not a psychic," Markus said, standing up, Phillip guessed, by the sound of a quick strain in the old man's voice. "I have my weaknesses."

Phillip thought about that, then said, "Don't we all."

"You didn't want to come here, did you?" Markus asked. "This must mean something is amiss and you need my help to resolve it. Thus Christopher sent you."

"Thought you said you sucked at psychic stuff."

"Yes, but I'm brilliant at common sense."

Phillip faced the old man, determined and ready, deciding that he need not be intimidated. But those eyes gleamed, like a painting that stared at you from all angles. Phillip glanced away. "You're right; I didn't want to come out here. I heard how you handled the Vatican case with the wolves four years ago. I thought it was... excessive."

Markus, who had been leaning on a cane that resembled a rotting piece of driftwood, eased himself back into the porch swing, apparently deciding this subject would take a few moments to discuss and he wanted to be comfortable doing it. "Perhaps it was," he said, "and it will undoubtedly do me no good to try and convince you otherwise, but I can assure you... *you* having not *been* there... it was much more complex than blind rage and destruction."

Asshole… so what if I wasn't there? He'd still heard what happened. He heard about it from Alexis Jade who *was* there. "Alexis said you didn't need to kill as many people as you did. She said you acted prematurely."

"Alexis is very good… and very young. I've heard from Christopher what she's said about me. I saved her life, you know. If she'd contacted me earlier, perhaps much of the bloodshed could have been avoided, but her pride resulted in her procrastination. I can assure you young man, she would've been killed."

Phillip winced because though he'd never admit it here, Alexis's pride cast shadows on many things. He'd been in love with her since the moment he'd met her. He'd heard the story of Markus's methods from her. She'd failed to mention anything about Markus saving her life. Those were the kinds of details she always left out.

"Didn't know that did you?" Markus stretched a humorless smile across his wrinkled face.

"She didn't mention it." And he wished he didn't love her so much, because why love someone who wasn't completely honest? Goddamn it.

"She wouldn't."

"Yeah, well, I guess that's her prerogative. Anyway, this isn't about Alexis." Phillip fought a brief urge to have Markus explain further. He wanted to know more about this, but it would have to wait.

"Very well." Markus clasped his weathered hands together and studied them as if he wondered where they'd come from.

Phillip stepped closer. "Have you heard of Nathaniel Smith?"

Markus's eyebrows shot up. "I met him years ago," he said. Phillip thought he detected fear in Markus's eyes, just a brief flash. Gone like a flicker of light that might never have been there to start with.

"Well, he's here now, in the United States, and the Society needs you to capture him."

Markus stared straight ahead, past Phillip and into the distant corn fields. "You need me to capture him? Why not Alexis or Jobe? They are very competent."

"I was told to get you."

"I'm an old man. I told Christopher to leave me be. I want to live out my final days here in Taylor County. Now you're asking me to go after yet another one of your bad guys. Then you chastise my ways? Not off to a good start there, pup."

"I said I was *told* to get you. I probably would've asked Alexis if it was up to me."

Markus chuckled. "Lucky for her, it isn't up to you."

"Look, I'm flying back to Houston tonight. I need to tell Christopher that you'll be there in the next few days. Or I can tell him that you said no and that you chose to stay here and do puppet shows for the local brats. Doesn't really matter to me."

Markus said, almost in a whisper, "I see."

"Well, what—" Phillip's words stopped dead in the air.

An unseen force slammed him back against the dry wood of a door frame, his chest burned from the crushing weight of an invisible hand. He struggled to breathe, to scream, but the pressure only increased. His hands began to shake, and his knees knocked. The loafer on his right foot fell off onto the wood floor with a hollow thump. *Jesus Christ*, his feet were off the ground!

"I think," Markus lifted himself with a grimace from the porch-swing, "that what we need to establish here are a few ground rules. You will not insult me in my house, Phillip." He leaned on his cane and hobbled closer. Phillip watched him, his vision beginning to blur.

The old man stopped in front of him and cast his cold gaze. Phillip trembled as the icy stare sank deep into his bones. His feelings of contempt melted to horror as he stared into the vacant eyes of Markus Blue.

· · · · · ·

For Markus, it was always the same with these young little shits. They thought they knew everything and that the world revolved around them. Hell, maybe it did, and he was just too old to see it. Only an old bastard would think something like that.

The young man's mouth hung open, giving the impression that he'd just started to yell *Oh shit* and got stuck. Phillip's hair was combed neatly back and blessed with a youthful thickness that prevented the sight of scalp through the grooves made by the comb. *Was my hair ever that thick?*

He turned away. The sound of the man crashing to the porch floor sparked silent amusement. *You're a schmuck Markus Blue*, he thought as Phillip gasped desperately for air. Poignantly, lessons must sometimes be taught for progress to be made.

"Now... shall we start again?" Markus faced Phillip who was just starting to pull his feet hesitantly beneath him.

Phillip got himself into a crouch and stopped there, maybe for fear of toppling over if he stood up too fast. Markus didn't think he'd actually hurt the young pup, not too bad anyway. But he was getting old; maybe he was losing his touch at gauging restraint.

Still gasping, but more under control, Phillip stood up. His lower lip trembled, and his skin paled. Markus understood the hesitancy and repeated, "Shall we start again?"

Phillip nodded and rubbed his chest.

Markus said, "You mentioned you needed my help to capture Nathaniel Smith, that he was here in the United States. I think I may have gotten us side-tracked." Markus leaned back against a large, white pillar. "Please continue."

Phillip touched a shaking hand to his forehead where beads of sweat gleamed like teardrops. His breathing hitched and he kept his gaze down at the porch floor. Finally, he cleared his throat and spoke, his voice scratchy like someone who'd just woken up. "We think Nathaniel has created a vampire Legion. No one knows how large or how powerful." He coughed. "Christopher sent someone to New York to investigate a lair that was thought to be in Manhattan. No one in The Society has heard from him in two weeks."

"Why is Christopher convinced that this is Nathaniel?" It was good hearing Christopher's name again, good knowing that his old compatriot - and leader of The Society - was still alive and kicking.

"He didn't say."

"Hmmm." Markus glanced down at Phillip's feet - noticed the right foot was without a shoe - and then back up to his face. "Surely Nathaniel would know that if he created a Legion, the Society would come after him."

"Christopher thought that too. The Vatican investigated Nathaniel's community just south of Hamburg and confirmed that he'd left there several months ago. A report from London suggested evidence of a Legion, somewhere in the southern part of that city. But there was nothing there except for a dozen or so corpses left in an apartment."

"Were the bodies decapitated?" Markus rubbed his chin. He was an old player in an even older game; most things didn't amount to shit. But experience taught that the little things made the difference between a false alarm and a dance with the Devil. Markus knew the little things.

"Yes."

"All of them? Please be sure."

"Yes, all of them."

Markus nodded. This was a pretty big little thing. Certainly, an apartment full of headless bodies wasn't something little, but when establishing the existence of a Legion, that was a red flag not to be ignored.

Phillip continued. "The Vatican didn't find anything. They kept watch in London for several weeks. Nothing happened for a while until a similar case popped up in New York. It was a lot smaller, only about four headless bodies. The Vatican called Christopher to investigate. He sent Jonathan, and he hasn't heard from him since."

"Nathaniel seemed very arrogant when I met him years ago. He certainly had no fear of me," Markus added.

"Christopher is worried about Jonathan. Plus, if it's Nathaniel..."

"Then you have a rogue vampire on your hands." Markus shot Phillip an accusing stare.

Phillip nodded.

"And, you may have lost a Wizard."

Phillip nodded again.

"And now you want me to hunt down Nathaniel and capture him?" Markus asked and chuckled. "God help us." He laughed and instantly felt the all too familiar wheeze deep in chest, like blood puddled in the bottom of his lungs. He cut off the laugh to avoid a nasty coughing fit.

"Christopher said to get you." Phillip cast his gaze down at his feet like a puppy after it just shit on the carpet.

"If I were to guess, Christopher is aware of much more than he has told you. In fact, I'd bet he wants me to kill Nathaniel and his Legion. That would be my guess."

Phillip glanced up and said, "I don't know."

Markus thought about it. He wanted no part of this. He liked the quiet life he'd built here – Friday night card games, Law & Order in the commons, and breakfast cooked by the sweet Daisy Howard. He was just another old guy, and no one here knew his past, and there was peace in that. This is how he wanted the rest of his life to be, no matter how much, or how little of it was left. Last December he told Christopher he had to stop, that he was too old to continue and wanted to live out his final months quietly. *Months?* Christopher had asked. And when Markus didn't elaborate, Christopher's lips pressed to a thin line, and he'd simply said, *go in peace, old friend.*

Now Christopher was calling on him yet again, ostensibly because he had the most experience and was the most powerful. *What a fix you're in*

Christopher if a dying old man is the best you've got. Goddamn Christopher for doing this to him, for putting him in this spot. A vampire was no match for a competent Wizard, but a Legion of vampires could be a different story entirely. There was a good chance that none of the young tykes in the Society had ever dealt with one.

And this was Nathaniel Smith they were talking about; not just any vampire and God only knew what his real name was.

Markus closed his eyes and listened. The birds sang, the breeze softly lapped his gray hair. The faint aroma of sweet corn drifted on the air and Markus thought, only in Indiana does the air smell like that.

Damn it, Christopher.

Markus sighed and said, "You can tell Christopher that I'll be at his ranch by week's end."

Phillip nodded.

"You have a good trip back, Phillip, and I do hope we get off to a better start next time."

"Yeah." Phillip picked up his loafer. He slipped it on and trudged down the steps. He looked so defeated that Markus almost felt bad for him.

At the bottom, Phillip stopped, then said, "Can I ask you a question?"

"Sure," Markus said.

"How did you know my name?"

Markus hobbled back to the porch swing. A perceptive young pup, this one was. "Lucky guess I reckon. Like I said, I'm not good at psychic stuff."

Phillip stared at him, either satisfied with the answer or perhaps deciding it wasn't worth the energy to pursue it (Markus guessed the latter) and ambled back to his car.

Well, this day turned to shit in a hurry. Better enjoy the solitude here before he left. He could not shake the despairing feeling, creeping up from the shadows of an abysmal pit in his aging mind, that this may be his last stay at the Taylor County Nursing Home.

CHAPTER 2

Sitting at a coffee shop in downtown Pittsburgh was the last place Liam Balsing expected to see the woman of his dreams.

She emerged from a limousine and took his breath away. Striking, with brown hair flowing down past her tanned shoulders, which were bare except for the straps of her black tank-top. She strode confidently around the front of the car and for a very brief moment where his heart shot a jolt of blood through his already constricted veins, she walked straight towards him.

Then she veered off in the direction of the Marriott Hotel's front door. A tall man, wearing a black suit and sunglasses, followed behind carrying a suitcase. Just before she passed the doorframe that would end Liam's fixation, the woman glanced in his direction. Her eyes were dark and green, portholes to the greatest pleasures a man could imagine. He sat frozen, unable to even blink. Her lips transformed into a genuine smile. She smiled at him! Before he could break his paralysis and return it, she was gone beyond the door and into the foyer of the hotel. The tall man glanced at Liam with palpable indifference, and then he was gone.

Jesus, Liam thought, returning to his senses. He glanced down at the dirty concrete and then back up toward the limousine. The young bellhop that had opened the car door for her gawked in the direction the woman had gone. His mouth hung open, and his eyes were glazed as if hypnotized by an invisible swinging watch. *I get it, dude.*

He took a long swig of his coffee. *I'm such a jackass*, he thought, amused by his own stupidity. *She smiled at me, and I just sat like a toad.* He was quite positive that if she had asked him his name, he wouldn't have remembered what it was.

By evening, he'd be back home in Houston, back in his empty apartment, tossing his keys onto the table, plopping his travel bag on the bed and watching TV, alone. Like always. By then, he'd be back to feeling like he was wasting his life chasing the elusive dream of being a writer, a *real* writer, one who published books and received royalty checks and had to contact his agent before making any decisive career moves. To hell with the cheap supermarket tabloid he currently worked for, to hell with his editor, to hell with everything that made up what he felt was a sorry excuse for a life.

Get a hold of yourself, you'll never see her again. Dream about her maybe, but never see her.

Grace be to the almighty for his ability to make miracles happen because three hours later, Liam met the girl of his dreams.

• • • • •

He was in the throes of a stupid accident when it happened.

He leaned back in a large chair sitting inconspicuously in the corner of an open area just off to the side of the hotel foyer. Fancy hotels always tried to make these areas look so inviting, but in Liam's opinion, they existed for the extremely bored or the habitual loner. Liam didn't know which category he fell into, but could make a good case for either.

He picked up his computer bag with the latest article he'd written stuffed neatly into the side pocket, slung his clothing bag over his shoulder, and grabbed his briefcase, then made his way to the front desk, thankful he didn't have one more thing to carry.

The hotel receptionist took one look at him and asked, "Would you like for me to call you a cab, sir?"

"To the airport, yes please."

Liam listened as she picked up the phone, pushed one button, and said, "I need a cab at the Marriott on Pine Street," then a short pause followed by, "Thanks," and she hung up. "It should be here within ten minutes."

"Thanks. Guess I should've just hailed an UBER before picking up all my stuff," he said. He couldn't explain why, but he felt stupid for saying it.

He turned toward the main entrance and took about two steps before the strap on his computer bag give way, sending the bag and its contents onto the floor. Thank goodness the computer itself was in a zipped compartment and didn't fall out. That asshole Jeremy, his editor, would've killed him, then taken it out of his tiny paycheck. He watched the pages of his article slide across the tile floor like an unfolding accordion.

"Shit." He sat his stuff down and started picking up pages. It was going to be a pain in the ass carrying the bag now with the strap broken, and it was the actual clasp on one side that had snapped off, so there was no fixing it. "Just my luck." He'd be glad to get out of here.

"Oh my goodness." Her voice drifted into his ears, and somehow, he knew immediately who it was.

She was squatted down, plucking papers off the floor. She still wore the black tank-top and a smile spread across her face. He watched in shock as her fingers closed on each item, seemingly in slow motion, and he noticed the manicured fingernails and smooth skin of her arm.

Absolutely angelic.

"Strap on my bag broke," he said. "My computer bag," he blurted. *Oh, I'm such a dumbass.* He'd never been good at talking to women.

"You looked like you had your hands full." She pushed her dark hair behind her ear. "Are you staying here at this hotel?"

"Yeah." He didn't see the need to elaborate that he was on his way out.

"Me too. I think I saw you this morning outside." She picked up the last of the papers and held them out to him. They both stood up as he took them.

"Yeah, I saw you pull up." He pushed the pages back into the side pocket of his computer bag. *My god, she noticed him this morning? This was starting to feel dreamlike.*

"Yeah. You were right out there." She pointed and then looked back at him. He had trouble concentrating on anything but her eyes and lips and the gentle slope of her throat as it met with her chest in a small, perfectly formed crevice.

"Yep, I was." He smiled, felt clumsy. *Say something!* "How long are you staying?" he asked.

"Don't know, but I think we're here through the night," *We're... so she wasn't alone. She must be staying with the tall guy that walked in with her.* "My friend and me, we're here on business together." Now she blushed, maybe feeling like she was explaining too much or maybe too quickly.

An awkward silence sprang between them, and he expected her to bid her farewells and be out of his life forever, but she didn't. She seemed to be waiting for something. *Dear god...* did she like him? It seemed impossible, and he nearly panicked in a pool of his own screaming thoughts. He pictured his cab about to pull up outside, any minute now. Was he prepared to leave?

Maybe. It was more likely that this little encounter would go nowhere. But *what if?*

All of this shot through his head in the space of about three seconds. His heart pounded as if pumping sludge. The tall man stood at the edge of the foyer, watching intently. *My friend and me*, she had said.

"You want to get some lunch or something?" The words were in his throat and out of his mouth before he even knew he was ready to say them.

"Sure." She stammered. "I'm not from around here. Are you?"

"No. But I've been here for a few days… I know a place to get good burgers." Burgers might be taking a chance with a girl like this. She might only eat healthy shit.

"That sounds good. I could eat anything. We didn't eat breakfast and left Houston at like 3 AM." She turned to the tall man. "Wasn't it like 3 AM when we left this morning, Jobe?"

Houston? Hey now.

Jobe nodded and yawned. *That's a weird name, Jobe.* Like the guy in the Bible. He wondered if it was spelled the same. He also wondered if 'ole Jobe would be joining them for lunch.

The awkwardness dwindled as his confidence swelled. They shook hands, and hot blood rushed into his cheeks at the touch of her skin. She introduced Jobe who checked his watch, as if bored. *Fuck him,* Liam thought.

He held her gaze and said, "Let me go drop my stuff in my room."

"Yeah." She flicked her hand, "Might not want to carry that stuff around."

He grinned and said, "Yep. Be right back."

He hurried up to the counter. "I need to reserve a room for another night," he said, keeping his voice low, "and could you cancel my cab?" The receptionist crinkled her eyebrows but didn't ask anything. As he paid, he wondered how pissed off Jeremy would be about him staying another night. And he'd have to change his flight, which would be another $150 to explain. Too bad. Liam felt like he was doing something now that actually mattered.

He was back down in the lobby in less than five minutes, and to his delight, the girl was still there and alone. Jobe was nowhere to be seen. She sat on a sofa along the edge of the foyer and stood up as he neared. She smiled and, in that moment, he was completely at her mercy.

"Where's Jobe?" he asked.

"He decided to grab some lunch here in the hotel, so I guess it's just you and me."

Sweet! They strode out the front doors and into the bright sunlight that bathed downtown Pittsburg.

"I'm Liam," he said, "Can't remember if I told you."

She shoved her hands into her back pockets. "I'm Alexis."

Alexis.

It fit her perfectly.

CHAPTER 3

Phillip gazed through a large picture window with his arms crossed over his chest. The rain-covered glass distorted the outside world, like looking through the bottom of a soda bottle. Across the lawn and pasture, a rustic old barn stood nestled among Cedar trees. A few cattle loitered close to it, not giving a shit.

The world couldn't be more wrong for him right now. His chest fluttered when he thought of Alexis, of her out there away from him, possibly in harm's way. Did anyone around here ever consider his thoughts or opinions? Or feelings? Because it sure as fuck didn't feel like it.

"What time is he supposed to arrive?" Phillip asked, referring to Markus. Markus was another shit-show event he wished he could forget.

"Said he'd be here by 3 o'clock." Christopher's voice had always been rough, like an old smoker. "Something bothering you?"

The first thing that popped into Phillip's head was *what the hell do you think? I told you what happened when I met him.* Christopher's question was bullshit if Phillip was being honest. But of course, he couldn't speak that way to Christopher. No one could.

"I don't think he likes me," Phillip said.

"I wouldn't jump to that conclusion."

"I didn't think he was supposed to treat me like that." Phillip licked his lips. He didn't like how his words sounded, dancing precariously close to whining and that wasn't the effect he was going for.

"I'll discuss the situation with Markus when he arrives," Christopher said. Phillip sensed the accommodating tone of the words. *I'll tell Markus to quit picking on the baby because the baby is whining.*

He wished he hadn't brought any of this up. "I'll be fine. You don't need to say anything to him. I'll talk to him." He turned from the window and stepped over to where Christopher Gray sat in a leather loveseat with his legs crossed and reading an article from some cheap tabloid called The Unexplained Truth. Phillip sat down in a velvety maroon chair across from him.

He felt like he needed to say something. "Anything interesting?"

Christopher continued to read. He turned a page. Then, "Yeah, if you must know, there's an interesting article here about a boy named Charlie Black in Pennsylvania. Moves things without touching them and stuff like that. We may need to check on this one. Perhaps he's a sorely needed addition to the Society."

"Maybe." Phillip wanted to scream, *Who gives a shit about a kid named Charlie Black who might have powers?* What about Alexis? That seemed a far more pertinent thing to discuss because that's all Phillip cared about. Everything else was just pretend. Just to be in her presence, to be in the same room, was all he needed and no one got that. Not even her.

Christopher looked up from his paper, those sharp eyes finding his. "What else is bothering you?"

"Honestly," Phillip placed his elbows on his knees. *Okay, here it goes.* "I wish you would have told me you were sending Alexis to Pittsburg. I didn't know about that."

"And what would you have done if I'd told you?" Christopher's eyes maintained a steely gaze that made Phillip look away.

"I would liked to have known, is all."

"I know how you feel about her. Most men feel the same way; you're not alone in that aspect."

Phillip hated those words. Despised them. He'd heard it before. Anger flared deep in his chest because it was asinine statements like that which proved no one truly cared about him. If they did, if Christopher *truly* did, he wouldn't make such a nonchalant comment about the girl he loved.

Christopher continued, "She is a member of the Society and the Society is under *my* discretion. It isn't that I don't want you involved, but you must also remember your place here. I got a tip that Michael, one of Nathaniel's main spooks, was in Pittsburg. She said she wanted to go. So she went."

The words of Markus echoed softly, *She is very good... and very young. I saved her life.*

"I would like to have known, that's all I'm saying," Phillip said. "And I don't care how other men see her." That whiny feel crept up again, but he ignored it. When it came to Alexis, he didn't care how he sounded.

Christopher clamped his jaw tight and clasped his hands together in front of him. "I'll tell you what, I need someone to go to Pittsburg and work with Alexis on the public front... just in case things get ugly and the police, the newspaper, or whoever gets involved, I need a PR guy there. I've got Jobe with her, but he is not good with that." Christopher held out his hands with the palms up. "You up for that?"

The question sprang out and slapped him across the face. Would Alexis know Christopher had sent him because of this discussion? Would she wonder why *he* was the messenger chosen and not Eric? Would she know he was in love with her? Would it be so bad if she did?

And why in the hell was he even hesitating on this?

"Yes. I would."

A forced smile spread across Christopher's face. "There, you see, we're all happy now. I need you to leave first thing in the morning. Alexis is staying at the Marriot in downtown Pittsburg close to the baseball diamond. I'll get word to her and Jobe that you'll be there as soon as you can."

An image formed of Christopher regurgitating this entire conversation to Alexis and of them both laughing their asses off. He pushed the thought away.

"Keep in mind," Christopher said, "this particular issue is bigger than anything you've been involved with. I told your father I'd take care of you, so don't go up there and do something stupid. You're there as a messenger and nothing more." The words hung in the air for a few awkward seconds, then Christopher went back to reading his paper.

Again with the *your father* crap.

"I want you on the 5:30 out of Hobby so you can get to Pittsburg before noon."

Phillip stood up. He felt better. Genuinely better. Not only would he be seeing Alexis tomorrow, but he would be involved in investigating a possible Legion. Real work! Not being sent to retrieve bitter old men from creepy looking old folk's homes.

Christopher didn't look up, but added, "and I'll be sure and mention your... uh... mishap to Markus since you won't be here to inquire of it yourself."

Phillip got the jab and considered saying *I'd be happy to wait here until Markus arrives* (which, of course, was a lie), but decided the opportunity to leave immediately was a much better prospect. Besides, he didn't like the idea of being here discussing it when Markus arrived, which could be any minute.

"Thank you, sir." Phillip strode to the door and left the room. He had an overwhelming urge to break into a run back to his quarters but decided a brisk walk was sufficient.

•   •   •   •   •

Markus was relaxed as the limousine rolled down the driveway to Christopher's ranch house. He could barely feel the occasional dip or bump while looking out the rain splattered window at the pastures. Did Christopher still have those half-dozen Texas Longhorns that used to draw stares from passers-by? He remembered the anxious faces of children plastered against car windows. *You can always tell who ain't from Texas*, Christopher would say in a manner very uncharacteristic of his usual sophisticated demeanor. *It's like someone from Canada seeing a wild alligator for the first time.* Maybe so and maybe it *was* obvious, but Markus still found them to be amazing creatures with the massive horns spreading out from their heads like a prehistoric animal. He could give a damn if anyone knew he wasn't from here. He didn't like this place anyway. Too damned hot.

They passed a shed leaning heavily to one side looking as if it may collapse in a huge sigh of relief. He helped Christopher build that old shed well over thirty years ago. That was back in the days when he could move without his cane and sleep through the night without taking his regular dose of heartburn medicine, or waking up and having to piss three or four times due to a swelling prostate. His doctor had said they had some new pill out that may help alleviate that inconvenience as well. His life seemed less like living now and more like a goddamn pharmacist's Guinea Pig. He had nothing else to do but wait for his number to come up and relish that glorious day when he would simply not wake up. He possessed magic that most people would find incomprehensible but still didn't have the first clue of how to circumvent nature's relentless assault at killing him.

The car rolled to a stop, and Markus waited as the driver got out. A few seconds later, his door opened. The humid air wafted in with a stench that reminded him of stale pond water.

"Do you need some assistance Sir?" the driver asked. Another one of Christopher's messengers.

"I think I'll manage, though not as fast you might wish." Markus slid his legs over the edge of the seat and placed his feet on the small, wet rocks of the driveway. He heaved himself up, pushing his cane into the ground to steady his balance.

"Very well sir." The driver took Markus by the elbow to lead him toward the door.

Markus almost objected to having this young man hold his arm like he was some sort of blind cripple, but then decided to put up with it.

"How was your trip, sir?"

"As good as expected, I suppose."

"Indeed, sir."

"Too many people at the airport, though. I don't like crowds."

"Yes, sir." The young man opened the front door and led Markus into the tiled foyer. Markus remembered it being bigger for some reason. He caught the scent of brewing tea, and it sparked a comforting familiarity.

"I think I can manage now." Markus patted the kid's hand.

"Yes sir." The young man dropped his hand and escorted him across the foyer toward an oak door that stood ajar. "Christopher is waiting inside." He pushed the door open.

Markus said nothing. He knew where Christopher was waiting. Christopher was waiting where he always waited. He stepped into the room and Christopher's face lit up with a smile. *Oh, my old friend.* Perhaps family was too strong a word, but if Markus were to say what he felt at that moment, family would be how he'd describe it.

"Sir... Mr. Markus Blue," the young man said, making it his job to say shit everyone already knew.

"Yes Eric," Christopher said. "I'm quite aware it's Markus. You may go now."

The kid backed out of the room leaving Markus alone in the doorway staring at his oldest living friend who seemed unsure of what to do next. Markus returned the smile, a genuine smile, full of love and bad memories that only old friends knew.

"Markus." Christopher stepped towards him, his arms held out. *Jesus, I think he's going to hug me*, and for a second, Markus wished he was still young enough to run. But Christopher stopped a few feet from him and only touched the upper part of his arms. "I'm so glad you've come, Markus. I was worried that you'd tell Phillip to get the hell away and never return."

"It's good to see you too, Christopher, and I considered telling your messenger just that." He didn't bother to add that he still might. Nor did he state his need to understand the purpose of all of this travel – from what he could tell so far, a simple phone call would have sufficed just fine.

Christopher would get to that soon, he hoped, and all of this secrecy would be clear.

"Well, I'm glad you decided to only scare the shit out of him and come see me." Christopher strode to a leather sofa and motioned for Markus to join him. "Please. Let's sit down."

As Markus followed, he said, "Phillip told you about that, did he?" Dear god, what a story that must have been. He couldn't help but wonder how it was told.

"He did." Christopher sat down. Markus eased himself into the maroon chair that Phillip had occupied twenty minutes prior. Christopher said, "I don't suppose he deserved it?"

"Of course not. I just find amusement in pushing the messengers around." Markus relaxed into the chair. After the hour of luxury in the limo, this chair was more comfortable than he thought it would be.

Christopher interlaced his fingers. "Phillip has a lot to learn. I think you taught him some respect, he gets frustrated that he's not higher in the pecking order." Christopher seemed to think about this and then changed the subject. "It's damned good to see you, my friend, even though I doubt you're happy about it."

"I thought I was done. Waiting for God to pull my number, so to speak." Markus offered a smile but didn't hide the strain behind it, maybe showing too much teeth. *Get to the point*, he wanted to say, *because I only came for you, because you needed me, and for nothing else.*

"I wouldn't have sent for you if it wasn't important." Christopher's mouth straightened out to a serious line and he glanced down at the floor. "I'm in a bit of a pickle."

"Phillip told me it had to do with Nathaniel Smith."

"He was right. Maybe a big problem with Nathaniel."

Markus didn't like the sound of that. "He also mentioned evidence of a Legion."

"More than one Legion I'm afraid." Christopher looked up and his concern was etched deep. "To be honest, I don't know how many."

Markus raised his eyebrows. "That's not a good thing to be unsure of, old friend. I see now why you sent for me." Markus quickly summarized what Phillip had told him, ending with, "and you sent Jonathan to investigate, and he hasn't been heard from since. That's about all that Phillip told me."

Christopher nodded, looking solemn. "Good. That's everything that he was told. However, there's a little more."

Markus leaned forward. "I thought there might be."

"Jonathan is dead. His body was found about a week ago in Florida."

"Florida?" Jesus, it's like every conversation involved a different location. Markus was having trouble keeping up.

"Yes. I have no idea how he got there, but I can tell you it was a mess. He was made an example, I'm sure of it. His body was found in a swamp just south of a little town called Arcadia. He'd been tortured. There have also been four Legion ceremonies in Florida, that I know of." Christopher held up four fingers as he said this, reiterating the point.

"Who found him?"

"Some old couple on a morning stroll found the body. The police identified him, and of course, I'm listed as the next of kin."

"Strange that the body was left in a place like that and that the Legion didn't eat it." Markus still searched for something that might suggest a different reason for all of this, something less abominable. But with each passing minute, the options dwindled.

"Almost like a taunt, I would think," Christopher said.

"Sounds like it. So now we five Legion ceremonies and the murder of Jonathan. Good Christ." Markus had not known Jonathan except through discussions with Christopher, but any murder of a Society member displayed a blatant disregard for order and authority. A symbolic spit in the face by someone determined to start serious shit.

"Twelve Legion ceremonies."

"Twelve? My god, Christopher! That's a goddamned army!"

"The four in Florida. Seven in New York. And one in Castle Rock, Colorado."

"Colorado, Florida, and New York... why so spread out?" Markus clasped his hands together and rubbed them briskly as if washing off some sticky material. His irritation at being summoned to this place had dissipated and was now replaced with frustration that Christopher had not called on him sooner. "Surely Nathaniel knows that the Vatican is going to send us after him? Or *them* I guess it's now safe to assume."

"It is safe to assume *they* since it is quite obvious that he is building an army with these Legions. Multiple ceremonies all at once, an attack on the Society, all in the face of the Vatican and us... actions like these have not been witnessed in well over three centuries. They obviously do not fear the wizards and seem to have found a way to kill them since Jonathan's dead."

Markus shifted in his chair, feeling as if the cushion under him was becoming harder, like sitting on concrete. The air was stuffy with the fragrance of old books, as if the air was literally thickening with it. He wanted out of this room. The world seemed to have fallen askew, and he couldn't straighten it.

"Any ideas of why Nathaniel's doing this?" Markus shifted again and feared he may have to stand up if he couldn't get more comfortable. It was his hip that hurt so bad.

"I do, but they're just theories. This is all leading up to something, but damned if I know what. Nathaniel has been alive for centuries... no one knows for sure how long. Perhaps he's very patient and has been planning this for years." Christopher leaned back in the couch.

"Planning what?" Markus asked.

"Just a theory, mind you, but I think he means to reignite that Slovene War from centuries ago," Christopher said. Much of the color seemed to drain from his face as he said it.

Markus stared at him and brushed a hand through his gray hair. "Christopher... that seems highly unlikely. Nathaniel is the only one we're having the problem with, correct?"

Christopher shook his head. "He is the one who appears to have started it, but over the past few weeks three more powerful vampires have come up missing; Michael, Sydney, and Christine. I believe they are under the leadership of Nathaniel and following his orders."

Markus glared at Christopher. "Why didn't you call me earlier, goddamn it?" He slapped his fist against his thigh as hot anger flooded his face. "It should never have gone this far!" He spat the words. All vampires were disgusting creatures, but the order has always been kept, the truce has always been upheld. Yet one rogue vampire can spark a war as one did almost three centuries ago that ended with death and destruction to entire territories. Markus had read the stories, he'd studied the journals – the Society existed to prevent this very thing from happening again.

And now there was not one rogue vampire, but four! Damn Christopher for letting it go this far.

"We took action, Markus!" Christopher's face hardened, and his hands clenched to fists. "It's not as though we all sat around on our asses and waited. We acted, and now I've got one wizard dead. I've got Alexis and Jobe in Pittsburg and who knows in what danger they're in. I did not ask you here to criticize me!"

Markus's tension ebbed and he dropped his glare. This was Christopher and not some politician without the balls to do what needed to be done.

Christopher leaned closer, holding his gaze, and said, "I don't know what to do next, Markus." He shot his hands out to his side. "There you have it." He pointed a rigid finger at his own chest and growled, "I don't know what to fucking do next, and I'm afraid I've lost already." His cheeks trembled and Markus felt fear emanating from him.

This is a place we've never been. In all our years and all our trials, my god, we've never been here, defeated like this. Markus reached out and touched Christopher's forearm, gently grasping it. "I'm here now, old friend."

Christopher clasped his hand, gripping it. "I'm sorry, Markus."

The moment lingered with Christopher's sweaty hand on his. Their eyes exchanged deep truths that need not be spoken, and then it was time to get back to the subject at hand.

"Has anyone tried talking with Nathaniel?" Markus asked.

Christopher released Markus's hand and leaned back on the couch. "There's been no opportunity to speak with him, but here's what I really think Markus, and I may be wrong, so let me know what *you* think. This is an unorthodox theory, and I've not spoken of it to anyone outside of this room." Christopher cleared his throat. "I think the real question is why start a war in the first place? The world, the Vatican, us... we've lived with the vampires for centuries in a fairly harmonious state. We leave them alone, and in return, they don't go outside the boundaries of reasonable activities to maintain their existence. However, Nathaniel is the oldest of his kind. He was alive a thousand years before the Slovene War, hell, maybe longer."

"I'm quite aware of history." Markus did his best to avoid sounding impatient and felt like he pulled it off reasonably well.

"Okay." Christopher took a deep breath. "This all sounds like madness because that's exactly what I think it is... I believe Nathaniel has gone mad. He's suffering some deep level of dementia. Specifically, I'm convinced he's lost his grip on reality and is suffering from severe Schizophrenia. He's gone crazy, Markus. Plum crazy."

CHAPTER 4

Markus recalled meeting Nathaniel in Germany thirty-some years ago and tried to remember if anything had struck him as troubling at that time. Nothing in particular stuck out other than Nathaniel's profound arrogance. The creature had barely spoken and had not stood upon Markus's departure, which was particularly insulting considering every other vampire in the room had come to their feet to bid him farewell. Perhaps, Nathaniel had been considering an uprising at that time, maybe for years in secrecy. That was the major problem with vampires, especially the old ones, they were ludicrously patient. Bram Stoker had it right; vampires possessed the weapon of time. If Nathaniel felt he was in danger, he could hide out for a century and wait for his enemies to die off, and then reemerge to continue his quest, whatever the *quest* was.

"What makes you think he's crazy?" Markus twisted, winced, and then stood up.

"You okay?" Christopher's eyes narrowed.

Not a conversation I want to get into right now. Not even with you. "I'll be fine. Please elaborate." Markus walked to the large picture window facing the barn and pasture, the same place Phillip had stood earlier.

Christopher nodded. "It's a hunch. Stems from an interview from Vatican officials with a pastor from one of the Lutheran Churches in London. This was shortly after the discovery of the Legion ceremony in London and would have been around the time that he allegedly came to the United States, which we believe was less than a month ago. Apparently, the London police found the pastor, not a very old guy I might add, lying on the floor of his sanctuary and muttering something about a demon asking him for atonement."

"Like a confession?" Markus asked.

"Yes. Apparently, it wanted to confess." Christopher shrugged his shoulders.

"Bizarre." Such strange events. And Markus knew that Vatican *officials* meant it was the Vatican Chasers who'd talked to this pastor. Markus had never liked dealing with them. Wizards and witches assigned directly to the Vatican to protect the Pope. Pompous assholes.

"Indeed, it is. They're keeping the pastor for observation at the King's College London mental health facility at the University of London. The University has cooperated fully with the Vatican and allowed the Chaser's access to talk with the man, which is, of course, how I came by my information. According to the London police, the minister is talking nonsense, but I don't think so. He's mentioned several times about how the temperature inside his church dropped to freezing in a matter of seconds when the strange man entered, and that he saw horrible images."

"The projection of vagaries."

"That was my thought as well," Christopher said, "but I'm not as knowledgeable on it, which is another reason why I needed you. I'm in some unchartered territory here. What is the projection of vagaries, exactly?"

"It's a gift," Markus said with a humorless smile. "Apparently Satan didn't see it enough to give vampires immortality and strength, so he gave them the ability to project vagaries as well. A vampire's very presence spawns horrid and shameful thoughts in the mind of the mortal. But with age, vampires learn to control it, like the volume of a radio, turning it up or down when needed, but never actually *off.*"

Christopher nodded as if this explained everything. "According to the Vatican, there are not supposed to be any vampires in London."

"Strange that Nathaniel would enter a church." Markus had never heard of a vampire entering a church before. In fact, he had to admit to himself that he wasn't aware that they *could* enter a church.

"I agree. Very strange," Christopher said. "And now to go one further... last week, two pastors in New York, neither of them Catholic, had similar experiences. One of them committed suicide over the past weekend."

Jesus... what kind of vision had that guy seen? "So, we have Nathaniel entering churches and seeking confession, then leaving without killing the pastors." Markus considered this carefully. Ideas swirled in his mind like pieces of a jigsaw puzzle floating about, waiting to coalesce and form that clear picture. Perhaps his mind was not as sharp as it once was since the clear picture eluded him. "And seeking confession from non-Catholic ministers. Odd."

Christopher scooted up in his seat. "He's insane, delusional, mad, all of the above... whatever word you like."

"No," Markus said, perhaps more sternly than needed. "This is not unpredictable insanity. This sounds like madness with logic and purpose and obsession. Perhaps you've started out already underestimating Nathaniel." Markus faced him and said, "I want to hear the rest of your theory, but keep what I said in mind."

Christopher hesitantly glanced down at the floor. "He's been alive for centuries. I think that he's been alive for so long, that he's lost his mind. Maybe he's confused as to what his purpose is and questions his existence. I'm still stumped by what he's doing going into the churches and seeking confession but avoiding the Catholic Churches. I believe that is a vital part of the mystery we must unravel... I think it is the crux of his motivation."

Markus ambled back over to his seat and sat down, keenly aware of Christopher's gaze upon him. The jigsaw pieces floated faster, and he tried desperately to grasp the idea which danced just out of his reach, like trying to think of the words to a song you've sung hundreds of times. Something about the churches. "Do you think the recent death of the Pope ties into this?"

"It could, but I can't piece it together. Not yet anyway."

Markus braced his elbows onto his knees. "How 'bout me? Does he know that I'm here?" he asked, "Where did you say I went when I left the Society?"

"I did as you wished. I told the Vatican that you left the Society to... uh... go in peace." Christopher pursed his lips.

An awkward silence sprang between them where Markus knew that Christopher had not told the Vatican *to go in peace*, he'd said *to die in peace*. Not a huge difference, but enough to drive home an unspoken truth. Still, the point was the same – Nathaniel likely thinks that Markus is either dead or at the very least, not a factor in this game.

"So we have a lot to think about," Markus said. "You have Alexis and Jobe in Pittsburg about to close in on Michael, correct?"

"Yes," Christopher said. "They plan to strike first thing in the morning before word can travel that we know about them."

"You don't plan to kill Michael, do you? You plan to take him alive so you can see what he knows." Markus reached over and picked up his cane lying against his chair and propped it in front of him.

"What options do we have?" Christopher held his hands out to his sides.

"This is a dangerous game you play, Christopher. We don't know their numbers, their locations, and most importantly, we don't know their true intent. Your actions are panic-driven." Markus stared hard at Christopher.

"Markus, I've got one wizard killed. It's as if they are taunting us, daring us to act. Why'd they come here to the United States rather than Europe?" Christopher looked to Markus.

"I'd guess it's because they want to destroy the Society before they do anything else." Markus shrugged. How did Christopher not think of this? "How did you find out that Michael was in Pittsburg?"

"A Catholic Priest said he was visited by someone, or something, walking back to his Rectory a few nights ago. He said it was very disturbing, and described a creepy looking man dressed in an old Army uniform; which Michael is famous for wearing. He also said the air around this man was cold and that he was overcome with immoral sexual images. He reported it to his Bishop who reported the incident immediately to the Vatican. We followed up by sending Alexis and Jobe to Pittsburg. It could turn out to be a false alarm, but at this point, I'm taking no chances. We just have so damned little experience, and it troubles me a great deal. I feel like I'm sending children to battle. I'd have joined them myself, but I'm scheduled to fly to London tomorrow to meet with the Vatican."

Markus didn't like this. "Are they supposed to report to you before they move against Michael?"

"Yes."

"I need to be part of that conversation. They are not to do anything before speaking to me."

"Sure. Anything you wish," Christopher said. "This is why I needed you here... to help me." His expression grew concerned, and he said, "There is one thing; Jobe contacted me earlier and mentioned that he and Alexis planned to use the daylight to scout the area, maybe get a glimpse of the warehouse Michael is allegedly hiding in."

Markus tapped his cane, thinking, and then said, "Tell them to stop immediately and return to where they're staying. Not sure what it is, but something doesn't feel right about this."

"I'll contact him now and tell them to stand down." Christopher pulled out his phone and furiously typed out a text.

I'd have just called, Markus thought, but kept that opinion to himself. "Tell me when he responds."

Markus rubbed his chin considering whether there was more he needed to know and decided he was satisfied. For now. Not much to do until they spoke to Jobe and Alexis. Plus, he needed to rest. It had been a long day already.

A moment later, Christopher confirmed that Jobe had responded with *we're heading back to the hotel*, and then he and Christopher parted ways with a warm handshake. Christopher told him to call for anything and he'd send a messenger right away with whatever he wished.

A short while later, while sitting alone in his dark room perched uncomfortably on the edge of his bed, he had a brief recollection of the Taylor County Nursing Home and of the quiet pastures that surrounded it. He pictured himself walking through the knee-high grass and dragging his hand along a row of sweet corn that bordered the pasture.

He would've liked to have held the image for a little longer, but a violent coughing fit left him feeling dizzy. The serene picture in his mind fled away as quickly as it had come.

CHAPTER 5

Alexis considered telling Jobe that he could leave her alone if he thought she was being so careless for having lunch with Liam but bit the words off before they flew from her mouth. She stewed in her anger, and then said, "He went back to his room." She didn't bother to check Jobe's expression and frankly didn't care. Damn his opinion anyway. Men and they're egotistical bullshit.

Besides, it was time to work.

They strolled down a worn sidewalk in downtown Pittsburg, keeping their pace slow and deliberate. It was strange how the characteristics of a city could reflect its foundation and mimic the personality which created it – though she couldn't put a finger on exactly what it was, the blue-collar roots were evident by its very demeanor.

"Should we be out like this?" she asked, genuinely curious. She got that Jobe wanted to get a feel for where things were while the sun was still out, but strutting around in the open seemed a bit precarious, maybe borderline irresponsible.

"We're not going far," he said. "The address Christopher gave us is across that river." Jobe pointed to a bridge several blocks ahead of them. "I don't want any surprises in the morning."

Alexis didn't like it. He should've told her he wanted to scout the area. Just all the sudden, they had to go. Pretty damned ironic that it cut her afternoon with Liam short.

They crossed the bridge and walked along the Monongahela River. She and Jobe, both strangers here, watched street signs closely. In the intense sunlight and cloudless sky, this part of the city contained a quaint beauty as the river flowed past. A large paddle boat drifted lazily with people lining the rails.

It sparked the memory of a vacation she'd taken when she was a little girl to Galveston Island aboard a paddle boat called the The Colonel. Her dad took pictures of her and her mom while she held cookies and a stuffed animal he'd bought for her at a petting zoo. Sea salt in the air and sunshine on her mother's hair. Wide, screaming mouths and bleeding gashes. Her father's throat torn open to reveal something wet and slippery. And then the teeth. *Stay quiet, Alexis, and don't come out, no matter what happens.* Screaming…

"Keep your eyes open," Jobe startled her.

She swiped a bead of sweat that trickled down her cheek.

"Stay alert," he said. "We need to remember how to get around."

Fine, she could do that. She *was* doing that. "Did you tell Christopher about this?"

"Yes, I spoke to him this afternoon. He agreed we should at least have an idea of the terrain before tomorrow."

She doubted it had gone exactly like that. "And he wasn't the least bit concerned that we might be spotted out here?"

Jobe shrugged and said, "By who? Have you ever seen a vampire?"

"You know I haven't."

"Trust me, they're not out here strolling around in the sunlight. Besides, we're just out for an afternoon walk, that's all. There's people everywhere. We're blending in."

Blending in, huh. She supposed they were. She'd like to know Jobe's history with vampires, if there even was one. The Society hadn't dealt with vampires in over thirty years, well before she was born. She didn't know how old Jobe was. Did he speak from experience or was he just being a pompous ass? Likely the latter. She considered telling him how she'd fought the wolves and won and that Christopher was amply satisfied with her work there, but she decided that exasperating Jobe wouldn't help a thing.

He said, "Besides, the only image we have of this place is from Google Maps, and that could be years old. I just want to see it from a distance. The plan is still the same when the sun comes up tomorrow."

Ah yes, the plan; which also seemed flimsy, other than the agreement that they'd approach on foot, hence this ridiculous scouting escapade. "Yeah, well, I still don't agree with it."

They passed a park where two rivers met. The crowded buildings eventually gave way to houses and strip malls as they continued their walk, gradually getting farther from downtown. Now they were the only two out here and everywhere they looked seemed abandoned.

"I didn't think it was this far away," she said.

"Me neither." His pace had slowed. "Maps said it was only two-and-a-half miles." She didn't like the way he kept scanning the area. He seemed nervous.

She stopped. "What the hell are we doing out here, Jobe? This is stupid."

He faced her. "I told you already, I want to have an idea of what this place looks like." He dug his phone out of his pocket, tapped the face, and stared at it. "This says it's only a quarter mile from here."

"This is close enough. We're going back." She glanced at the sun which had settled low in the sky. She swore it was moving faster in its downward arc.

Jobe's phone buzzed, and he said, "I'll be damned, Christopher just told us to get back to the hotel immediately and not to scout the area." He scratched the corner of his mouth.

Okay, that message made perfect sense to her. So why were they still standing here?

"This seems weird," he said. "Not sure I agree."

"Well, it's Christopher, so let's head back." She crossed her arms, growing nervous and frustrated. Surely, he wasn't contemplating ignoring Christopher.

As he stood there, glancing around, she knew that's exactly what he was doing. Another thing suddenly occurred to her.

"You haven't either, have you?" She glared at him.

He stepped out to the edge of the street as if trying to read the street signs. "Haven't what?"

"Seen a vampire," she said. "You haven't actually seen one either."

At first, he didn't answer. He just stared at his phone until finally, he said, "No, I haven't. But I've heard a lot about them. Christopher said we should be okay doing this."

"I'll be damned," she held her arms out to her side.

"Look, Christopher agreed it was a good idea that we scout the place out."

She shook her head. "I'm going back before someone sees us." She lingered for a bit. "You coming? We can walk through the plan one more time before tomorrow."

His gaze found hers, and she read something she'd not seen in his eyes before. A mixture of puzzlement and fear. She asked, "Did Christopher say why Michael was here? Seems arbitrary."

She knew that if she could get him talking, especially out here by themselves, he'd start moving and he did just that. They strolled back toward downtown as Jobe answered her question. "He said that Michael was from here, apparently born in Pennsylvania. He met Nathaniel during World War I, in Bohemia. Information was sketchy on that part. Michael was reported missing in action during the war but was later found on a merchant ship entering the United States sometime in the nineteen-thirties. He was escorted back to Germany by the Society."

That seemed flimsy to her. "So he thought he'd come to Pittsburg and hang out? Doesn't that seem odd?"

He shrugged and she couldn't help thinking he felt the same way she did, but wouldn't say it.

• • • • •

Four hours later, long after the sun had set, she flipped through the pages of a Cosmopolitan Magazine while seated cross-legged on the floor of her hotel room. The TV blared the news (to which she paid no attention), and she snacked on a bag of chips she'd picked up downstairs. She stared at a page with a pretty girl sitting down to a bowl of cereal, eating it seductively, and a caption stating; *Hold Back Flabbiness to Keep Your Happiness.* Who thought of these stupid stories? Like eating a bowl of that shitty cereal would keep you from getting fat.

She couldn't sleep. Her nerves sizzled, and twice she'd thought someone was standing outside her door, but when she'd checked, there was nothing. She hated this. Vampires frightened her, and she knew they scared Jobe too. The idea of facing them sparked a thickening dread that swelled and grew heavier with each passing hour.

She glanced at the phone and debated. *Don't contact that guy tonight, you need to get your rest and stay focused.* Now there was a joke!

Liam had been so swept away by her. Different than the other men, like Phillip Sawyer, who could be sweet in his own haughty way, but also arrogant. Same with Jobe. All of them with something to prove, like little snot-nosed boys playing king-of-the-hill on the playground. So dumb.

She could relax and be better prepared for tomorrow if she didn't have to sit alone and feed her anxiety. She flipped the magazine closed and crawled across the bed to the telephone.

Calling him would be better than just showing up at his room.

CHAPTER 6

Markus's eyes fluttered open and adjusted quickly to the darkness. Objects stood out like gray ghosts—the dresser, the nightstand, the ceiling fan. He stared at the rotating blades. Something had awakened him; a bad dream. He'd seen Nathaniel standing out in the pasture like a decrepit statue; cloaked in black and tall. So real.

He glanced at the clock on his nightstand - 11:30 PM. He'd been asleep for just two hours! He hated nights like these. The best remedy was to trudge toward the coffee-maker. Naturally, the doctors frowned on him drinking coffee. At some point he'd tell the doctors to go fuck themselves and not worry about it – ain't no getting better for this old man.

He hoisted his legs over the edge of the mattress (with what seemed like more effort than it should have been) and placed his feet onto the thin rug. He scrunched his toes against the velvety surface, waking up his feet. It felt shockingly good.

A thought occurred to him - something Christopher had said yesterday. Nothing big really, but lingering, like the words of a bad song, stuck in your head. The man who reported seeing Michael in Pittsburg was a priest, a Catholic, and yet according to the accounts Christopher went over, Nathaniel was avoiding Catholics like the plague and entering Protestant churches. Maybe Michael had no problem with priests. Perhaps the issue with Catholics resided with Nathaniel only. Just seemed odd to go all the way to Pittsburg and talk to a priest on the street. Not very stealthy.

Surely Michael knew the priest would talk to someone about it. And if word reached the Vatican…

Clarity dawned on him as he finished the words aloud, "…they'd send the Society looking for him." Christ on his throne, how could they have missed that! *Because I'm an old fool, that's why!*

Markus placed his wrinkled hand on the bed, ready to push himself up when heavy footsteps thudded down the hallway. His door burst open. Christopher stood wide-eyed and breathing heavy. "We need to talk. Nathaniel knows we're coming."

• • • • •

A few minutes later, Markus followed Christopher into the same room they'd met in earlier. It was different at night, reminding him of the inside of a log cabin, deep in the woods, where only the lights from lanterns filled the space. Christopher wore his pajamas and red robe and as he walked, the robe spread out behind him like Superman's cape.

"I received a call from Bishop Anderson in New York." Christopher strode toward a large oak desk, his hair askew. "He seemed quite anxious and called me first since he knows that we're involved in this."

"Bishop Anderson?" Markus asked.

Christopher reached the desk and flipped on a small lamp and then looked up at Markus. "He's our contact in New York who has direct access to the Cardinal in Rome who obviously has direct access to the Pope."

"Ah." Markus clasped his hands in front of him. Thank goodness Christopher kept up with all these people.

"He called, quite frantic, stating that he'd received a phone call earlier this evening and it sounded like something similar to the occurrences in London and New York with the ministers who were visited by Nathaniel." Christopher seemed to be talking more to himself as he ran his hand through his thin hair. "I just don't understand why Nathaniel would have risked us finding out if he already had us tricked."

"Tricked?" Markus felt eerily sure Christopher's rantings were along the same lines as his own worries. *They're spreading us out.*

"If he had us tricked, why would he expose himself? Unless..." Christopher rubbed at his chin, and his eyes got bigger as an explanation must have popped into his head. Markus thought Albert Einstein might have had a similar expression when the idea of relativity first sprang into his mind. "Unless, he *wanted* us to know he was there. Which would mean he's already gotten to them."

"What the hell happened?" Markus asked. They needed to speed this along.

Christopher plopped into a chair behind the desk and spoke almost too quietly to hear. "There was another minister who met Nathaniel, in a similar

DAVID ODLE **33**

situation as the ones I told you about earlier where he was seeking confession. It was a Lutheran minister, a man named Acosta. Just happened late this afternoon."

Markus's feet grew heavier, and he inhaled deeply before speaking. "It was in Pittsburg, wasn't it?"

Christopher nodded. "My God. Nathaniel is in Pittsburg... he lured us there. Alexis and Jobe don't know. He is taunting us, Nathaniel is. He *does* mean to start a war."

"Contact Jobe right now and tell them to get the hell out of there." Markus leaned onto the desk looking Christopher in the eye. "Stay with me, old friend. We've got work to do."

Christopher looked like he'd aged ten years in the past hour. "I tried calling Jobe, his cell phone is dead. Alexis isn't answering hers either. I called the hotel and got nothing."

Markus didn't hear the rest. He was out the door. If Christopher could have the jet ready within the next thirty minutes, he could be in Pittsburg within four hours.

It was the best he could do.

CHAPTER 7

"Thank god for good Thai food," Liam said. He held the door open to the hotel lobby, and Alexis walked through. She shot him a shy smile as she sauntered past. "There's a few places in Houston like that." They strode across the lobby toward the elevators. He took her hand, grasping her warm skin with his own damp palms, and her grip tightened.

"I don't go into town much," she said, "I live on the outskirts, more towards Dayton." She stopped outside the elevators, and her gaze found his. He blinked, totally lost in her dark eyes, every cell in his body buzzing like supercharged ions.

The awkward moment. *The moment when I'm supposed to kiss her!* He hadn't expected it to pop up right then. He wasn't ready. But he had to do something or the moment would pass and possibly never return. Her eyes, that deep shade of green, invited him in and he wanted to taste her, to become part of her, to have everything he could of her. He bent down hoping his lips weren't too wet.

His confidence surged as he felt the unmistakable press of her mouth against his, her sweet breath on his tongue. The tenderness of her body pressed against him and his belly tingled. He could have said *I love you* right then and never regretted it, even if it meant the last words he'd ever speak to her.

Their lips parted, and she smiled. Since meeting her this morning, Liam had not given the slightest thought about deciding to stay another night in Pittsburg with the most beautiful woman he'd ever met. He could care less if Jeremy at The Unexplained Truth fired him. He'd told Alexis during lunch that he was a writer (he'd left out the part about the shitty tabloid he worked for). Her eyes widened in amazement as she'd asked him so many questions. For the first time in a long time, maybe even forever, he was truly alive. There was no explaining how that felt, not even for a writer.

He glanced at his watch. "Can't believe it's ten o'clock already. What time are you leaving tomorrow?"

"I'll be busy." She glanced away, and a look of reservation crossed her face, a thought hidden that only she knew. "Are you leaving tomorrow?" She reached out and touched his arm.

Still in utter disbelief that this could even be happening, he answered, "I'm supposed to," he chuckled and added, "I was actually supposed to leave today."

"You were?" Her smile lit up her face. "That is so sweet."

"I couldn't help it," he said. "You can't tell me I'm the only guy to ever do that?"

She shook her head as if dismissing the statement, then pushed her hair back behind her ears, "As a matter of fact, you *are* the first one to ever stay an extra night to go out with me."

Go out. That had a nice ring to it. She'd called earlier and asked him if he would like to go do something. But *going out* was more than something. *Going out* meant it was more than *just friends.*

He said, "I'm either stupid or a hopeless romantic." He pushed his hands into his pockets.

"I'll take hopeless romantic." Goddamn, that smile. He knew right then he'd never forget this image of her

Liam laughed. "I never saw myself that way."

"You know, my room has a little mini-bar in it. You could come up and have a drink if you want." She bit her lower lip adorably.

The question slapped him like a wet glove. Of all things he might have guessed would happen, Alexis asking him to come to her room wasn't one of them.

"A drink sounds good," he said, trying to sound cool and casual, but not sure he pulled it off.

She threaded her arm through his and tugged him toward the elevator. "Just a drink, I have to get up early in the morning." She pressed the elevator call button.

"I wasn't thinking anything else," he lied.

"Oh, I see." Her playful smirk was too cute.

The doors to the elevator opened and they stepped inside as he said, "I swear."

"I'm sure." Her voice echoed slightly in the small space as the doors closed and they started moving up. Thank god she couldn't read his mind because if she could, she'd likely think he was a shit for the fleeting image of pressing her against the wall and kissing her as deeply as he could.

"Besides," she said, "Just in case I don't see you in the morning I want —"

The elevator doors slid open, and two morbid figures loomed in the hallway. Liam grasped Alexis's hand. An awful hum, unlike anything he'd ever heard, echoed in his ears. Blood oozed down the elevator walls, seeping from the creases along the ceiling and the floor.

Liam scrunched his eyes shut, sucking in a harsh breath. He rubbed the heels of his palms against his eyes hard enough to see stars. The bloody image disappeared, and then something hit him hard in the chest, slamming him against the back wall of the elevator, rattling the panels and the floor. He collapsed forward, onto his knees, but couldn't breathe, he couldn't scream, he couldn't move. A white face descended toward him; its red mouth crammed with jagged teeth.

Alexis? He had not even heard her scream. He pictured her dead, her dark hair fanned out on the floor, her green eyes open and sightless.

A second later, heat erupted inside the elevator and the hairs on his neck and eyebrows singed. He smelled it. An orange glow engulfed him. Fire. Their attackers clambered backward into the hallway. Alexis faced them, now standing in front of Liam with her back to him like a mythical warrior protecting her young.

•   •   •   •   •

She knew that she'd messed up about a split-second before the elevator doors opened. She'd let her guard down. A smell foreign to her. A mixture of old earth and dead flesh, tainted the air. Liam's face paled. The moment the doors opened, a gnarled hand shot through and struck him. He rebounded from the wall and landed heavily on his knees. She'd hesitated too long already.

She lurched in front of him and extended her arms, exerting all of her energy toward the open doors. A massive heatwave swelled like a bubble, then blew forward. The air rumbled and then ignited into a screaming wall of fire.

Do not hesitate, Alexis, when killing a vampire, the words of Christopher from just prior to her departure from Houston last night, *they are relentless and will not stop, and, if it is a Legion, there will be many.* But she was not totally inexperienced. She'd fought the wolves several years ago utilizing similar techniques. She knew what she was capable of.

Horrid wails from the hallway penetrated the roar of the inferno. She pushed harder, now unable to see anything except fire. Within seconds, the fire alarm blasted and the corridor filled with a high-pitched squealing noise. She prayed this would not cost anyone their lives.

She glanced at Liam. He coughed and struggled, his hand clasped to his chest. *I'm sorry for this.* And she was. He should be home right now, not here with her.

"Liam... get up!" she yelled. He placed his hand on the side of the elevator wall, making a shaky attempt to stand.

She focused back on the doorway. One of the creatures was fighting its way through the fire, its mouth wide, the teeth bared, and it was wailing. Just before it reached her, she screamed too.

Maybe these weren't like the wolves at all.

CHAPTER 8

Jobe was as surprised as Alexis, but not as unprepared. There was a reason he'd followed her tonight. Since they'd received the text from Christopher, he suspected that Michael knew they were here in Pittsburg. Christopher had said to return to the hotel immediately, and they'd huddle in the morning before doing anything.

All okay? Jobe had texted.

Maybe not. Christopher responded, *but blatant attacks on the Society are highly unlikely.*

Christopher had been wrong.

Jobe's elevator halted on Alexis's floor, and a soft ding sounded inside the carriage. A rumbling noise rattled the walls, and orange flames flickered through the crease in the doors. A horrid scream tore through the small space, and his heart plummeted. *Oh, Jesus Christ.* He readied himself as the elevator doors slid open.

The first thing that hit him was a wall of fire. He jumped out into the hallway, forcing a wall of energy around him, like a red-tinted bubble, to protect him from the flames. It was chaos. Alexis was focused – spewing fire, Liam on the floor, someone (no, *something*) pressed against the opposite wall of Alexis's elevator, nearly burnt to a crisp, but still kicking. Another was at the doors, suffering a horrible blast of fire, but still fighting to reach her.

Vampires.

Two more crouched in the corner, waiting. One of them held a long, cane-like thing and Jobe guessed that it was some sort of a weapon, but wasn't sure, he'd never seen it before.

He glanced behind him and nearly stumbled and had to catch his balance. His heart fluttered. Michael leaned against the far wall, a lurid smile spread across his shadowed face. He wore a dark robe, with a hood draped over his head, but underneath was the old Army uniform. One of the medals reflected the fire like an obscene eye.

"I've been waiting for you," Michael said.

Jobe spun and dropped to his knees, forcing his magic to the center of his body, then thrusting it out through his palms in a thick, red light, exploding outward in a rippling cascade. The smile on Michael's face vanished. His arms swooped up to cover his face but did nothing to halt Jobe's onslaught that struck him dead on. The power flung Michael back. His entire body disappeared into a collapsing mess of paint, plaster, and splintering wood.

Jobe whirled back toward Alexis. He fired another burst of red light and struck the creature trying to get into the elevator, slinging it back against the wall, burnt to a crisp. The remaining two backed down the corridor, one still holding that cane-like thing, and out of sight. Why weren't they attacking? This all seemed wrong. Thick smoke roiled within the corridor. Jobe crouched. They had to get out of here.

"Alexis!" He kept his eyes open for any more surprises that may lurk in the shadows. There was no response from the elevator. The flames died out.

"Alexis!" This time he screamed her name, reaching for the opening of the elevator doors and praying he wouldn't look inside and see her corpse lying strewn on the floor.

"Jobe... we have to get him out." Her voice echoed within the darkness and relief washed through him.

"Hurry up," Jobe yelled. The hotel sprinkler system kicked on dousing him in cold water. It actually felt refreshing in the smothering smoke and heat. In the distance, he could hear sirens. "We need to get out of here, now."

Liam got shakily to his feet and stumbled out into the corridor. Emergency lights flickered in the thick haze. Jobe grabbed Liam's arm and hauled him toward a door with a faintly lit EXIT sign above it. He heaved it open, pushing Liam and Alexis into the dank stairwell. The door swung shut behind them as they hurried down the steps; their hoarse coughs echoed in the narrow passageway.

"What the hell is going..."

Jobe clamped a hand over Liam's mouth. "Shhhhhhhh."

Scuttling from somewhere, like feet dragging on a sandy floor.

"I hear it. It sounds like it's above us," Alexis whispered.

Above was good.

Jobe whispered harshly into Liam's ear, close enough that he caught the whiff of perspiration on the guy's skin, "Don't say a word." He slid his hand away from Liam's mouth. Goddamn it, they just needed to get down to the bottom floor and get out of this damned hotel.

"You should've left him alone," Jobe hissed and shot a finger at Liam.

"Shut up and listen," Alexis stopped moving. "There's something in here."

It sounded as if someone were scraping their fingernails down a blackboard. Jobe's muscles tightened. *Oh Christ*, they're everywhere.

"Go now!" he yelled and plunged down the stairs shoving Alexis ahead of him and dragging Liam by the arm.

•   •   •   •

Jobe's hand grasped him roughly around the elbow and hauled him down the steps. Liam scrambled to keep his footing. *What the Christ is going on!* He couldn't breathe. What the hell had hit him in the elevator? The teeth. And then the fire. He didn't have a clue where that had come from.

He tripped and caught himself.

"C'mon!" Jobe yelled.

This couldn't be happening. Then it dawned on him, and his legs felt like concrete pillars. A goddamn terrorist attack, people wearing masks. Panic danced in his chest and a sudden urge to vomit surged into his throat. *Get out, they had to get out, now!* He moaned, terrified, and took the stairs as fast as he could.

A loud bang echoed as something landed on the platform in front of them. A man, dressed in an all-black robe, towered at the base of the steps. Where had he come from? Liam halted clumsily. A stairwell door was just out of reach, and he wanted to dive for it, and he might've if Jobe weren't still gripping his arm. The man in black, his face shadowed by a hood, didn't move. Bizarre images materialized, and Liam clamped his free hand over his eyes. Corpses lay strewn on the floor and even with his eyes closed, Liam still saw them. Sticky blood and rancid guts squished under his feet. He flailed and tore away from Jobe's grasp.

Someone forced him back against the wall, pushing him away. He opened his eyes.

Alexis.

A rush of air swooped past him. He glanced at Jobe who had his hands out before him. For no apparent reason, the man in black tumbled backward against the wall.

And then, more people jumped down around them, crowding the space, and screaming so loud that his ears might burst from the strain. Jobe stepped in front of him and lifted his hands. A murky wall appeared with smoke swirling on its surface. It was like it just formed out of nowhere. People crashed into it, trying to claw through it, but rebounded as if they were trying to break through unbreakable glass. But these people, they looked strange, like they were –

"Get out the door!" Jobe yelled over his shoulder, "I can't hold this forever."

Liam whirled and heaved the door open, bursting out into the corridor. Something heavy collided against his back, and he stumbled forward. He turned and saw Alexis sprawled on the floor; half in the corridor, half in the stairwell. He reached for her.

She stretched out her arm, and he grasped her hand, but something inside the stairwell tore her away from him. She caught herself on the doorframe. "Get out of here, Liam," she said with a weakening voice. "Find Phillip Sawyer. Tell him the Legion..." and then she was gone, yanked into the blackness.

The stairwell-door slammed shut, and he plopped down onto the carpet, alone. The hotel fire alarms blared. His hands trembled, and a fat tear slid down his cheek.

"Alexis?" His weak voice shocked him as if spoken by someone he didn't know. Then he screamed, "*Alexis!*"

Nothing.

He scrambled to his feet and charged the stairwell door. It slammed open, and he gazed into the dark. No one. Just smoke and that retched blare of the alarms.

"*Alexis!*" His voice echoed lifelessly. She was gone.

He spun away from the stairwell and charged down the hallway, nearly tripping and sprawling onto his belly, but regained his footing and ran.

"Help me!" He prayed for anyone to hear him.

CHAPTER 9

Markus placed his coffee mug, only half full, into the cup holder built into the arm of his seat and gazed out the window into the darkness. They'd been flying for two hours. Phillip Sawyer sat in the seat across from him with his legs crossed, nervously jiggling his foot. Poor kid was asleep three hours ago, then jolted awake and ordered to go to Pittsburg tonight with Markus rather than waiting until tomorrow morning.

He knew Phillip was worried. With Nathaniel already there, things could get messy. Most likely, they already were. If it were not for Jobe, Markus would have told Phillip earlier that Alexis was most likely dead, but stayed silent knowing that Jobe's experience may save them. And, Markus reminded himself, there was no proof that anything bad had actually happened yet. *Don't worry about anything until happens.* A thing he used to say. He didn't think Phillip would want to hear that, though.

"Do you remember what I told you about Alexis when you visited me in Indiana?" Markus asked while picking up his coffee cup. He wasn't sure why he felt compelled to speak; perhaps it was the distraught look on the young man's face.

Phillip appeared stunned at first, then answered with haste, sounding bitter. "Yeah, you said that her pride nearly got her killed."

"Yes." Markus sipped his coffee, wishing he had not used the word pride to describe Alexis, it would have been more accurate to say *stubborn.*

"And you said you saved her life," Phillip said. "Are you trying to make me feel better?"

"Yes. As a matter of fact, I am. If you remember, I said something else about her."

"What?"

"I also said she was very good." Markus kept a stern gaze on Phillip's face and waited patiently for the words to sink in, then he went on. "She is one of the best I've ever seen with fire. I saw her fight the wolves and she fought valiantly."

Phillip stared as if waiting for the punch line of a sad joke.

"If she and Jobe have encountered trouble, she will not go quietly. And Jobe is very powerful; the two of them would be a formidable force in any encounter."

"He hasn't fought against a vampire," Phillip said, "Let alone a Legion."

"But he *is* powerful."

"Not as powerful as you."

Markus stayed silent. He wasn't sure if Phillip's statement was a compliment or just another step on the ladder of pessimism. Phillip was in love with Alexis, and young love almost always played tricks on the mind and made men think in extremes – never in moderation. Everything was either as bad as it could get or absolutely fabulous.

"Not as old either," Markus said.

Not a trace of humor touched Phillip's face; he turned and stared absently out the window. The young lad's girl was in trouble, and until it was clear that she was okay, he would be the eternal nay-sayer.

"Well," Markus said, "we'll be landing within the hour, and we'll go straight to their hotel. Most likely, we'll find them sound asleep, and they'll wonder why we're there checking up on them."

Phillip raised his eyebrows but still didn't speak. Time was the best ingredient in these situations, and if enough of it passed, Phillip would be fine. *There is no pain or hurt that time will not heal.* In Markus's opinion (which may be outdated – he certainly would not discount *that* possibility), the greatest downfall of the younger generation was impatience. Simply allowing time to take its course was no longer acceptable.

Markus shifted his gaze to the window and watched the darkness zip past.

•　•　•　•　•

What does he know? Phillip thought and was glad when the old man stopped talking.

Markus could try to bullshit him that everything was hunky-dory, but Phillip knew better. He'd known it by the tone in Christopher's voice a few hours ago and by the hasty departure in the middle of the night and most importantly, by Markus's silence when they'd left. Add all that up, and Phillip would say something was *very* goddamned wrong.

And Alexis was at the center of the wrongness. Her image filled his head with thoughts that were warm, but devoid of comfort as he thought of her hurt, dying, or maybe dead. *Jesus, would Nathaniel kill her?* He understood that Nathaniel was the bad guy here. But to kill Alexis… how could any man want to hurt her? Nathaniel was not a man and hadn't been for centuries. But he *used* to be. Surely that had some bearing on how creatures like Nathaniel behaved and interacted. Wouldn't a beautiful woman still be beautiful? Perhaps the appeal changed to appetite, and allure was the taste and not the person.

Phillip had seen a real vampire once when he was thirteen and that had been from a distance. When you got right down to it, he knew nothing about them. Whatever they were, whatever they'd been, equated to an entity still capable of coherent thought and actions since they co-existed with ordinary people and maintained order agreed to between them and the Society. Surely the core of our common humanity shared by both vampires and people meant something, didn't it?

The thought of anyone hurting her prompted despair, even anger. And sitting on this goddamn airplane, totally helpless and waiting on it to land, was the worst. God knew what may be happening and all he could do was –

"We messed up." Markus's words cut the silence and startled him. The troubled look on the old man's face was unsettling.

"What?"

Markus glared at him, glared *through* him. "Christopher sent us to Pittsburg because we have an eyewitness that Nathaniel is there." Markus sat up straighter, gripping the arms of his chair as if preparing to launch out of it.

"Yeah," Phillip said growing more uncomfortable. "He sent everyone to Pittsburg early this morning." He recalled Christopher's hasty briefing before they'd left. Jason, one of the wizards working in Colorado, and William, a wizard currently assigned with the chasers in London, had already been given explicit orders to converge on Pittsburg immediately.

Markus's eyebrows furled and his fist clenched around his cane. As he spoke, his eyes seemed focused on something far off, as if talking to himself and unaware that Phillip was sitting four feet away. "Christopher was very distraught this morning about Nathaniel being in Pittsburg. He was equally certain that Alexis and Jobe would be dead by morning if we didn't get there. He even said he didn't understand why Nathaniel would make his location known; it seemed like an odd mistake for him to let it slip out that he was in Pittsburg. Why wouldn't he have killed the minister, the Lutheran minister named Acosta, to prevent him from telling anyone? Nathaniel may be insane, but he isn't stupid."

Markus stopped speaking. Phillip waited for what seemed like eternity and finally asked, "What are you saying?"

Markus settled his cold gaze on Phillip and said, "I don't think Nathaniel's meeting with the Lutheran minister was anything genuine... I think it was a setup."

Phillip uncrossed his legs as dread crept into his belly, "A setup?"

"I think Nathaniel very cleverly got us all to converge on Pittsburg," Markus said and slammed his cane onto the floor of the plane, scowling.

Phillip looked at Markus, confused, and then it dawned on him.

Christopher was at the ranch, alone.

CHAPTER 10

Thought projection. A skill possessed by the most powerful.

It was somewhat effective when sending a single thought – it was like having a gun with one bullet; the shot had to count. Markus waffled on projecting to Christopher. He feared sparking unnecessary panic since the projection could not be wrapped with any sort of explanation or clarity. However, neither did he want Christopher's death on his conscience if he could prevent it.

"Check for messages," he said to Phillip. "Perhaps I'm over-reacting." If there was nothing from Christopher, thought projection would be his only option.

"Still no cell signal," Phillip said. He held his cell phone out in front of him. "But..." he started tapping the face of it. Markus found the wait excruciating. Finally, Phillip said, "This plane has wifi, and I got an email from Christopher. It's mainly to you."

"Read it." Markus leaned back in his seat and listened as Phillip read.

Phillip said, "It's a long-ass email." He cleared his throat and read it:

"Markus, I'm worried that Nathaniel may have gotten the better of us. Call it intuition, but it occurred to me, I am here alone, and I continue hearing noises outside the walls. It's imperative that I impart my key initiatives onto you in the event I am killed. I do not mean to be the eternal pessimist, but I must face a possibility never considered before... that we may lose."

Phillip paused and glanced up. Markus waved his hand for him to keep reading. He needed to hear it all. Phillip continued:

"A couple things you must know and I'll start with the most important which is the Vatican's message to me regarding Nathaniel's motivation, hence the reason I'd planned to get to London later today. Here is the key piece from the Archbishop's message received tonight pasted into this email:

Four vampires were found dead in Hamburg, but not at the hands of the Society or the Chasers. Apparently, they had been killed by their own kind in a small hostel located on the outskirts of the city. A major disagreement had transpired, and factions had formed. Potentially, Nathaniel's faction met fierce resistance by those who refused to disrupt the current co-existence between the world and vampires. And for that, Nathaniel had killed them. The bodies were found today, but the killing took place days before.

It is without any resignation that we speculate this is the work of a Legion given the destruction – clearly, the victims had barricaded themselves into the basement as a last resort to ward off the attack. Decapitations were rampant. We speculate the attack was merciless and allowed no negotiations, providing further evidence that Nathaniel is far more organized and controlling more Legions than originally anticipated. Our fear is that Nathaniel's objective is to remove all resistance to ensure he can move without interference or opposition. It is quite evident he is moving aggressively against the Society in the United States and against the Vatican in Europe. If he is successful, he will establish an imbalance of power where mankind will be at the mercy of the vampire."

Phillip looked up from his phone, his eyes wide, and said, "Dear god, I didn't know any of this."

Markus raised his eyebrows and said, "I'm not sure anyone did. Christopher was scheduled to go to London today where I assume this was planned to be the topic of discussion." He rubbed his temples as a headache threatened to creep in. "Is there anything else in his message, Phillip?"

Phillip nodded and said, "Just a little." He scrolled with his fingers and read the rest of the message:

"I fear that Nathaniel's insanity has driven him to seek domination and his experience gives him an upper-hand. His existence spans centuries, wars, and the rise and fall of nations. The Society and the Vatican only have written accounts concerning the actions of the old vampires.

"I must step away now, old friend, as these noises I hear are not arbitrary. I do hope you receive this before arriving in Pittsburg. Collect Alexis and Jobe and return to the ranch at once so we can regroup. Stay safe, Markus."

Phillip slid his fingers across the face of the phone and said, "That's it."

Markus had never felt more helpless than he did at that very moment. Nothing he could do but sit and wait. His hand crept down to his chest, and he massaged a dull ache in his left side; a habit he'd developed over the past few months knowing the rot that festered inside. Nothing but a dying old man with no more tricks up his sleeve and no more cards to play.

He stared at Phillip whose slack face concealed nothing of the fear etched behind it. What must this young pup be thinking after reading that note? Christopher was the closest thing he had to family. Good Christ, what must be happening at the ranch right now? He could still hope that everything was okay, but that seemed less and less likely as the night drew on. Dawn was still an hour or more away and much could happen in that much time.

Think, goddamn it! You old fool, do not drift away now!

Markus glanced away from Phillip and said quietly, "Be it our triumph to impeach the vampire of existence rather than have him utilize his greatest weapon of immortality against us, his ultimate efficacy."

"What?" Phillip's shaky voice.

Markus forced a humorless smile. "Those are the words of a great warlock named Nostradomas from the sixteenth century."

Phillip nodded, then asked shakily, "What the hell are we gonna do? We have to go back!"

Markus heard the pup's words but ignored them. He said, "Did you know that Nostradamus actually tried to annihilate vampires in the 1500s?"

Phillip shook his head, exasperated, and said, "No, I didn't. What does this have to do with anything?"

Markus shifted his gaze toward the ceiling of the plane. "The vampires fought him relentlessly, and the war had cost many lives. A truce was reached to end the bloodshed with agreements on both sides to co-exist peacefully. But perhaps Nostradomas had been right, and the truce had been nothing more than a 300-year hiatus."

Phillip tossed his phone down on the seat next to him and buried his face in his hands. "What in the fuck are you talking about? We need to do something now!"

Markus lifted his cane and pointed it at Phillip. He shoved the end of it against Phillip's chest, forcing him upright and back against his seat. The young man's eyes widened, and his mouth fell open, as if to yell, but thought better of it. Goddamn impatient little shit. If he was to keep Phillip alive, then it was time to lay the ground rules.

"Listen to me," Markus said, "You are nothing but a child, and you know nothing of the enemy we face, and you're too damned foolish to learn. The beast we pursue is centuries older than you with eyes in the back of its head. It knows all and will kill you with joy to feed on your flesh!"

Phillip blinked back tears and Markus leaned toward him. "We will not panic. Do you understand me?"

Phillip nodded.

"We will keep our wits about us, and we'll regroup. We're going to collect Alexis and Jobe, and we'll hustle back to the ranch. That is our mission here. Do you understand me, Phillip?"

Again, Phillip nodded, and this time a tear slipped from his eye. Markus withdrew his cane. "You will do exactly as I say when I say it."

The plane started its descent into Pittsburg with a jerky shudder, and a small ding filled the cabin. "Now listen to me," Markus said. "Before we land, I want to ensure…"

Suddenly a voice blasted in Markus's head, filling his skull. His teeth smashed together in a sickening crunch. He slumped back into his seat and eased his eyes open. Holy Christ. The plane jostled again, about to land, and he questioned whether he should have turned back to help Christopher, a choice that would haunt him for days.

Phillip scooted forward and touched Markus's arm. "You all right?"

"A projection," Markus said quietly. His mouth was dry. "From Christopher."

The plane bumped against the runway, followed by the loud roar of the reverse thrusters. He reached out and took Phillip's arm, gripping it to offer some sort of reassurance.

"Christopher will fight valiantly," Markus said, "Nathaniel would be foolish to underestimate him."

The plane slowed to a crawl and rolled toward the terminal. Phillip looked lost. "So, Nathaniel *is* there. And they're fighting as we speak?"

Markus shifted in his seat, preparing to get up. He was anxious and wanted off this damn plane. "We'll go to the hotel immediately and confirm the whereabouts of Alexis and Jobe. We'll also need to locate Jason and William. I assume you can contact them?" Phillip affirmed that he could.

"What did Christopher say?" Phillip pleaded.

Markus pressed his lips to a thin line, debating. He knew damned good, and well Christopher's message was one of desperation, likely projected as his oldest friend was on his last stand. A painful thought.

He glared into Phillip's imploring eyes and decided to hell with it. Nothing good would come from withholding information now.

Markus's voice hardened. "Christopher's message was… 'Kill them, Markus. Kill them all'."

CHAPTER II

Liam stood at the bottom of the stairwell staring up the steps with his teeth clenched so hard his jaw ached. How in the world could this place be completely empty?

Officer Kyle Morris lingered next to him along with two firemen decked out in full gear. This had to be the craziest goddamned thing he'd ever experienced and to be here so helpless infuriated him most of all.

"Mr. Balsing," Officer Morris's voice echoed, "this is our third look in here… there's no one here."

Liam said, "She *was* in here. They drug her into this stairwell, and now they've all just disappeared? What the fuck?" He spat the words.

Officer Morris, whose patience should be commended, touched Liam's shoulder with a firm consolation. "We've searched everywhere, every floor, every room, and every road and alley around this place. I'm sorry, but she's not here."

Liam turned to him, then to the firemen. They all regarded him with blank expressions. "She was here," Liam pleaded. "They dragged her away from me."

Officer Morris nodded and asked, "But you didn't get a good look at them?"

Liam shook his head. "Like I told you, they were wearing some sort of masks. All of them were." The writer in him conjured words for description – nefarious… monstrosities perhaps - *how would I write what happened in here?* Explaining things should be his strength, but right now, he'd never felt more inept.

The fire had been out well over an hour, but a burnt smell, like hot plastic, still hung in the air. The raspy sounds of his breaths echoed in the cramped space, and finally, Officer Morris said, "Let's go out front, maybe walk through it all again and see what we missed. Maybe we overlooked something vital... the devil's in the details on these kinds of things."

Liam stuffed his hands in his pockets and fought an overwhelming urge to cry. Was this all he could do? Just walk out front and talk to a bunch of strangers about the same shit again? It hardly seemed possible. How on earth could someone just disappear like that... just totally gone as if they'd never existed to start with. Only the ripples of the lives they'd touched proved anything at all. Signed receipts, a magazine lying on her hotel room floor, a few snacks perched on the edge of her nightstand, and her lifeless clothes, what few there were, stuffed into a backpack plopped onto a chair.

"Mr. Balsing?" Officer Morris urged. "Let's step out front."

And tell the same damn story again. He was starting to think Kyle suspected *him* of having started the goddamned fire! And Alexis was still out there, somewhere.

Liam followed Kyle out the door and through the hotel lobby. People gathered in small groups, clumped together doing whatever it was they were doing. His eyes darted from one person to another, irrationally expecting Alexis to be standing somewhere... *Oh, there you are.* But of course, that was fanciful. Earlier, Kyle explained that roadblocks were established within 4 city blocks of this place and that police were pulling over and questioning anyone suspicious.

Outside, four large fire-trucks were parked jaggedly in front of the hotel with red lights flashing like beacons. He and Kyle stopped next to a parked ambulance. Liam wiped his face with his sleeve. Black char clung to his arm, and he could only imagine what his face must look like.

"What type of work did you say Alexis did again?" Kyle asked. He took out a cigarette and lit it.

"I don't know, she didn't tell me," Liam glanced down at his shoes and noticed the dark smudges across the top. "She only mentioned this guy named Phillip Sawyer."

Kyle nodded, then shrugged. "This is the goddamn-dest thing."

Liam said, "I just don't know how they could all just disappear like that."

Kyle raised his eyebrows. "If I'm guessing, they had a solid plan of escape. I'm just at a total loss as to what they wanted or what they were trying to do. I mean, why light the place on fire? Why snag this girl and the guy she was with? I'd guess the fire was a diversion, it's still just not adding up. I don't know..."

Kyle stopped and just stood there smoking as if waiting for Liam to speak. The quiet hung awkwardly between them for what seemed like ages.

He's waiting for me to say something, he still thinks I had something to do with all this. Or at least, that's the way it felt.

Liam leaned back against the front fender of the ambulance. He thought of calling Jeremy, his editor back in Houston, but he didn't have Jeremy's cell phone. Besides, what the hell was he going to say? He sure as hell wasn't calling his dad, not yet. That was the last thing he needed right now.

That's when a strange man stepped up next to them, and Liam was struck by how tired the guy looked. With his shoulders slumped and dark circles under his eyes, the man walked right up to Kyle Morris and, with his hand extended for a genuine shake, said, "Mr. Morris, I'm Phillip Sawyer."

• • • • •

Kyle Morris's hand rose slowly.

Phillip shook it. The usual barrage of questions would soon follow – *how did you know my name? How did you find us? How... how... how...* Never an easy explanation when you could read minds. Kyle's hand was warm. The skin unexpectedly soft. *Kyle Morris. Kyle suspected this man standing next to him. Liam Balsing. Kyle didn't like Liam. Liam had been here. He'd witnessed everything. He'd been with Alexis... Liam had been in the elevator with her and was going up to her room...* What the fuck?

Phillip said, "I came as soon as I heard. I need to talk to this gentleman." He shot a thumb toward the man named Liam, who had his arms crossed over his chest. 'Ole Liam here had better have some goddamn answers. This situation was completely out of control, and the thought of Alexis hurt somewhere horrified him.

Kyle's eyebrows scrunched together. "Did you say, Phillip Sawyer?"

"Yes, sir." *Here we go.*

Kyle shot Liam a look, then said, "Isn't that the guy she asked about?"

Liam nodded and uncrossed his arms, his expression was one of shocked recognition, and Phillip thought he looked quite stupid if he was being honest. Liam said, "She told me to find you."

"Alexis did?" The immediate urge to ask Liam what the hell he was doing with her danced at the back of his throat. He swallowed it back. *I'm not supposed to know that yet.* Too many red flags and Detective Kyle Morris might bring more people over here. It was Alexis's life he feared for now, and in the scheme of things, nothing else mattered.

"Yeah," Liam said.

Kyle held his hands out to his sides and with a cigarette dangling from his lips and said, "Wait a damn minute here. All this shit happens, and then you just stroll up and say hello? Who the hell are you?"

Hurry up and don't horse-ass around, Markus had told him when they departed the airport. *Horse-ass around...* that was a new expression. The old man had hobbled away on that ugly cane of his, exiting the main terminal doors and disappearing into the crowd outside the airport. Despite their differences, they were completely aligned on not *horse-assing* around.

Phillip peered into Kyle's eyes, all the while feeling Liam's gaze crawl over him, observing him, probably wondering who Phillip Sawyer was and why Phillip Sawyer was here to talk to him and most importantly, how Phillip Sawyer was going to get rid of Kyle Morris. The sooner, the better on that.

Phillip opened his senses and felt a strong emotion emanating from Kyle, one buried and hidden from all the world. Shame. He penetrated Kyle's tough exterior and reached into his mind, like long, invisible fingers dipping into a mound of soft clay. Deep in Kyle's brain, in the place where his fantasies lived late at night with the lights off, Phillip found a secret (as he so often did while performing this bit of magic). Kyle Morris was addicted to cocaine. Though no words would be spoken, Phillip knew this and Kyle, even though he'd never be able to explain how, knew that Phillip knew.

You're done here, Phillip's unspoken suggestion drifted to Kyle like radio waves. *You can return to your precinct and begin organizing your documentation for a report of what you have found here, you will even deliver it early.* Phillip waited, keeping his telepathic fingers wedged into the recesses of Kyle's mind, making sure the man reacted correctly – sometimes it took an extra effort.

Kyle's eyes softened, and his shoulders slumped. He turned to Liam and spoke almost too quiet to hear. "I think I've got what I need for right now, but I may need to contact you if I need more information."

Phillip withdrew. Kyle was doing fine.

Kyle trudged away from them looking defeated. Phillip and Liam stood next to each other and once again, Phillip was keenly aware of Liam's glare upon him.

"Did I miss something here?" Liam asked.

Phillip shrugged as Kyle walked away. "It's all I know how to do. Others start fires, or create lightning – but not me, I get to persuade dip-shits like Kyle Morris to leave. Some talent." Phillip shook his head. *I'm rambling.* He turned to Liam, "We gotta go. Now."

Liam gawked at him with questions swimming in his eyes, but there was no way they were going to stand here and have some long conversation. Too much at stake. Markus was waiting for him. Alexis was in trouble, maybe worse. And, goddamn it all to hell, what was Liam doing here with Alexis to start with?

"I'm not full of shit, you know," Phillip said, "I can assure you of that. Let's get a cab." He stepped away from Liam, heading toward the street.

"Where you going?" Liam asked. He didn't move at first, and Phillip decided if the guy decided not to come with him, so be it. Phillip honestly didn't think Liam would be of much help anyway, even if he *was* the last person to see Alexis.

"First, we have to find Markus," Phillip said over his shoulder. "Stay here if you want."

"Who's Markus?" Liam scrambled up next to him.

"You'll meet him," Phillip said. He pictured Markus asking *why in the hell did you bring this man with you?*

"How do you know Alexis?" Liam asked.

Phillip hesitated a moment, then decided what the hell, it didn't help Alexis to keep secrets from anyone who could help. "Trust me, I know her and I know Jobe, too."

"Who the hell are you? What do you people do?" Liam asked. "I've never been close to a terrorist attack before."

Terrorists? Then Phillip understood and said, "Those weren't terrorists. They weren't even people." He glanced at Liam whose blank expression signaled a new slew of questions brewing. "I'll explain in the car."

They caught a cab about a block down from the Marriot. As they pulled away from the curb, Phillip dug his cell phone from his jacket pocket and started dialing Markus's number.

CHAPTER 12

Her father presses his bloody finger to his lips and says, "Shhhhhhh."

Tears sting her eyes, and she nods. She draws her knees up to her chest and wraps her arms around them, squeezing them, trying to make herself smaller, wishing she could disappear.

"Don't come out, Alexis, no matter what you hear," he says. She's never seen him cry before and she hates it; it scares her more than the monsters.

"Okay," Alexis whispers.

Her mother hasn't made a sound for a long time; maybe she escaped. Or maybe she's dead. Alexis squeezes her eyes shut. Daddy said not to cry. If she cries, the monsters will find her.

She doesn't like it in here, but there's nowhere else to go. Her daddy always keeps those big round heavy things in here that he called propane tanks, along with a spare tire and some tools. Alexis barely fits.

His lips contort into a painful smile, and she can see blood in his teeth; a gash in his cheek gapes open like he has another mouth on the side of his face. "I love you, sweet pea. Stay quiet and don't come out, no matter what happens..."

And then he's gone, closing the small door to this cramped little space, leaving her alone, shrouded in darkness, to sit and to listen. She hears the monsters again. She can hear their breathing and the sound of their heavy feet as they pace and plan. They're here to kill us.

That's when the screaming starts. Her Daddy's screaming. Alexis hugs her legs tighter. She doesn't want to cry, doesn't want them to hear her, but doesn't know if she can help it.

Burn them, Alexis.

Her eyes fly open, and she looks at the small door her daddy just closed, a small ribbon of light frames the edges.

Burn them! You know how.

But she's not allowed to. Never to start the fires, never ever. But she knows this is different, she knows this doesn't count. She wants the screaming to stop. She lets go of her legs as her heart thumps madly inside her small body. She wants to burn them and the wanting sparks rage.

She remembers her mommy saying that if she starts the fires, people will come and take her away. This doesn't count, this is different. She crawls toward the small doorway on her hands and knees. She's sweating and dimly aware of the rising temperature as her fury builds.

The screaming stops. Alexis listens. Nothing happens for what seems like forever, and then something hits the door to her hiding place; the hiding place her daddy put her in knowing that he would die. She cries out and clamps a hand over her mouth, trying to stifle the sound. But the monsters heard it.

The door rips away, and she looks into the hideous face that will haunt her for the rest of her life. It peers inside, the snout wrinkled in a snarl revealing teeth dripping with fresh blood. Its ears are laid back against its massive skull.

She stays on her hands and knees, not scrambling back into the corner, not doing anything but glaring into the eyes of the creature she hates. Burn them. Burn them all.

It reaches through the tiny space and grabs her, latching onto her arm, pulling and yanking, and biting. Her fingers and toes tingle and she feels something else, something inside her that she's never felt before, even when she'd started the fires in her secret place in the backyard. Like a weight inside her belly, growing heavy and hot.

The monster stops and gawks at her. It knows. Its snarl fades, and she has a moment to relish the terror in its eyes. When the air ignites, the monster doesn't have time to blink. The fire rockets out like a torpedo, consuming everything.

And as the air around her blazes a furious orange glow, Alexis Jade screams and...

...and the bad memory faded as she awakened.

A rancid smell – air stuffed with a rotten mixture of ammonia and shit. She coughed and when she did, a heavy pain spread through her chest and belly like thick fingers squeezing her insides. The swimmy residue of unconsciousness lingered, and she was unable to move anything except her tongue across dry lips. An instant sting of pain shot through her cheeks as her tongue brushed against warm, swollen flesh. Dried blood caked her teeth.

She was upright, somehow, with her back against a wall. She opened her eyes to a blurry sight of the floor. *I'm hanging.* A crazy thought indeed, but was she? Her head lulled, too heavy to raise, and her sweaty brown hair hung in her face. She tried to wiggle her fingers but couldn't feel them. *Christ almighty...* her arms were bound, stretched out like on a crucifix. Her legs were bound at the knees and ankles, spreading them. She couldn't budge. Her hands and feet were hard asleep, and as she awoke, prickly needles stung her fingers and toes as blood seeped back into them.

She coughed, and it echoed. Her eyes adjusted achingly slow to the dim light. Finally, she saw the ropes wrenched painfully around her thighs, just above her knees, securing her legs to what appeared to be a metal frame of some sort.

"Finally awake, I see," a deep voice, a man's voice, from directly in front of her.

Alexis's first impulse was to shield her body. She pulled weakly against the binding ropes. Everything hurt.

"You were out for nearly three hours." A chuckle, then, "sometimes I don't know my own strength. Plus, I must admit, that I do love hurting the pretty ones. Do you think that makes me less of a man?"

The feeling in her fingers and hands was returning. With some effort, she was able to clench her fists.

"I will tell you from experience, dear one, that the blood of pretty girls *does* taste better. It's like a fine wine, not too bitter, and I think it has a slight sweetness in it – like the succulent taste of a purely aged Vinho do Porto straight from Portugal. I'll bet you will taste so sweet, like the nectar provided by God himself. In fact, I probably won't be able to drink it from you fast enough."

Footsteps scraped on concreate, moving closer, and she anticipated cold hands descending upon her. She squirmed and pulled harder. Nothing gave. She grimaced and summoned the strength to lift her head and found no shock at seeing Michael, his mouth spread in a wide, horrid smile. A lump of revulsion caught in her throat, and she swallowed hard. Her anger sparked. *You sonofabitch!*

"Ah." Michael moved to within a few inches of her face, "you really are beautiful. Those eyes! I see now why Nathaniel said to keep you alive. Men will die to save you. Even the great Markus Blue."

Her mind reeled at the mention of the name... *Markus*. Her savior from the wolves. But Markus Blue died months ago.

"He's dead," she huffed.

Michael chuckled again. His rancid breath wafted into her face, and she twisted her head away to escape it. "*Contraire*, my dear, Markus is very much alive."

Michael's words sank into her mind. Had she been told Markus was dead? She didn't think so; she'd just assumed. If Markus actually *was* alive...

Why would Michael risk bringing Markus to them?

Because they planned this. She was bait. A surge of panic gripped her. Where was Jobe? Were William and Jason in Pittsburg? Was Phillip here yet? Did Liam make it out of the hotel? She was so stupid for bringing Liam into this.

Too many questions, too many errors. Her carelessness may cost them everything.

"Jobe was most powerful," Michael said. He sighed, as if in deep thought. "He underestimated the Legion, however."

Her eyes snapped to Michael. Through clenched teeth, she hissed, "What did you do with him?"

Michael glared at her, then tilted his head, as if perplexed. "Most fascinating," he said and furrowed his eyebrows. "I find your common humanity, that which you share despite your differences, to be beautiful." He gazed past her, his white eyes focused on something unseen, as if in deep thought. "It is what I miss most about being among you if I'm honest. I've nearly forgotten how it felt."

He reached down and lifted something off of the floor, then held it front of her. He cradled Jobe's severed head like a bowling ball. Jobe's mouth hung open, and one of his eyes had rolled back in his head while the other peered lifelessly at her.

Hot vomit lurched into her throat, and she gulped it back, unable to draw enough air to manage even the slightest whimper. Was this her fault? Warm guilt blanketed her, and a single tear streamed down her face. Goddamn this all. Her rage blossomed, and her eyes found Michael's.

"I'm going to kill you," she said. Her taught muscles protruded like ribbons and hate consumed her.

She would ignite everything, free herself, and save Michael for last. She wanted to see his eyes as he burnt. But Michael was not the only one in here with her. Taunting laughter echoed out of the darkness.

They were everywhere. Their presence lurked in dark corners, along the walls, and in the rafters. Their lustful gazes fueled her rage deeper. Their end would be the same as his.

Michael turned his back toward her. She focused all of her energy to her center. The fire would be horrific and relentless, more massive than anything she had done before. Nothing in this place deserved mercy.

Just as she was about to act, a jolt of pain tore through her. Her muscles seized and her jaws clamped shut so hard she nearly broke her teeth. Her head slammed back against metal, and she wanted to scream but couldn't breathe. Her eyes squeezed shut. *I'm dying! Oh god...* anything to stop the pain.

Suddenly, it stopped. She collapsed with exhaustion, held up by the ropes binding her arms. Before another thought registered, a fist slammed deep into her stomach. Pain blossomed inside her like hot lead.

"I would strongly suggest not trying any magic," Michael growled. His cold breath brushed her ear. "As you can tell, the consequences will be most unpleasant." His words resonated as if spoken from another dimension, over a radio barely audible. She tried to gulp air and puked, dimly aware of the wet spats smacking the floor. "Your misery will end shortly as did William's and Jason's, and of course, poor Jobe."

Dread engulfed her. *Christopher... help me!*

But there was nothing. Just an empty void where Christopher's presence had always been.

CHAPTER 13

Markus's phone buzzed, and he swiped the bar to answer it. "Phillip?"

"Where are you?" Phillip asked. "We're on our way."

"In an abandoned building," Markus squinted at a shadowed storefront across the street. "Down by the river across from an Italian restaurant called Roma Campisi's." He hoped he was seeing that right. "Pull up along the street by the river. I'll come out." Markus ended the call and slipped the phone back into the pocket of his overcoat.

He leaned against a concrete pillar and wished there was a place to sit down without having to go all the way to the floor. Getting back up could prove arduous. The sun cresting the horizon created deep shadows and the stench of stale urine hung thick in the air. God knew how many vagrants lurked inside here.

Markus removed one hand from his jacket pocket and rubbed the left side of his chest, right at the bottom of his ribcage. That was the spot. The consistent reminder that not all was right with the world – something growing, consuming... wicked. Foolishly, he still had days when he thought it might go away on its own. Hell, sometimes he thought it *was* going away. Days would pass with no pain at all, and he'd think, *they had it wrong... not cancer at all*. And just as hope sparked, he'd cough, and that discomforting ache would flare and remind him with cruel certainty, that it was there to stay. He'd always envisioned himself laughing in death's face and leaving the world in admiration. A fanciful thought until you stood on the bastard's doorstep and fully understood how beautiful life actually was. How truly wonderful each sunrise could be. And how shockingly fast each minute passed.

If there was one thing Markus had learned, it was that none of us are what we perceive ourselves to be. Big, strong, handsome, courageous beyond all definition... it didn't matter. Once you looked in the mirror at the gray hair and wrinkled face staring back at you, reality hit home. *I'm not ready. Not yet.*

He wanted to be back in Indiana right now, relaxing on that old porch, staring across the green fields and savoring that earthly fragrance of summer. But oh, hell no. Thanks to Christopher, he got to stand in this empty building smelling piss.

Christopher.

Markus had not felt anything from him for hours and prayed that Christopher had somehow found a way out from whatever hell he must have gone through. *As slick as we thought we were, old friend, as great as we thought we were.* Nathaniel had prepared well beyond anyone's anticipation, and it seemed the punches just kept coming.

Buried in his pocket, he caressed the small paper between his thumb and forefinger – the paper with Michael's location jotted roughly by Christopher a few hours ago. Markus had to assume Nathaniel made Michael's location in Pittsburg known. He had to assume also that Nathaniel would count on any strike against his Legion to be in the daytime when it made the most sense to move against a vampire. And lastly, Markus had to assume that Jobe, Alexis, William, and Jason were all dead.

He was alone.

He considered what few options still existed. He could contact the Vatican and request help from the Chasers in Europe. If Christopher was dead, surely the Vatican was aware of it by now. It was his best option. To fight Nathaniel alone at this point would be both irresponsible and stupid with all of the unanswered questions still floating around.

Hence, why Markus's last assumption was that Nathaniel was here in Pittsburg, or soon would be. What was Nathaniel capable of? It was quite obvious he'd figured out how to kill wizards, and very efficiently from the way things were turning out. As Christopher had –

Help me Markus...

Markus's eyes snapped wide as the projection entered his head, like the soft waves of classical music. It was Alexis! Adrenaline surged through his veins. He sensed the pain in her thoughts.

Even though he would never have anticipated it, he found his emotions difficult to contain. Perhaps she meant more to him than he would have ever admitted, or maybe it was simply that he was not alone after all.

As Phillip's cab pulled up to the curb, Markus stepped out of the shadows, utilizing his cane to augment his walk, and into the infant sunlight.

Perhaps this was what the vampires wanted... perhaps it was a trap. It would lure Markus to them. As he clenched his teeth, making his way with heavy footsteps across the wide concrete sidewalk, he decided they would regret ever playing this game with him, and they'd wish to the evil that spawned them that they had never been born.

I am on my way Alexis.

If Alexis died on this day, Markus would not see it – he would be dead first.

CHAPTER 14

Just before the cab stopped to pick up the wiry looking old man...

"Markus is our only chance to get Alexis." Phillip used his hands to animate his words. "I'll explain later how this all ties together, but trust me when I tell you, this shit gets deep. Those things you saw in the hotel last night?" Phillip stared at Liam from his side of the cab.

Liam nodded, feeling as if he were in a dream; caught up in a whirlwind where he may only exist as a character in some bizarre Stephen King novel.

"Vampires. The real thing," Phillip said and wiped his hand across his mouth, then cast his gaze out the window. "Goddamn vampires."

Liam sat there, stunned. His first reaction at hearing *vampires* was to let out a fake laugh, but he couldn't, not after seeing what he saw last night.

"If you know where she is, why aren't we going there now?" Liam asked, feeling a bit nauseated. He didn't know if it was the totality of the situation or the lack of sleep catching up with him.

"Because we need Markus," Phillip shook his head. "Jesus, didn't you listen to anything I just said? And, you were there. You might think of something we can use."

Liam considered this, then asked, "Why not call the police? I mean, if you know where she is."

"How'd that work out for you tonight?" Phillip asked. "Why don't you call them now... dial 911 and inform them that you're fighting vampires and they took your friend."

"I wouldn't tell them *that*. But if she's being held somewhere, I could at least say she's been kidnapped."

Phillip nodded. "You could, but you'd be sending those men and women to their deaths since you can't tell them what they're up against and they wouldn't believe you if you tried."

Liam looked at his hands, out of things to say. Frustrated.

A few awkward seconds passed between them.

Phillip asked as the cab rounded a corner, "Did you get any good looks at what attacked her?"

"I saw three for sure" Liam stated, gazing out the window. "One in the elevator and two in the stairwell. I didn't get a great look at any of them. Alexis jumped in between me and the one in the elevator. It felt like they were everywhere."

Phillip glanced around the inside of the cab, looking nervous. "This whole thing is fucked right now. No one knows what's going on and I can't really explain the whole situation to you without taking two hours to do it. And not knowing if Alexis is alive or not just... I can't think of her hurt. I love her."

A million more questions flooded Liam's brain. Alexis had not mentioned him, Liam was sure of it. Not until she was dragged away.

"Are you and her..." Liam's words faded as he wondered what to ask – *are you a couple, engaged, married?*

"Yes," Phillip said without hesitation. "Not engaged or anything, but we're together. I have the ring. I guess I just always assumed I'd have more time to ask the question."

As the cab halted at a curb, Liam felt tangled up in someone else's life, especially when the strange old man got in on the other side of him and wedged him in the middle.

Liam contemplated just what in the hell he was doing between these two men who obviously knew each other and understood what each other was talking about. The cab skirted corners and weaved in and out of traffic as if late for the last space shuttle leaving a doomed earth. The man named Phillip had told the taxi driver twice that *we're in a hurry and need to get to Federal Street.*

"If Christopher's directions are right, the warehouse will sit off a side street." The old man spoke while looking at a small piece of paper with blue ink scribbled across it. Liam glanced at it, then shifted his focus back to the front, watching where they were going... wherever *that* was.

He wanted to ask questions, dozens of them, but Phillip's explanation on the ride to get the old man still hadn't fully sunk in. Vampires. What in the hell? He expected someone to say *surprise, we're just shittin' ya.*

Had he not seen what he'd seen last night, he might even laugh.

"Drop us off about two blocks from the address I gave you," Phillip said to the cab driver.

The cab driver nodded and said, "Okay."

Liam clasped his hands tightly together. *Oh, what in the Christ am I doing here?* Just stay focused on Alexis... we're going to help Alexis. And he wanted to be part of that. He wanted to be a part of her, despite this new wrinkle of Phillip.

"We have to take advantage of the daylight," the old man said and stared straight ahead.

"Shouldn't we do something now, then?" Phillip seemed surprised.

"We are." The old man lightly tapped his cane on the floorboard. Liam tried to remember what Phillip had said the old guy's name was. Mark, or Mike, something like that.

• • • • •

Remain patient, Markus told himself.

"Did any of them speak to you?" Markus asked Liam who was sitting right next to him, fidgeting with his hands in his lap.

"No. It all happened so fast, I don't think anyone did," Liam said. "Alexis said to find Phillip, that's the main thing I remember."

Phillip's eyes shot to Liam. "Makes sense. She knows me."

Liam shrugged and said, "That's what she said."

Markus shook his head. "Don't get the big-head there, Phillip. She said that because you're a Messenger and Messengers can be reached by civilians."

Phillip didn't respond and Markus was glad for that.

Markus focused his attention back to Liam. "Most likely, those that attacked her didn't care about you and hadn't expected you to be there."

"I'm pretty sure they would have taken me too," Liam said looking at Markus. Markus stared at him, into the depths of a soul who was, from what Markus could ascertain, a good man.

"Oh yes, they would've." Markus tried to smile, but only managed a small curve in his upper lip. "You can thank Alexis that you're not dead right now."

Markus glanced out his window, not caring to see Liam's or Phillip's reaction to his statement. He hoped to god he wasn't making a mistake right now by pursuing Alexis, perhaps becoming too emotionally invested in the outcome and clouding his judgement. There was no plan, no preparation – this whole thing seemed hodge-podge at best. But the vampires wouldn't expect Phillip and Liam. He could only hope that Alexis was being held at this location. The misery in her projection still lingered in his mind like sticky residue.

The cab sped over a bridge, the same one Alexis and Jobe had crossed the day before and barreled down Federal Street. Markus watched the buildings thin out, giving way to houses and older neighborhoods.

Fresh sunlight splashed the clouds as the horizon brightened. Wonderful sun.

"I don't want anyone making any sudden moves once we're out of the taxi," Markus said. "I will tell you what to do and where to go."

Phillip acknowledged with a nod.

Liam sat there, still wringing his hands in his lap. Markus said to him, "You don't need to be part of this." The kid probably wouldn't do much good anyhow, other than being another set of hands, which Markus wouldn't turn down.

"I want to help," Liam said, "Count me in."

Markus smiled and patted Liam's knee. Good man indeed. "I won't lie, I could use your help. I think I can deal with the vampires, but I'm not sure an all-out fight to the death is our best option right now. That's what Nathaniel will be expecting me to do. They'll be waiting for me, but they don't know about either of you. If we can locate Alexis, I'll distract them while you two get her out. Get her into the sunlight. Flimsy, I know, but it's all we've got if we're to act now. I can't risk losing Alexis. A wizard and a witch are much better than a wizard alone."

"A warlock," Phillip said.

Markus shrugged and said, "Magicians."

The cab eased to a stop.

It was time.

CHAPTER 15

A metallic shriek ripped through the space like throttling aircraft engines. Alexis blinked against wind full of tiny wasp stings slinging debris and dirt in a violent swirl. A chair flew across the floor followed by a table that flipped end-over-end and finally fractured into shards. A haze of blue light erupted. Screams, painful and furious, echoed out of the commotion.

Something tore loose from her legs. It fell to the floor and clanked onto the concrete. Someone stood next to her. Not Michael, thank god, but someone else. They had a knife. The effort to move was too painful, and she could do nothing but yield to their mercy.

One of her legs fell loose, swinging and unbound, then the other. There were two people. She blinked again and tried to speak. A dull pain filled her stomach, spreading through her chest. How bad had Michael hurt her? Something was definitely wrong down there. Very wrong. The idea of moving horrified her.

Suddenly her hands were free, falling like dead flesh, her fingers and hands numb. She fell and folded over and into someone's arms. The burn in her belly turned to fire. Her mouth opened, but no sound escaped. Something warm and sticky coated her cheeks and throat. It spilled out of her mouth in a gush and then subsided to a trickle from the corners of her mouth. *Oh god...* she was puking blood. *Stop moving me!*

Another sound erupted inside the warehouse, like crumpling glass and grinding metal. A heavy boom echoed from somewhere, and she dimly saw two dead vampires motionless on the floor, their skin seared black.

Someone yelled, "Don't drop her Liam, she's bleeding."

Liam. Liam, the writer guy who she'd met earlier.

Liam had her in his arms, and he was saving her. Just an ordinary man.

"Markus said we only have three minutes," the voice yelled again. Phillip.

And Markus. Markus Blue was here!

With that knowledge, the darkness engulfed her.

CHAPTER 16

Jesus, she was getting heavy. Liam struggled to keep hold of her.

He lumbered clumsily, his shoes clopping against concrete, doing his best to weave around the old crates, deserted desks, and piles of scrap lumber littered throughout the warehouse. He could barely see, which didn't help a goddamn thing.

Explosions swept past while bursts of blue and green light cascaded above and behind him, creating a strobe effect that made it even harder to reach the side door. A sulfuric, acidy smell infested his mouth and nose and seemed to stick there, like swallowing smoke.

Just keep running... just keep running...

Perhaps worst of all were the wails. Death had come to this place.

Smashing debris and wrenching metal reverberated inside the cavernous building mixed with a whistle of air, moving like a wall of water, blowing apart anything in its path – except for him and Phillip.

Liam focused on Phillip directly in front of him, leading the way to the mouth of this terrible place. Something hit his leg just above his knee, and he thought it might be one of Alexis's arms swinging limp and banging against him. He squeezed her tighter.

Phillip reached the door first and collided against it with his shoulder. Liam plowed into the back of him. He backed up a step and watched helplessly, as Phillip banged his fist against a green button with the word OPEN on the front.

"They won't follow us?" Liam gazed behind him and peered through thick fog. His biceps screamed in protest, but he held on to her, perhaps through sheer terror, he held on.

"Goddamn, this door!" Phillip growled.

We should've left the way we came in, Liam thought.

But the way they came in was a broken window, way in the back. They'd never get Alexis out that way.

Phillip slammed the button again, and this time it triggered the mechanism to lift the overhead door. It hummed to life. Liam stepped back, ready to shoot under as soon as it rose far enough. The heavy door ascended achingly slow, the rusty hinges squeaked and whined as they gave way to the laborious motor heaving it upward.

The door rattled, and as it did, a swath of sunlight bathed the concrete floor, growing wider. Liam nearly cried at the beautiful sight of it.

Finally, after what seemed like eternity, Phillip scuttled underneath. He stopped on the other side and waited, his arms outstretched. Liam bent down, trying not to topple over as Alexis hung limply in his arms. He fell to his knees and hoisted her, as gently as he could, through the opening. The creak of the door springs squealed as the door shuddered and stopped.

Phillip grasped Alexis's shoulders and pulled her out. That was when Liam heard scuffling behind him. He dropped to the floor and scooted out on his belly. He scrambled out into the sunlight, feeling as if he'd stepped into a world made of bizarre stories that might be published in The Unexplained Truth.

Glorious sunlight! Warm and wonderful.

"Get her legs," Phillip yelled at him.

Liam gripped Alexis's legs just below the knees and hoisted her up, so her ankles pressed against his hips. Phillip held her by her arms as they shuffled her off the short concrete platform and together they carried her out into the parking lot. Her head lolled back and her hair dragged against the filthy asphalt.

His heart ached for her. Blood, still wet, soaked her mouth and neck and the front of her shirt. Deep fear settled over him. How bad was she hurt? *We shouldn't be moving her like this.* But it wasn't like they could just stop and call an ambulance.

As they moved farther away, the sounds from inside the warehouse changed from what sounded like a barrage of mortars to a tumultuous rumble. He half expected to wake up right then and find himself asleep in his hotel room thinking he'd just had the weirdest dream of his life.

"There's Markus," Phillip yelled.

A cab raced toward them, the engine revved as it tore across the parking lot, like it intended to run them down. It screeched to a halt and Liam peered through the driver's window, not knowing what he would see: perhaps a dungy cab driver or maybe a pale-faced corpse glaring back at him.

Markus sat in the back-seat, his face crumpled into a frown that seemed to say *why in the hell are you standing there looking at me.*

Phillip found the rear door handle and flung it open. He climbed into the backseat pulling Alexis across his lap.

Liam followed and slammed the door behind him.

"Go," Markus said.

The cab lurched out onto the street and accelerated in the opposite direction of downtown Pittsburg. Alexis lay across their laps; her head on Markus's legs, her body on Phillip's, and her legs on Liam's lap. Liam noticed Markus gently stroking her hair, almost caressing it.

He didn't want to ask where they were going, not yet. The mood wasn't right, like sulking in a hospital waiting-room after someone has just died. He needed to calm down. He stayed quiet and stared out the window as tears stung his eyes.

He hoped to God it was over, that they'd made their escape and soon Alexis would wake up, and they could just go home and get the hell out of Pittsburgh.

PART II

CHARLIE BLACK

CHAPTER 17

Strange how life worked. The older he got, the less he knew. If he glanced back over his life, he had a litany of shit he'd do differently. Like a remorseful father painfully regurgitating horrible words spoken to his children, Markus's time alone with his own thoughts were often filled with regret. He hoped to Christ the decisions he was making now would not become one of them.

It seemed every action sparked a tiny voice inside him crying, *oh, don't do that.*

Not taking Alexis to the hospital; this was the decision he worried most about if he was being honest. He'd led them to one of the Society's 'safe houses' located just inside the Amish country of Pennsylvania. A quaint little cabin totally off the grid, completely hidden, and where Alexis could die if he made the wrong choice in bringing her here.

Don't leave Pittsburg; stay and ensure you kill Michael. Oh, don't do that.

Don't keep a civilian with you; drop him off at the nearest bus stop. Oh, don't do that.

Don't hide Alexis; get her to a hospital. Oh, don't do that.

Markus sipped his coffee and glared out the window. An arrogant old fool who'd believed his own bullshit and relished the hype about how great he was. Except now he was alone, and suddenly he felt smaller, and his failing body only compounded the despair.

Phillip walked in and sat across from him while Liam remained outside on the front porch. The mid-afternoon sun bathed the world in blessed light which he knew everyone relished and appreciated more than ever before. Doesn't take many run-ins with vampires to make a person love the sun.

"I can't believe that guy is still with us." Phillip crossed his arms over his chest and leaned back into the dining chair. The furniture may have been trendy back in the late fifties, but now it looked cheap and out of place. Another reminder of where they were.

"Maybe he can't believe it either." Markus placed his cup on the small, worn dining table.

"Maybe not," Phillip said, "I know I'd haul ass out of here like someone just threatened to cut my balls off."

Markus didn't reply. Perhaps it was their situation and the need to collaborate, or just little statements like that, but Markus was starting to like Phillip.

"How did you know about this place?"

"The Society has a few places like this," Markus said. He watched Liam through a small kitchen window sitting silently on the steps outside with his face resting in his hands.

"I suppose they do." Phillip paused and then said, "What do you think Nathaniel's next move is? Their big plan to kill you didn't work, so they've got to be pissed."

Markus was wondering the same thing. "Assuming that *was* their plan and that we foiled it, I'd think they're hunting us relentlessly right now."

"Any chance you killed Michael?"

"Doubt it." Markus didn't actually know but could make a strong assumption. He'd spent about 30 seconds in that warehouse – enough time to cause mass chaos and then get out. "I took out a few, for sure, but Michael's been around too long. He would have sent his Legion to the slaughter before endangering himself. Their only mistake was expecting me to be alone. So, now that they've lost Alexis, Nathaniel will be furious."

Phillip sat quiet, then asked, "So now what do we do?"

"I'll contact the Vatican; see if we can get help from the Chasers in Europe. They'll have found out about Christopher by now."

Silence stretched between them, each lost in their own thoughts, until Phillip asked, "You haven't contacted them yet?"

"I tried but was unable to reach anyone. I'll try again here in an hour or so." He considered adding that being unable to reach the Vatican was unsettling. He didn't want to worry the others with circumstances they had no control over, but likely Phillip wondered the same thing he did… how bad had things gotten?

The Vatican was like the white house, someone always answered the phone.

Phillip rubbed his eyes. "I'm gonna go talk to Liam and try to explain some of this. I'll check on Alexis while I'm up." He scooted his chair out and stood in a slow stretch. "Let me know if there's anything you need me to do."

"I will, Phillip. I'll call you first thing." Markus took another long sip of his coffee.

He listened to Phillip's footsteps echo on the wood floor, growing distant and finally coming to a halt somewhere in the back; most likely, right outside of Alexis's room.

He shifted uncomfortably in the chair and winced at the grating of his hip. It was like forcing open a rusty hinge. Twenty years ago, he would have stood inside that warehouse, even though he'd walked into the dragon's lair and the dragon had *wanted* him there. It was the fight he'd loved.

"It's the reason, Markus, you're not the leader of the Society," Christopher had once told him. *"Not a shred of talent for diplomacy."*

Christopher. *I miss you, old friend.*

Markus gazed out the window, alone with his own restless thoughts. Phillip had gone outside and stood next to Liam, talking. Markus considered going out to join them. But what would they think? *Ah look, it's the old man again.*

He brought his hand to his chest and placed it against his left side as a dull ache thrummed inside him.

CHAPTER 18

"A lot to take in." Phillip's words were flat, and Liam's immediate thought was *no shit Sherlock*.

Liam said, "You check on Alexis?" He scraped his foot back and forth on the wooden step. Buzzing insects and the distant bark of a dog drifted lazily in the humid air.

Phillip sat down next to him. "I did. She's fine. Still sleeping."

Liam nodded. "That's good." He gazed out into the lush green landscape of an open pasture. He *hoped* that was good. She needed a doctor. Period. Why the old man insisted they come here, he didn't know, but for damn sure, nothing about this felt right. She could die lying in there.

"Ya know," Phillip said, "We couldn't have gotten her out if you hadn't been there to help." Phillip's voice sounded tired but genuine.

Liam flipped his head toward Phillip and wrinkled his eyebrows. "I feel like I just stepped into the goddamn Twilight Zone. Hell, I don't even know if *you're* the good guys."

Phillip shrugged. "Fair enough. But for what it's worth, we *are* the good guys. And Markus knows what he's doing by coming here."

"So what if she dies or gets worse?"

Phillip didn't answer, and that pissed him off more.

"She's your fiancée or girlfriend, or whatever the fuck, and it doesn't bother you she could be dying in there?" They'd already had this conversation on the way here ending with Markus's declaration, *we're hiding her, and that's final.*

Phillip's lips pressed to a thin line, and he rubbed a hand through his hair. "Of course, it does," he said, "What kind of dumb-ass question is that? But if they find her, it'll make things worse. Don't you get it?"

Liam couldn't read Phillip at all. The sonofabitch better not be reading his mind either. He thought of saying that, then bit the words off.

After a few calming seconds, he said, "Look... yesterday I was a writer doing a story for a stupid tabloid called The Unexplained Truth. I met Alexis, we talked, I liked her, and the next thing I know, these..." Liam hesitated, grasping for the right word, still refusing to say vampire, and finally settled for, "...*things* are coming after us. The place catches on fire, and then Alexis and that other guy are drug off, and I never see them again."

Phillip maintained an irritating silence.

"Until you show up. And now here we sit at some old house in the middle of bum-fucked Egypt. Alexis is hurt and now that I know you and her..." his words trailed off. He didn't want to finish it. Finally, he just said, "Maybe I just don't know why I'm here."

The dark circles under Phillip's eyes seemed deeper. "Maybe just in the wrong place at the right time." A weak smile touched Phillip's lips.

"Lucky me." Liam's knees ached, and his eyelids weighed ten pounds. He needed sleep. Hell, they all did. What he *really* wanted was to go whisk Alexis away from here; to take her somewhere safe. It was as if the woman he met last night and the woman she actually was were two different people. He'd only known her a short bit, but he honestly couldn't see her with someone like Phillip. It seemed more and more that Phillip's relationship with her was only in Phillip's head. How much truth was in that, he didn't know, but that's what he thought.

He pictured his empty apartment back in Houston - the microwave dinners sitting in the freezer and the TV shows he would normally watch on Saturday evenings. Odd, but that almost seemed like a different life now. This was Saturday, his favorite writing day, and he'd normally spend several hours working on his novel and then maybe go have a beer somewhere near the Galleria. Perhaps it was a mundane existence, both uneventful and boring, but at least it was consistent, no vampires running around.

"Let me ask you something," Liam crossed his arms and leaned back against the railing. "Would you let me go if I wanted to leave?"

It took Phillip longer to answer than he'd hoped. "I think we would." Phillip shrugged. "I don't know why not. But I'd like to explain a few things. Will you give me that much?"

A spark of curiosity ignited and Liam rested his chin on his hands. "Go for it. This should be a hoot." Yes, a hoot for sure. *I think we would.* What the hell did that mean? But, however foolish, Liam wanted to hear this. He yearned to know this story.

Phillip leaned back with his elbows propped on the step behind him. "Basically, this is a war."

Liam raised his eyebrows. *Great hook.*

"I know this sounds unbelievable, but like I said earlier, those things you saw last night were vampires. They were in the warehouse too, even though you and I really didn't see them."

Liam recalled the scuttling noises approaching him just before he'd crawled under the door. He shivered.

"They were expecting Markus to come alone. And they weren't expecting Markus to leave so quickly, and they weren't expecting us – me and you." Phillip flipped his finger back and forth between them. "It was a trap set by Nathaniel and Michael to kill Markus."

"Who's Michael and Nathaniel?"

"They're the leaders of the Legions."

"Legions?"

Phillip shook his head and said, "Damn. Okay, so If you knew of all the things that actually exist in this world: vampires, werewolves, demons... you'd shit yourself. If those things had free run of the earth, I doubt the human race would have progressed much past the middle ages. But in addition to the bad things like vampires, there are wizards, witches, and even warlocks. Warlocks are the most powerful."

"Markus is a warlock?" Liam asked. He recalled their conversation in the cab earlier where Markus had said *magicians* after Phillip called him a warlock.

Phillip nodded. "Yep. They're also the rarest."

"Why don't they have wands and spells? Don't they need that?"

"Sort of," Phillip said. "This ain't Harry Potter, so they're not running around pointing sticks, but conjuring magic does require some finesse; sometimes they do say the ancient Latin words. It's more *within* them than anything."

Liam smiled but stayed quiet. He didn't know whether to laugh at this or to believe it completely. He teetered toward the latter.

"On occasion, a very rare occasion, someone is born with all of the gifts combined. They are like super-wizards, and they're pretty much unstoppable."

"Warlocks," Liam said. Several things made sense. The reason they had to pick up Markus before going to the warehouse, the reason Markus was in charge, all of this made sense and Markus being a warlock seemed the only logical explanation. If a person bought all of this, of course.

"Yes, warlocks. There are two known living warlocks in the world, one is a man named Christopher, the leader of the Society, and the other is

Markus Blue, the old man inside the house there." Phillip paused a moment, staring off as if lost in deep thought. "Actually, there's only one. Christopher was killed last night."

Liam let the silence hang between them until Phillip started talking again.

"The Society and Chasers are one in the same. Pretty stupid names if you think about it. You'd think it would be something fancier, but it isn't. The Chasers organized themselves in Europe well over 500 years ago to combat the vampires. They were, and still are, governed by The Vatican and solely at the Pope's discretion. I'm not positive, but I think there are about six wizards that belong to the chasers. The Society is the Chaser equivalent in the United States, but still under the Vatican's thumb. We had eight wizards up until a couple of weeks ago. Now, counting Alexis, we're down to two."

"Jesus," Liam said. The need to stay hidden made sense now. "How many vampires are there?" Liam asked.

Phillip shrugged. "Hell if I know. They're only allowed to live in designated areas in Europe. The chasers keep tabs on them. During the Slovene War, hundreds of years ago, it was evident that The Vatican couldn't kill all of the vampires since they can spread like cockroaches, which can lead to the formation of Legions. That war lasted for well over a century until The Vatican got an idea to compromise. They allowed the vampires to exist without being hunted as long as they stayed within their given territory. The vampires agreed, I guess deciding a life without being hunted may allow them to indulge in the one true gift a vampire savors... immortality.

"It was also agreed between The Vatican and the vampires that the existence of a Legion was forbidden. A Legion is a pack of vampires spread from one source and allows them to think as a collective mind. Put mildly, a Legion is probably the single most threatening force in the world. A vampire cannot overcome a wizard since vampires don't possess magic. Most of them don't anyway. But, a Legion can kill wizards due to their numbers and their collective thought process."

Markus's voice from behind them was rough and scratchy, "The key word used there is *most* when referring to vampires as having no magic." He hobbled over next to them, leaning heavily on his driftwood cane.

For Liam, the sight of Markus, his gray hair sweeping away from those icy blue eyes, brought everything home.

CHAPTER 19

Within the darkness, heavy breathing makes the space smaller. The hoarse rasps fill every void down to the last molecule and turns the blackness into a living entity.

It is the wolves.

Alexis knows she is dreaming but cannot stop the rising fear clutching her heart. I have to open my eyes, this is not real. But it is real, they are here, and she cannot see them. Their claws cut through the blackness, grazing past her face. She feels the whoosh of air, and she crouches.

Then silence

Her dream-world shifts and a comforting aroma settles around her, and she brings a trembling hand to her mouth to stifle a cry. It is the smell of Brut aftershave, and it shrouds her in familiarity. Her tears begin to flow.

"What do you have planned today, sweet pea?" Her daddy's voice. She reaches into the darkness, grasping for his hand.

"Me and mommy are going to do her scrapbook." She's little, six-years-old again, and she sits perched on the edge of the marble sink. Her daddy is shaving, staring into the mirror with white stuff smeared over his chin and cheeks.

"Sounds fun. Are you putting together our vacation pictures?" He presses the razor to his face and scrapes down, clearing a path in the white stuff. She wonders what it might taste like. He rinses the blades under the faucet and then returns for another swipe. This is their routine. Always.

"Yes. Are you leaving Daddy?" Alexis stares up at him. She wonders why she asked him that question and knows something is wrong. Terribly wrong.

Don't answer.

He splashes water on his face and dabs it dry with a towel. "I'm afraid I have to, sweet pea. They killed me a long time ago, remember?" He glances at her and smiles.

"Don't go, Daddy." She cries and his sad eyes prompt despair. He picks up a small, green bottle that is semi-transparent and tips it, so the narrow top spills clear liquid into his hands. Brut Aftershave.

"Oh baby, please don't cry. I didn't come here to hurt you." He sets the bottle down on the counter and briskly rubs his hands together. Then he slaps both his palms to his cheeks. "I just wanted to see you and to tell you something."

She can't speak. The wolves are here. Their presence lurks just out of sight, and she clutches at his arm. She wants him to embrace her like he always used to.

Within the blackness, the husky rasps turn to low growls. She is somewhere dark and scary.

This isn't real.

Of course, it isn't. I'm dreaming this.

She knows she is not a little girl. Her father isn't here. Neither is she in a dark space where the wolves are pressing in on her. The wolves are dead.

"Be mindful of the man who helps you." Her father's words fade like losing a radio station. His presence shimmers. The bathroom shrinks, and she realizes it is moving away. "He will betray you, Alexis. He doesn't know it, but he will."

The image deflates to a single, white dot and then disappears with a small pop!

The wolves surround her on the cliffs, in the trees, swarming like locusts. She stands in a familiar meadow, backed up against the cold rock of an overhanging cliff. Nowhere to run. They seem to anticipate her every move and have overcome her power with sheer numbers.

This was her battle four years ago.

She screams and ignites the earth, surrounding herself in a ring of fire, but still, they come. Too many. Even on fire and dying, they press forward, almost within reach now, she can hear their snapping jaws and painful howls. She has underestimated them. She should have killed them when she had the chance a short while earlier while still in the tunnels.

As the first scarred and hideous faces penetrate her fire, within inches of her skin, she accepts her fate in a wail of contempt.

She closes her eyes as their claws and gnashing teeth descend upon her.

Then the world fills with a slow rumble that builds to a roar of air that sweeps past her, extinguishing her fire. The wolves howl as she opens her eyes to see them flailing back, their hairy bodies torn apart, their mouths ripped open, and their eyes exploding in their sockets. Her hair whips around her face, but she is unharmed as the wolves explode in a cascade of blood and bone.

Within seconds, it is all over, and she stands gasping with her back against the cool rock. She glances around her, amazed she is alive.

Her eyes spot a figure standing at the top of the cliff, dark and motionless, leaning on a driftwood cane and staring down at her. It is the warlock. Markus.

Her eyes snapped open to a dimly lit room with a dirty ceiling. A light-cover hung loosely over an unlit light bulb. Alexis squinted as sunlight filtered through the window at the edge of the room. She was in a bed, but where? A dresser stood against the far wall with a soft ticking clock perched on top.

Her chest ached something fierce. What time was it?

Things came to her in spurts.

Jobe was dead. The warehouse. The electric shocks. Phillip. Phillip was there. And Liam.

And Markus Blue.

She tried to sit up but froze when a jolt of pain shot through her stomach and settled in her chest like a hot iron, making her feel dizzy. Words stuck in her head, though she couldn't remember for sure who'd said them.

He will betray you. He doesn't know it...

CHAPTER 20

"Vampires and Wizards have lived in relative harmony for centuries," Phillip explained to Liam. "But on occasion, one breaks the rules and has to be dealt with. The vampires have their own council, which the Vatican works with."

Markus cleared his throat. "The vampire council is notified about all issues and courses of action. It was part of the truce made in 1656."

"Ah," Phillip said, "There you have it."

Markus hesitated, then said, "Every member of that council was found murdered three weeks ago in Germany. The obvious assumption is that Nathaniel is behind it." Markus glared out across the pasture. Now more than ever, the murdered vampire council felt like the pivotal shift in their world, the unbalancing of power.

He didn't need to look at Phillip to feel the pup's eyes on him. "Yes, Phillip," Markus said, "Christopher did not divulge that information to you or anyone for fear of it landing in the hands of the wrong people. But, it's what prompted him to send you to get me."

"Nathaniel again? Who is Nathaniel?" Liam asked.

Markus glanced at Phillip who was staring back at him, likely waiting to see if Markus would answer the question. Perhaps it made the most sense to just fill in the holes and correct the things Phillip screwed up. He didn't come out here to be the center of attention, but oddly, he wanted the company.

He waved a hand at Phillip; a *you-go-ahead* gesture, and listened.

Phillip said, "Well first, let me tell you what the Society is, it'll make more sense that way."

"Oh yeah… forgot about that." Liam leaned back against the step behind him.

"So the Vatican is the big cheese in all of this. They pretty much run everything. In the early1800s, it became evident that the United States was a perfect place for rogue vampires to hide and, since the only mode of travel across the ocean at that time was about a month on a ship, it would take a shitload of time for any Chasers to get here. And if the vampires knew that, they may start creating Legions."

"Once a Legion has been formed, it can be hard to destroy," Markus added in.

Phillip nodded. Although this was a great history lesson, Markus wanted to get to the shit that mattered. He folded his hands together, leaned on the porch railing, and waited.

Phillip continued, "The Vatican placed a man named Zacharia Black in the United States. Zacharia was a warlock. He found other wizards and witches and was eventually sanctioned as his own organization that he called The Society. The name stuck."

Liam shifted in his seat, placed his elbows on his legs, and looked at Markus. Markus felt the young man's eyes crawling over him but didn't return the glance. He kept his gaze forward, listening, and letting Phillip lead the discussion on this one. By god, Phillip wasn't doing bad at all at telling the story, and Markus saw no reason to interrupt.

"Nathaniel is the oldest living vampire that we know of. He's lived in Germany for centuries and was forbidden, both by his own council and by the Vatican, to leave the country. However, a few weeks ago, no one knows for sure when, he left Germany. There are rumblings of Legions being formed in England. We believe there is a Legion here as well and that he is the creator of those Legions."

"How many?" Liam asked.

"Possibly more than one." Phillip nodded as he spoke.

"Twelve," Markus said.

"Twelve?" Phillip's mouth fell open. "You're shitting me?"

Markus didn't know whether Phillip was shocked that the number was so high or if he was embarrassed for not knowing. "There were some items that were best kept confidential – once again, we didn't want Nathaniel to know how much we knew."

"Not sure why *that* was kept a secret." Phillip's words had an edge, and frankly, Markus understood. Perhaps they shouldn't have kept any information from him.

An awkward silence hung on the breeze.

Liam asked, "How do you find a Legion and how many vampires are in them?"

Phillip tilted his head to Markus.

Markus said, "Depends. If a ceremony occurs in different parts of the country or the world, then one can reasonably assume it is two separate Legions. But, if the rituals are occurring in close proximity, then the most logical assumption is that it is the same Legion, making itself larger. As far as how many vampires are in a Legion, there's no specific number. The term Legion has always been used since one can assume it's at least one-hundred." Markus finished the sentence and began fumbling in his jacket pockets.

Phillip asked, "What are you looking for?"

"My cigarettes."

"I didn't know you smoked."

"I don't."

"Ah."

•   •   •   •   •

The screen door creaked open, and they all turned to look. Markus inhaled a drag from his KOOL cigarette and then removed it from his lips with wrinkled and calloused fingers. *Holy shit.*

Alexis stood in the doorway, her eyes squinting, adjusting to the sunlight, and her hair was askew and matted to her face on the left side. She had a large, purple bruise under her right eye and appeared unable to stand up straight, leaning heavily on the doorframe, favoring her left side. Markus noticed the red, raw rope burns on her wrists and a surge of anger flared within him.

Markus clapped his cane against the porch. "Someone get her a chair, you goddamn idiots."

Both Liam and Phillip scrambled to their feet.

"I'm surprised to see you up," Markus said. He'd never tell her, or anyone, the relief washing through him at the sight of her. Goddamn, he'd been worried. "How's the stomach?"

She shrugged. "I've felt better. How long have I been asleep?"

"About a day and a half. You need to stay off your feet."

He couldn't read the look on her face; either surprise that she'd been asleep so long, or perhaps the pain she was in. He still didn't like that she was up moving around. She'd puked blood for Christ's sake. What the hell even caused that?

"A weird dream woke me up." Her voice was scratchy like she'd just swallowed sand. Liam gently grasped her elbow, ready to assist.

"That happens." For a brief moment, Markus forgot he was dying. He loved those moments. He flipped his cigarette out into the yard. It tasted like shit anyway.

"What are you guys doing out here?" She hobbled forward, placing a timid foot onto the porch.

Phillip gawked at her, and said, "We were just bringing Liam up to speed."

Markus watched Alexis's eyes dart from Phillip to Liam and then settle there like they'd just discovered the right combination of letters to form an elusive word.

Liam hooked one arm around her. She smiled, though Markus swore it was forced. "I just want to sit on the bench. I needed some fresh air."

"Okay," Liam said. The two of them shuffled toward a small wooden bench against the wall of the house, a few feet from where Markus stood.

Markus discreetly waved his hand in a small arc in front of him, a movement no one noticed, but Alexis seemed to relax, and he was positive her grimace dissipated, not entirely, but enough to know he had eased her suffering as much as he could. He wrapped a thick ribbon of energy around her body, holding her. If Alexis had fallen at that moment, she would never have hit the ground. Not because of Liam—though Markus was quite positive the man would have made every attempt to catch her—but because she would simply have levitated in mid-air, held up by an invisible cloud of protection.

CHAPTER 21

Charlie Black hid in the ceiling rafters, wedged deep into the shadows. He wished he could melt into the wood. He shivered and prayed to God in heaven that the two men wouldn't see or hear him. They'd killed Father Nead and Mrs. Baker. Charlie willed himself to stay still. *Just don't move... just don't move...*

The tall man in the robe, freakishly tall, scared him most of all. His deep voice echoed lifelessly, "This is most disappointing, Michael."

"Markus didn't stay." The other man wore an old Army jacket, like one from the history books in Mrs. Ward's class. "He was only there a moment. He had others with him."

They strode side-by-side down the center of the church. The tall man limped and the side of his robe was charred black as if he'd plucked it from a fire. They stopped in front of the pulpit and stared up at the large crucifix with the body of Jesus hanging in frozen pain.

It kept getting colder. *Stop shivering... please stop shivering...*

He'd hidden in this spot before, last summer so he wouldn't have to mow the church lawn. Today, however, he was hiding to save his own life, and he prayed those men would leave soon. At fourteen-years-old, he was still limber enough to stay crammed in this space longer than most adults, but even youth had its limits.

"So," the tall man said, "after so much infallible execution, we find ourselves in a conundrum."

"Indeed." The Army man nodded. Charlie's skin crawled as he stared down at them. The tall man's face was shadowed by a hood draped over his head, but the Army man was in plain sight. His pale skin stretched over his skull, enunciating the dark eyes and the man's mouth seemed oddly misshapen. It was like staring at a picture of someone you knew yet finding the jaw too large or the eyes too big. A mimic of what it once was, perhaps, yet wrong in some profound and creepy way.

The tall man said, "We needed to kill the warlocks, most importantly, we had to do that. Our failure to dispatch them troubles me a great deal."

The Army man cleared his throat. "Nathaniel, if I may suggest, Markus is old and is surely close to dying, even without our interference. Perhaps it would behoove us to wait for that."

The tall man remained still, as if contemplating, and Charlie wished he hadn't of forgotten his phone at home. He always felt so disconnected when he didn't have it. He could be taking pictures of this.

Finally, the tall man, Nathaniel, stepped toward the front of the church and bowed his head as if in silent prayer. "Perhaps. But how much damage can they do until then? And Conclave to elect a new Pope is less than ten days away. Plus, we have another issue to contend with." Nathaniel's voice echoed in the cavernous space of the church sanctuary. "The warlock, Christopher, escaped from my grasp."

Charlie carefully shifted his position trying to stretch out his legs. He placed both hands onto a rafter that ran steeply up the angle of the ceiling and pushed his left leg out as far as he could without the risk of making noise or falling off. His eyes darted at the floor where Father Nead's body lay cold. He swallowed dryly and gawked at the bloody hole in Father Nead's chest where the tall man had torn him open and ripped out his heart. He'd watched in silent horror as the tall man, Nathaniel, bit into the plump, dripping hunk of meat.

"I wasn't aware that Christopher was alive," Michael said.

"He fled like a coward," Nathaniel spat the words. "He proved to be more resourceful than I had anticipated."

"How did he escape?"

"Does it matter? The witch, Alexis Jade, she escaped from you with the assistance of a warlock and were you any more effective at preventing that?" Nathaniel's voice rose on this last sentence, echoing ominously.

Michael shifted his gaze to the floor.

"We must pursue them." Nathaniel turned toward Michael, his expression hidden by the dark cloak of his hood. "We're close to them; I sense it."

"But we have the upper hand, Nathaniel, if we simply..."

"We have nothing!" Nathaniel roared.

"We have killed all but three!" Michael's voice thundered. "Alexis may be dead already. Markus is old and will die soon. You have destroyed their home! Let them make their puny attempts to pursue us. We'll kill them, one by one! I will…"

Nathaniel struck Michael across the chest. Michael crashed through the wooden pews and collided violently with an enormous pillar that ran from the floor to the ceiling. The entire building rumbled, and Charlie tightened his grip on the wooden beam. *Oh my God!*

Thick dust drifted lazily from the ceiling, settling amongst the destruction strewn across the floor.

Nathaniel's voice tore through the aftermath. "You goddamned fool! You have clearly never fought a Warlock!"

Eerie silence settled into the church. Nathaniel turned back toward the hanging Christ. Michael stumbled to his feet and hobbled back to the front, a snarl frozen on his face. Charlie expected a fight to break out and he didn't want to be here for that. Truth be known, he hated it when real fights broke out around him, even a school. Perhaps just the shock of it all. But Michael did nothing except stop obediently next to the tall man and remained still.

"For centuries I've lived." Nathaniel sounded mournful. "I have witnessed mankind's dismal existence, I've watched the destruction of entire civilizations, I've stood by silently as the dawn of time changed the face of the world. And in all of this time, I have waited patiently for the allusive answer to my most basic question… what is my purpose?"

Michael glanced around the room as Nathaniel spoke.

"I have dreamed for ages of a world where I could walk free among the living and provide their feeble lips one chance to grace the skin of my passing hand. My gift to mankind is immortality. But my Lord speaks to me now, Michael, as he has spoken to me for over a century. And do you know what he says?"

Michael cast his gaze back to the floor, staying quiet. Charlie knew that if it were him down there, he sure as heck wouldn't say anything either.

Nathaniel said, "He tells me to go forth and attain the role He has bestowed upon me. He tells me that I am to rule over this earth and He pours his blessings upon my brow, and He demands that I go about my Father's work. *His* work. He is my Father, Michael. My cup filled with His blood runneth over."

The words seeped into Charlie's mind with odd familiarity. He'd heard similar things spoken since he was a child by Father Nead, and even by his own father. It was as if the wrongness of everything here continued to escalate and whoever this was, *whatever* this was, stood at the center of it.

Nathaniel turned to Michael. "I am meant to rule, Michael, that is my destiny, and I mean to fulfill it. God ordains me. I have no end and no beginning. This is our time! But we have our enemies as well. We must destroy them or risk never attaining greatness that is within our grasp."

Michael asked, "How should we proceed?"

"Unleash the Legions. Lead them, Michael, as I will lead them. Mankind has outgrown myth – it has been replaced by their faith in technology. But I have outlived all of them and can attest to their greed. Many will join us."

"And what of the warlocks and the witch?"

"We must prepare. Tell the wolves to remain vigilant, they cannot have gone far. And we must be ready to strike relentlessly when they rear their spineless heads. Go now."

"As you wish." Michael strode briskly between the splintered pews and burst through the large doors of the church.

•　　　•　　　•

After what seemed like a silent eternity, Nathaniel started talking to himself. His voice echoed softly. Charlie thought Nathaniel might be praying, but wasn't sure. He just wished the guy would leave. He knew, with absolute certainty, that he could not stay wedged in this spot all day.

Charlie's gaze crawled to the center of the church, and he saw one leg, plump and covered in dark pantyhose, protruding from beneath a large sheet of wood that tore from the wall when Nathaniel had smashed her against the upper portion of the balcony. Mrs. Baker, the lady who arrived every Saturday afternoon to vacuum the floors and dust the furniture, had barely acknowledged Nathaniel's entry when the terrible man had seized her neck and tossed her, as a child might throw a toy. As soon as Mrs. Baker landed with a heavy thud onto the floor, Charlie jumped into his hiding spot, his heart thundering in his chest and a scream stifled behind a fist thrust hard against his mouth.

That felt like hours ago. Maybe it was.

"Christopher and Markus," Nathaniel spoke to himself at the altar. "I will find you."

The devil had come to the small town of Pheasant Hill, Pennsylvania, where nothing ever happened, where the front page of the local newspaper rarely contained anything more dramatic than a lost dog or a stolen bicycle. And the nightmare was not over, not by a long shot.

Minutes ticked by with cruel slowness, and still, Nathaniel mumbled. Outside, the sun darkened, giving way to what would have been, under any other circumstances, a beautiful evening. The fireflies would begin to flicker soon and the local movie theatre, showing some cartoon flick that Charlie didn't care to see, would be opening. Of course, that would have been under normal circumstances.

As it was, Charlie heard something outside that was even more disturbing than what he'd witnessed here. It was people screaming, muffled by the walls and windows of the church. People were dying out there. The chaos grew, and as it did, the cacophony of death seeped deeper into the stone walls. Gunshots. Sirens.

And something else. A moan, low and steady.

Fat tears swelled in Charlie's eyes, and as he stared at Nathaniel, he wondered if the carnage outside was Michael. The Legions they'd talked about maybe? It must be. Had to be. Legions of what?

Markus and Christopher... who were they and could they help him... dear God, could anyone help him?

CHAPTER 22

I think I want to fall in love with her. Liam sat with his arm around Alexis's shoulders, savoring the feel of her body leaned against him. He'd stopped demanding she see a doctor. She said it looked worse than it was and that the blood she'd vomited was not from her stomach but from the bleeding in her mouth where Michael had struck her while still in the hotel stairwell. She said, *I think I'll be fine*, but Liam caught a slight grimace on her face as she'd said it.

Markus leaned on the rail of the porch. A small framed old man, but Liam found himself captivated by his presence.

Trying to digest the reality of real-life wizards, warlocks, and vampires was equivalent to understanding the mathematical formula to relativity. Despite how ludicrous it all sounded, Liam found he was fascinated with Alexis, Phillip, and Markus. Maybe he'd finally cracked up and totally lost it. Didn't that happen to writers sometimes? But my god, what a fantastic story this would make!

Markus had called this place *Amish country*. How convenient that they had this hidden house stuck out here. Who in the hell thought of that? It was nice though, and in the silence, Liam pondered what he'd been told. A few things, actually a *lot* of things, still didn't make sense. Perhaps some of them never would.

He peered up at Markus and debated if asking a question was appropriate. Surely they expected him to have questions. "So vampires have killed nearly all of the wizards?"

"From what we know, yes." Markus faced him.

"How many wizards were there?"

"Four wizards have been killed," Markus said. "Jobe, Jason, William, and Jonathan. And one warlock, which was Christopher. That leaves me and Alexis for the Society."

"How many vampires?"

"Not sure, maybe hundreds, depending on the Legions."

"Two wizards against hundreds of vampires? That doesn't sound good."

"True enough," Markus said.

"So if you die, and not saying you will, but if you do, there are no more warlocks? And there are no more wizards, except for Alexis?"

"It would be safe to say we were caught with our pants down." A dry smile spread across Markus's face, and he glanced down at his feet. "I most certainly *will* die since I am an old man."

No one on the porch spoke. Everyone stared at Markus thoughtfully. Even Alexis raised her head. Liam wished he had not brought it up.

Markus glanced back up at them, looking first at Phillip and then to Liam. "But, I think those are my worries and not yours. For now, I feel fine, or as fine as a man can feel at my age. No guarantees though."

Liam stared into those icy blue eyes that pierced something deep inside him, deeper than his soul, as if he were the only person on earth right now and Markus was not something greater than a mere human being.

"It is not that there are no wizards. They're not a dime a dozen, but they are out there, usually born, as I said before, with the ability to summon magic. There is no pattern to it; it's as random as a tornado. The challenge is finding them. One has to be mindful and look for signs. Believe it or not, many of the cheap tabloids sitting at the magazine stands can provide a lead to someone."

Ha, Liam thought, *someone actually does read that shit. And with a purpose!*

"We got Alexis from an orphanage in Nevada. We read a story in a newspaper, a small clip really, that told of a young girl who could start fires out of nothing. The story told of how she believed her parents were killed by werewolves. Christopher read it and went immediately to meet her. She was just seven-years-old then, and her parents had no magic, at least not that anyone knew of."

Alexis stirred slightly against Liam's side but remained silent.

"Had that story never been printed, we may never have known about her. There are others, I'm sure. But we haven't found them. It doesn't take a great number of wizards to keep vampires under control, but seven was the lowest number of wizards we've ever had in the Society."

A disquieting pause lingered for a moment – a moment in which an uneasiness crept into Liam's thoughts, or perhaps more of a realization, that of everyone here, he, himself, was capable of nothing.

"Jobe was a warlock." Markus's words spilled out as if spoken into a closet, they just hung there and were absorbed by the group around him.

"But he…" Phillip began, he sounded surprised.

"Was killed by the vampires," Markus finished. "Yes, I am quite aware of that, Phillip. Jobe was also inexperienced."

"How come no one knew he was a warlock?" Phillip asked.

"You mean how come *you* didn't know," Markus shot Phillip a look. "Christopher had not given Jobe the official title yet. If you look it up in a dictionary, warlocks are evil. Sorcerers, some call them. With great power one must be trained and groomed, that's what Christopher was doing with Jobe."

Liam pulled Alexis closer to him, hugging her. He noticed out of the corner of his eye, Phillip staring at them. This was so goddamn weird.

"I just can't believe this is all really happening," Liam said. "Wizards, vampires, warlocks… I mean, Jesus Christ."

Alexis's hand moved to his leg, just above his knee and rested there. "I'm glad you're here."

Really, he thought, *because I'm not so sure I am*. What value could he possibly contribute? Witches, Warlocks… and the powerless man named Liam. What the hell would he do against vampires… throw rocks at them?

"I'm gonna go take a nap." Phillip stepped up onto the porch and moved to the door. "I'm so damn tired I can't think straight." He hurried past and went inside.

Liam felt like he'd caught a second wind. He knew he was tired, knew he needed to get some rest, but found himself more alert now than he was an hour ago. "So now what do we do?"

"I wish I knew for sure." Markus rested against the pillar of the porch.

"Will Nathaniel come after us?"

"I would think so, yes," Markus said, "but the reality is, he doesn't have to. He could slip off and wait me out, knowing that I will die soon."

"Great." Liam stared out into the pasture. The thought of Markus not being here was terrifying. "I wish I could help. Doesn't any of that stuff from the old stories work – silver bullets, crucifixes, garlic… stuff like that?"

"Certainly," Markus said, "But, last I checked, I can't shit silver bullets, and I'm not really sure the crucifix thing actually works." Markus seemed to think seriously about that for a moment, then said, "Hell, I don't know, maybe it does. But, we *do* have an advantage… Nathaniel doesn't know where we are. At least, I don't think he does."

"What will he do next if he can't find us?"

Markus opened his mouth to speak when his phone chirped in his coat pocket. He dug it out and stared at the face with a slight scowl. "The Vatican," he said, "You should go in and get some rest. I'll wake you in a while." And with that, Markus swiped the phone and said, "This is Markus."

As Markus hobbled off the porch, down the steps, and into the open lawn with the cell phone pressed to his ear, Alexis sat up and attempted another smile.

"We should go inside," she said and strained to stand up.

Liam slipped his arm around her back. He helped her to her room and to her bed where she lay down carefully, grimacing until her back was flat on the covers.

"You can lay with me." Her eyes were barely open, but her hand gripped Liam's wrist. Of all the places he could be right now, being here with her felt shockingly right.

He moved to the other side of the bed and carefully laid down next to her, placing one arm awkwardly under her head. He longed for everything about her; the scent of her, and even the sound of her breath as she lay next to him. He caressed her arm and closed his eyes, praying that she was okay and wondering if this was going anywhere. The thought of Phillip popped into his head, but he was asleep before it could materialize into anything that mattered.

CHAPTER 23

This small space, tucked under the barn, was designed specifically for why Christopher now occupied it – hiding. The aroma of hay, tainted with rat droppings and dust, infested the air. Long, yellow strands of loose straw lay spread over the floor and under his legs. Most troubling was the rhythmic splat of blood squeezing through his bandage and dripping onto the wooden floor. *Splat... splat... splat...*

He thought it might be slowing down. He hoped.

His chill was to the bone, and the shivering wouldn't stop. He may have lost too much blood already, though he had no way of knowing anything for sure. Continuing down the path of death may actually be the easiest thing to do right now. Anything else would waste valuable energy that could be better spent savoring his last moments.

Through clattering teeth and a rising nausea, he wondered if the sun was still up. *Probably be raining outside, just my luck*, and at that thought, even in his misery, a faint but detectable smile touched his lips.

He shifted his feet, trying to get more comfortable, but achieved little more than wishing he hadn't tried to move to start with. He leaned his head back against a wooden beam. His side hurt and the horrible throb in his arm pushed him dangerously close to passing out. During his fight with Nathaniel *(how long ago... a day... two days?)*, the evil bastard had seized his arm and nearly torn it off as easily as snapping a branch from a rotted tree. He'd felt the sickening rip deep in his flesh.

Don't pass out, he kept repeating it until the dizziness either passed or let up enough so that he could think. Sometimes he spoke out loud, keeping his voice low. For a while, he'd heard *them* shuffling inside the barn above him, searching. There'd been nothing for a while, though. Maybe they'd given up and left. It was one thing to die facing your enemy. But to die slowly, like a wounded deer in the forest, in a hidden room where no one may ever find you, sparked dread that seemed worse than hiding with his arm torn to shreds. Much worse.

"Keep awake, old buddy," Christopher said to himself. Markus knew about this room and the tunnel from the house. He'd helped build it. Markus would find him... dead or alive. Assuming Markus lived long enough to do such a thing.

The sound of his own voice was oddly comforting and reassured him that he wasn't dead yet. His blood looked black in this dim light, like cooling tar on a hot rooftop. The belt he'd used for a tourniquet and the rag placed awkwardly over the gaping wound had slowed the flow to a trickle. But it still dripped.

I have to get out of here.

Death loomed in front of him like a mirage as if God himself stood pointing at a little sign nestled discreetly along a dirty path, *his* path of life. The sign said DON'T CROSS THIS LINE. Because once you crossed that line, there was no coming back. That gallant ride into the sunset. Dead at last. *I must be dreaming now, passed out.* But he was getting closer, unable to stop putting one foot in front of the other; walking as if that was the only direction he needed to go. And God wasn't saying a damn thing; just letting him come. Christopher glared past the sign, past God, and noticed a light, very subtle at first, but growing more vibrant and beautiful, and calling to him. It was a warm light, alluring. The light was the end of misery and suffering and would render death to a mere stepping-stone and expunge its finality. The end of his path.

So strange this all was. He thought of his mother from so long ago, her gentle hand caressing his cheek, and her soft words, *you're special, Christopher, my little Christopher, you will change the world.* Her comforting scent of fresh coffee, a fragrance he'd forgotten over the years. He dream-stepped closer.

But I survived. Goddamn right he did, and he got away. He stopped walking. God still glared at him and maintained that same resolute posture while pointing at the sign. *I am not dead. If I am to die stuffed into a cubby hole beneath a mound of hay and boards, then what was the point?* And what of the cost if he could not help Markus?

And if Markus dies, who would ever find me down here? Who knows of this place? My corpse would rot for ages in a dingy room for the rats to feed on.

And most importantly, I now know what Nathaniel is. What he truly is.

And if he releases the Legions with neither I nor Markus to stop them...

"I get it," Christopher said aloud. He opened his eyes. God was gone, the path was gone, and that wonderful light was gone too. Only this shitty little room.

He had to find Markus and tell him. Warn him.

And projections were not an option since he'd learned the hard way that Nathaniel could *hear* them.

Christopher rolled onto his side, being weary of his right arm - he sure as shit didn't want to get the blood gushing again. He flopped onto his belly and began to crawl awkwardly to the trap door a few feet away.

CHAPTER 24

"These are dire times, Markus." The raspy voice spoke slow and contained an accent. *Deze are dyer times, Morcus.*

"I agree." Markus hobbled down the steps. He managed his cane with his left hand and pressed the phone to his ear with the right. The grass was so green and the weather so perfect that it hardly seemed possible anything could be so wrong in the world.

Markus had spoken to Bishop Pepe twice in his life, both times having the same struggles to understand. "We hab not receibe word from Chriztopher seence last night. He said he would be in London today to meet with ze chasers. Heze prezence has alvays bean strong, but I hab feel nutting for hours, I'm afraid."

"We should assume that Christopher is dead." Markus rarely spoke to The Vatican, and no one at The Vatican ever identified themselves; he only knew it was Bishop Pepe because he'd spoken with him before. Dealing with the Vatican was Christopher's job.

"Ze chasers hab been destroid," The voice said. "It vas ze wolves and ze Legions."

"The wolves?" Markus stopped. Vampires and wolves co-exist fine, but they have never collaborated.

"Yez." The voice on the other end coughed and then continued. "Nathaniel has ordered ze releaze of ze Legions."

Markus felt his options dwindling and a void inside him began to form as the possibility of losing this war weighed heavily.

"How do you know?" Markus asked.

"Two accounts zo far. One in Germany and one in Poland, of all places, azking for help from ze church. But we hab no chazers to zend. Ze few zurvivors are guarding Vatican City." The voice huffed. "I fear great turmoil,

Markus. Conclave is only ten days away! All of ze Cardinals will be in Rome and if Nathaniel attacks, ze church will be in chaos."

Markus struggled to grasp the totality. In all his years, in all his battles, in all his experience, he'd never been a spot like this. Hiding in an old farmhouse on the brink of a dark war with the vampires, a war that seemed bleak, and, most disheartening for Markus, it was a war he may never see the end of.

"Do you have any idea how many Legions there are or how large?" Markus walked close to a small, wooden shed. Weeds and small trees shrouded it, and the sound of insects grew louder the farther he got from the house. An ocean of grass and bushes lay splayed between the house and him, and if he kept going, he would be in the pasture.

"We don't know," Bishop Pepe sighed and continued, "We only know ze number must be large. I would zay Nathaniel has been building and preparing these Legions for over a century."

"Perhaps." The good news just kept rolling in. Markus stopped, pulled out his depleting pack of KOOLs, and lit another cigarette. So stupid that a man with terminal lung cancer would even consider a cigarette, but goddamn it, this was just not a good time to do without them. Like it would do a lick of good to quit anyway.

A Cicada buzzed lazily in the distance, and a chirping cricket made him feel even more isolated. "It's obvious he's planned well. He's decimated the Society and the Chasers in a few short days, and none of us saw it coming."

"If we kill Nathaniel," the bishop said, "ze remaining Legions will become disoriented and ze wolves will abandon ze effort altogether." The bishop coughed and made a slippery smacking sound, like someone wetting their lips, and then said, "Can you kill him, Markus?"

Can I kill him? Yes, he thought he could. But Nathaniel was not alone, he had his Legions, and the Legions first priority would be to protect Nathaniel. Their numbers could be in the hundreds, even thousands. What then? Throughout history, great armies had proven the effectiveness of superior numbers.

"The Legions could be a problem," Markus said.

"Agreed."

"If Nathaniel disappears, we'll need to stand down and begin building our own forces for when he resurfaces,"—Markus took another drag—"which could be years or decades from now."

"We will begin taking action on this immediately by zeeking out the potential wizards we know of already. But this procezz takez time, and without ze chazers, it will take longer. We will need you, Markus, to train them and to help rebuild the Society." The voice fell silent.

Markus grimaced. Right now, his own army consisted of himself, an injured witch, a messenger and a guy named Liam. Dear God, this would be a miracle.

"It will take me a day, maybe more, to allow Alexis time to get well enough to fight," Markus said, wishing like hell that he possessed the coveted magic to heal, something not seen for centuries. "If you hear anything about the Legions, the wolves, or Nathaniel, contact me. Hopefully, once I find one, it will lead me to the other."

"We hab ze church as our eyes. Word shall go out immediately to maintain vigilance."

"That'll work."

"Dere is one other item. I'm not sure how theze affects uz for zertain, but Chriztopher was adamant that we discuzz it at our meeting today."

"What's that?"

"He believed Nathaniel to be insane."

Markus reflected on his and Christopher's conversation the day before. Was that just yesterday? It seemed impossible. "Yes. He mentioned that theory to me as well. He said Nathaniel may think he is God or at least some version of God. Not sure it makes a big difference now."

The bishop mumbled, "Most troublesome."

Markus dropped his cigarette into the grass and stepped on it. "Keep me informed and notify me immediately if you hear anything on his whereabouts."

"We will," Bishop Pepe said. "Stay cautious. Do not azzume you are zafe, too many hab done 'dat already and paid ze price."

"I make no assumptions." Markus ended the call and stuffed the phone into the pocket of his coat. A lot of good that call did. A bunch of shit he already knew. Except for the Chasers – according to Bishop Pepe, their situation was as dire as his.

Goddamn it all to hell, he needed something to go right; just a small nugget of good news for once.

A scent of sweet corn hung in the air and the humidity felt thick in this secluded part of the world. It was amazing how quiet it was here.

Too quiet.

He gazed into the thick cluster of trees lining the property. Behind him, the soft dings of a wind-chime drifted lazily on the breeze. Something was in those woods. He stepped toward the tree line tightening his grip on his cane.

His chest tightened, and he stopped; his breath became shallow and difficult. A cough, hoarse and deep, seized him and he had to slump over in a hacking fit. Goddamn, those fucking cigarettes. He'd been able to quit a few years ago by escaping all of this madness. But now, he was right back in the thick of it with mankind's destiny hanging in the balance. No damn pressure. Quitting smoking—a habit which had sustained him through the decades—was no longer at the top of his priority list and to hell with anyone who condemned him for it.

The coughing passed as quickly as it had come but left him out of breath and his chest ached like hell. He righted himself and wiped his hand across his mouth. A slobbery, blood-tainted mucus streaked his jacket sleeve. Shit.

A rustling from the trees. He peered into the green line of trees and tall grass. He sensed eyes glaring at him. Damn it all to hell.

The wolves had found them.

CHAPTER 25

"Forgive me Father," Nathaniel stood alone at the front of the church.

Charlie squeezed his eyes shut and grimaced. The disturbing noises outside had faded. Only sporadic screams drifted in from outside. Some were close to the church; others distant, maybe all the way across town.

He prayed desperately for Nathaniel to leave.

Charlie's tears spilled from under his clamped eyelids, and he wanted to see his dad. What if one of the screams he'd heard *was* his dad? He forced the thought away, but it kept nudging back in.

"I accept your judgment," Nathaniel's lurid voice echoed and dug into every crevice of the building.

Charlie pressed his fist against his mouth. Was Nathaniel the devil?

Nathaniel folded his arms in front of him "Hear my prayer and provide your protective embrace upon my Legions. We will restore the days of miracles and myth. The perfection of your creation will be realized, and I will rule at your right hand."

Please God, Charlie begged silently. Would God hear the prayers of someone like him? A teenage boy cursed with *the devil's gifts*. A boy who had taken the fifty cents his father gave him every week for the Sunday school tithe and pocketed it, on more than one occasion, for a can of pop during the inevitable Sunday afternoon boredom. Or the time when he gazed at a magazine showing the picture of a pretty girl dressed in a tank-top that cut off just above her navel. Would God punish him for that?

Charlie thought that God just might.

And maybe this was it. He prayed it wasn't. As soon as he got out of here, *if* he got out of here, he'd take the back alley to Front street, then cut through the woods to his house. He wanted to be home. Now.

The front doors of the church rattled and burst open. The man named Michael marched at a brisk pace between what was left of the pews.

"We've found Markus and the witch," Michael said.

"A bit of good news." Nathaniel did not seem fully convinced.

"The wolves found them."

"How?"

"I don't know. From the messenger, would be my guess."

"Where?"

"Not far from here. They're staying in an Amish farmhouse, the one we were told about. You were right to have the place watched."

A tingle of recognition swept through Charlie. Was that the same abandoned place he'd seen before, not far into Amish country? He knew of it from when he and his father had traveled, on several occasions, to buy hogs or a side of beef from the Amish. *They've got the best meat in Pennsylvania*, his father would say and as they'd pass that house set back far from the road, his dad would add, *you stay away from that place... very dangerous, a lot of abandoned wells and cisterns. You fall into a cistern, which is an underground tank full of water, and we'll never see you again.* Those words had horrified him as he imagined drowning in a black pit, never found.

"If it's true, at least we know our information from the messenger is good." Nathaniel faced Michael. "And you believe the wolves?"

"I do." Michael nodded. "The witch could not have traveled far. It makes sense."

"Tell the wolves to wait for us. We'll attack as soon as the sun sets, while Markus believes they are safe. We'll need everything at our disposal. That gives us one hour to prepare."

"We'll be ready."

"Be cautious," Nathaniel said. "Markus Blue is not to be underestimated. We will lose many of our Legions this night, mark my words." The two strode side-by-side down the sanctuary's middle isle. A second later, they were outside, and the door closed behind them.

The silence was immediate, and so was Charlie's relief. A small whimper escaped his lips as his muscles relaxed. One of his hands trembled and he breathed a quivering breath. A sudden urge to burst into open sobs seized him, and he swallowed it back for fear that Nathaniel may come strolling back in.

He waited a few more agonizing moments in the gloomy quiet. Nothing but the occasional noise from outside. He leveraged his magic, a levitation trick he'd performed several times over the years in the solitude of the barn behind his house, and floated down to the floor, landing softly next to

Father Nead's body. He glanced at the priest, whose stiff and puffy skin had turned a morbid shade of gray. Charlie knew that if he touched it, it would be cold and that thought made him shiver. He moved quickly up to the altar.

The church had a restroom in the foyer, just outside the sanctuary, but to hell with going out there! If those freaks came back, he had no desire to be standing there, caught using the restroom. The restroom in the basement would do just fine and the door to get down there was only few feet away.

Stepping onto the raised floor of the altar and communion area, he became aware of the echo of his own rapid breathing. An unpleasant odor hung about, and he did not want to think about what *that* was. *Bodies rotting... that's what they smell like at first... Shut up!* Hot vomit lurched into his throat. He had to get out of here. He charged for the basement door and burst through. His hands trembled as he entered the dark stairwell. The short flight of steps exited to a tile floor in the basement hallway. The restroom was at the end.

Pee and get home as fast as you can. The door to the back alley was in the basement, and he'd already planned his route.

The door opened with a squeak to the shadowed room. He hurried to the urinal, undid his fly, and let it flow. *Oh, sweet Jesus.*

What time was it? It had to be close to sunset.

They're all dead, Charlie.

The small basement window at the top of the wall offered a dingy gray light. The sun was nearly gone for the day. He pictured the route he'd take home and what it would look like at this time. His house wasn't far, but the woods would be creepy.

They are all dead.

No. He needed to get home and tell his dad what had happened. Maybe he could levitate himself over the woods. It was a small patch. But he'd never gone that high or that far. He didn't even know if he actually could. He'd never considered himself able to fly. He would run, that's what he'd do. He would run his butt off as soon as he exited this door and not stop until he was home.

Remember the screams outside while hiding and the sound of animals, horrible animals, growling...

The screaming outside.

Dead.

The people of Pheasant Hill are all dead, Charlie. You're the only one left. His mind whispered, and he tried to ignore it.

"He has the devil's gifts," his dad had said while standing in the confession room of this very church ten years earlier talking with Father Nead. *"He was born with them."*

Father Nead had hooked his large hand under the chubby chin of little Charlie's face and smiled. *"Maybe they are God's gifts,"* Father Nead had said. *"The devil has enough already."*

A heavy sob rose from his chest. His eyes clamped shut, and snot dripped from his nose. He buttoned his jeans and backed away from the urinal, against the wall behind him, and slid down to his butt in a fit of dry, lurching cries. He pictured his mom, long since passed away, knitting in her favorite recliner with her glasses pushed to the furthest point on her nose before they would slip off. His locker at school located right next to Becky Mae, the girl that made his knees weak and his heart flutter. His dad's smile, warm and comforting. All of them no longer existed.

The devil's gifts.

Charlie clenched his fists and the sound escaping him began as a low bellow, a sound he didn't even know he was making until it swelled to a wail. His voice cracked, and he cared less if anyone heard him. He hated this void, this hole that had formed inside him.

The image of Nathaniel slinging the woman against the balcony enveloped him. Her eyes widened during her death as if she realized what was happening to her and the horror had driven her mad.

That was when the pressure building inside him let loose. Pressure that threatened to tear him inside out.

The floor rumbled and cracked, splitting the tiles like jagged fingers. The walls pulsated, and concrete shattered like porcelain, falling in heaps, followed by clouds of dry dust. Violent crashes echoed above him and seeped through the floor. God knew what those sounds were; perhaps the rafters crumbling or the large crucifix Nathaniel had been so focused on crashing to the floor.

Charlie didn't care. He'd never felt more alive or more present. As if every cell inside him burst in dazzling explosions, like fireworks, showering and growing, and he craved more. Let the world rot as long as this power remained his.

Stop, Charlie.

Dust swirled and rose around him in a tornadic cloud. Yes, this was his destiny.

Stop NOW. You're losing control. STOP NOW!

The destruction stopped as suddenly as it had started.

He blinked against a suffocating cloud of dirt, then coughed. The urinal had fallen off the wall and now gushed water onto the floor. The light above the collapsed sink flickered and hummed, hanging on for dear life.

Strangely, he felt better. Focused.

He clambered shakily to his feet. He had to get out of here. He had to get home.

And he had to find the man Nathanial spoke of... Markus Blue. Nathaniel wanted to kill him, which made Markus an ally. *The enemy of my enemy is my friend.* He couldn't remember what book he'd read that out of.

He hurried to the basement door stepping carefully over the piles of crumbled concrete. He would stay hidden and move quickly. Once he reached his house and verified his dad was okay, they'd take the old truck that was always parked in the barn with the keys in it out to Amish country.

He slipped out into the open basement and hurried to the outside door. He pushed it open, staying quiet. All clear, thank goodness. The sun was down, but the waning day still provided enough light to see by.

He hopped from the church door to the shadowed alley and was running as soon as his feet touched the ground as only the youthful could. An eerie silence blanketed the coming darkness, and he shivered.

Please god, let my dad be okay.

He ran faster.

CHAPTER 26

Christopher heaved the wooden trapdoor open and peeked out.

Damn. Night had fallen. How long had he been hiding down there? *Fucking brilliant, Christopher... wait until dark to come out.* He considered holding out until sunrise, but time was of the essence.

The pungent smell of old hay and cow manure tainted the air as he scanned the inside of the barn. The place looked normal, but normal was an illusion. A mound of hay, some loose and some still in bales, lined the right-side wall. An old John Deere tractor sat parked in the middle like a gloomy ghost. The opposite wall had a large opening for the cattle to come inside and munch leisurely on the hay Christopher piled for them each morning.

There were no cattle inside the opening now, which was odd since they had not been fed anything since this morning. Another indication of how wrong things were, as if he needed another reminder. He wanted to get the hell out of here, get his arm stitched up, and then find whoever was left in the Society. *God, tell me there is someone still left out there.*

He trudged up the small ladder and crawled awkwardly out of his hiding place, then stood up. He shuffled across the open space to the tractor, a spot that allowed better cover. His only light came from the moon waning through the open door and the windows. He could see shockingly well; attuned to darkness thanks to time spent in his hiding space.

He fought a brief spell of wooziness and for a crazy moment, thought he might throw up. He peered through a small window not far from where he stood and sighed.

His house lay in ruins, decimated by his own hands, and a wave of emptiness swept over him. Sadness.

Hollow footsteps thumped across the barn roof, and he froze. Damn it, just as he'd feared, the Legion had been waiting for him to emerge. Now that they'd found him, he only had a few seconds before they converged on this barn. He wondered if Nathaniel was still out there.

If Nathaniel wasn't here, then Michael or Christine likely would be.

To hell with it. If it was a fight they wanted, then it was a fight they'd get. *If I gotta go, you bastards, then I'll go down swingin'.*

Christopher whirled toward the center of the barn and was met by the pale face of a creature flying at him, its arms outstretched. It was the eyes that Christopher hated, there were no irises and no pupils, just a dim, white bulb tucked into the socket.

Christopher's hand shot up, and the vampire stopped in mid-air, held by an invisible grasp, its hateful grimace melting to terrified surprise. He slung it backward, and it crashed through the rear wall.

Christopher scuffled a few steps from the tractor and stopped. If Nathaniel was here, which Christopher had to assume he was, the best chance to defeat him was to fight from a location where he could protect himself from all sides.

Vampires flooded into the barn like a swarm of hornets. They flew above him, floating like hawks, preparing their descent. They climbed the walls like hellish spiders.

Christopher stretched his left arm out in front of him with the fingers spread and clamped his eyes shut against the blinding light that materialized in front of him. At first, it looked like a small halogen bulb floating strangely a few feet from his hand. It spread out and stretched into a circle of white, then swirled like a tornado. It moved up and over him, forming a dome. This is what he'd tried to do while battling Nathaniel, but to his shock, Nathaniel had jumped through it, penetrating the barrier that *should* destroy anything that touched it.

The vampires attacked. Christopher watched them through his wall of light, their faces horrid, and their mouths open to reveal those wretched teeth. How in god's name these used to be people simply confounded him. Proof of a world beyond our own ability to grasp it.

He read their expressions; both confused and furious.

"You are pathetic." Christopher forced a smile, taunting them, trying like hell to conceal the pain. He leaned his head back and laughed. For some reason, doing that actually *did* make him feel better.

Let go, his mind screamed, *let it all go!* Christopher laughed harder and gazed at the those who were within a few feet of his spinning dome of light. They leaned closer, trying to peer through the cloudy haze.

Nathaniel had not appeared yet. Perhaps he would wait until the battle with the Legion was underway.

The time had come. Hordes surrounded him, and the opportunity to kill as many of them in one shot would never get better.

The first cracks of lightning shot out from the dome in jagged beams and blew holes through bodies big enough to climb through. The beams found their targets with deadly precision. The thick stench of burning flesh overwhelmed him, and he retched.

His mouth grew ridiculously dry, and he ran his tongue against the coarse roof of his mouth. Perhaps the blood loss was affecting him more than he'd realized.

Wailing cries erupted, but he couldn't focus on each one. He caught glimpses of those that didn't die outright, some crawling away, others lying on the barn floor with pieces torn off. A male wearing tattered pajamas lay screaming a few feet from the dome wall. Another, what appeared to have been a woman at some point in the past, scrambled away on all fours, trying to reach the open door to the pasture for escape. One of her legs was gone, and from here, he thought she might have been wearing a military or police uniform.

He concentrated on the magic holding his dome together. The dome was an effective weapon, but it required an incredible amount of energy to sustain it. He couldn't keep up this intensity for much longer. Fresh blood oozed through the bandage around his arm.

One of his knees wobbled and threatened to give way. *Damn it! Not yet, I cannot go yet.* The vampires streamed through doors, windows, and around the eaves of the roof, flying in through the hay loading door in the loft, and they showed no sign of stopping. They soared close to the ceiling like hawks, awaiting their moment to descend. Greater numbers to overcome superior firepower was proving effective. His beams continued streaming out in waves, finding their targets and annihilating them. Their assault would continue until either they were victorious, or every last one of them was dead.

His hand trembled, and he clamped his spread fingers into a fist to hold it steady. Finally, his legs buckled and he fell to his knees. His extended arm felt like it was made of lead as he strained to keep it out in front of him.

The vampires kept coming.

If he stopped to change tactics, they'd would swarm him like wasps. He'd need a few seconds to summon the magic for a different weapon... the vampires would be on him in less than one. Life could be so goddamn shitty sometimes.

Markus! To hell with it if Nathaniel heard him. Nothing to lose now. He projected as hard as he could. *I cannot hold the dome!*

CHAPTER 27

Phillip jumped awake when the door burst open.

"Get out to the car!" Markus's voice ripped through the house.

Something was wrong.

Phillip sat up and the world swayed, threatening to go black. He glanced at his watch. *Two days without sleep and I get a half hour nap!* What the hell did Markus want? The footsteps, rapid for an old man, thudded heavily on the floor, and the rap of the cane on the wood reminded him of someone hammering nails.

"We've gotta go *now*," Markus yelled. "The wolves are here. We have to leave right-goddamned-now."

"Wolves? Here?" Phillip's fog cleared. He sprang to his feet and hurried out of the bedroom. He'd never seen the wolves before, and he didn't want to.

"I'll wake up Liam and Alexis. Go get the car, pull it around," Markus said.

"I don't want to go out there." The words were out of Phillip's mouth before he could stop them.

Markus stopped and glared at him. Phillip didn't want to know what thought lurked behind that expression. "They're still in the woods." Markus continued his trek to the back of the house.

"What are they waiting for?" He followed Markus down a small hallway.

"Nathaniel would be my guess," Markus said.

"They won't attack me if I go out there?"

"I don't think so. They didn't attack me." Markus reached the doorway to where Liam and Alexis slept.

Well, of course, they didn't attack *you*. Phillip kept that thought to himself.

He and Markus peered in at Alexis, sound asleep next to Liam who had his arm tucked under her head. It couldn't have been more than a second that Phillip watched them. But in that second, he didn't know how to stand. He didn't know whether to put his hands inside or outside his pockets.

Dreams die, sometimes right in front of your eyes.

Phillip thrust his head through the open doorway, in front of Markus, and yelled, "Liam, Alexis... out of bed, now!" The sound of his own voice irritated him. It was as if everything he did felt wrong.

Liam stirred, blinked his eyes, and then looked at his watch. "What's going on?"

Phillip thought, *you motherfucker*. He knew it was irrational when he thought it, but he thought it just the same.

Markus's gruff voice cut in, "Phillip's bringing the car around. We need to be ready to go as soon as he pulls it out front."

"Okay." Liam hoisted himself up to one elbow.

Phillip asked, "You got her?" He felt stupid talking to Liam, smaller somehow.

"Yeah... we'll be out there." Liam slipped his arm out from under Alexis's head and swung his legs over the edge of the bed.

We'll be out there.

Phillip caught one last glimpse of Alexis moving and whirled away. He hustled to the front door. Fucking Liam. *I should have seen this coming*. But he'd trusted she wouldn't actually *like* a useless shit like Liam. Anger flared and he clamped his teeth together, gnashing them. He pictured himself infiltrating Liam's weak mind. *Put the gun in your mouth.... Take a knife, slice your throat...* And Alexis, you little –

Markus gripped his shoulder and stopped him dead in his tracks.

Phillip glared into those cold, blue eyes.

"You're not the first to feel this," Markus said to him.

Phillip blinked, and his rage subsided, like tossing water on a hot fire and watching it sizzle.

"Focus," Markus said. "We might be in a jam here. Get out there and get the car."

Phillip nodded. Yes, he had shit to do.

What was outside that door? Markus said the wolves were staying in the woods, but *would* they once he stepped out and ran toward the car? How tall were they? What did they look like? Were they fast? Surely Markus would be outside to protect him.

He reached the front door and grasped the doorknob. His heart thudded like an animal inside him. In all honesty, this would be much easier if ole' Liam wasn't there at all. Then *he* could take care of Alexis himself. *He'd* be the one lying next to her in the bed with his arm under her head. *He* would show Alexis that she could depend on him, unlike relying on some guy she'd just met yesterday.

Phillip took a long, courage-building breath, and opened the door.

• • • • • •

Markus hobbled out onto the porch and glared into the trees lining the back pasture. The breeze seemed to have stopped in anticipation of something wicked. Nothing moved. But he knew they were out there, watching.

Phillip exited the front door, shot a quick glance toward Markus, and then broke into a sprint toward the car. Markus had insisted they park next to an old shed where the tree cover would conceal the vehicle. A car parked in the driveway of a house in Amish country drew attention.

Not like it mattered now.

Markus scanned the area. He considered attacking right then, but there were too many unknowns that may prove fatal if he underestimated the fight. How many were there? Whether or not the wolves were acting in accordance with Nathaniel was undeniable, but why? What was in it for them? And of course, how long before Nathaniel arrived? The Vatican had warned him, but he thought he'd have more than five minutes to think about it.

The front door opened with a squeak. Liam and Alexis shuffled out; Liam with his arm hooked under hers, helping her along. Everyone was moving. He heard the car start up over by the barn. Good, good, good.

Liam and Alexis stopped close to where he stood, close enough that Liam could ask, "Where are they?"

Markus nodded toward the woods and said, "Damn things aren't as cunning as vampires, but they're strong. Ferocious too. They like colder weather. Here's the thing," he glanced at Liam and caught his eye, "they're not immortal, in fact, just the opposite. Once you're turned, it shortens your life by thirty years or more." Markus shrugged. "Maybe more, depending on how old you are when you turn."

Alexis said, "It's too dark. We need to get out of here."

"Indeed," Markus tapped a finger on his cane.

He thought Alexis looked a little better; some of the color had come back into her face and her eyes...

Markus!

The projection slammed into his head like a steel fist.

I cannot hold the dome!

He winced and his knees threatened to buckle. He reached out and gripped the wooden rail to steady himself.

Christopher!

Goddamnit, where was he?

Christopher was losing the dome which meant he was in the midst of battle and in trouble. Markus thought hard.

Wait just a damn minute...

You were never as good in battle as you were in politics, old friend, Markus thought as the feather of a smile touched his wrinkled lips.

He had an idea.

CHAPTER 28

Charlie snuck across the road and hid in the cornfield. He peered at his house through the drooping green leaves. Everything looked normal at first, but then he heard something that made his heart *ka-thud.* The fine hairs on his neck and arms tingled. A growling noise, deep and horrible, was coming from inside.

He crept closer through the tall corn stalks and surveyed an open window while dimly aware of the annoying sweat trickling down his face. *Get up there! Get up there now!* But he couldn't.

He was scared.

Charlie pressed his fist to his mouth, like he'd done while hiding in the rafters of the church, and bit down on his knuckle. That sickening, deep-throated growl seeped from the dark square of the screen window to his dad's bedroom.

A small whimper escaped Charlie's throat, and he muttered the word, "Dad?"

The day's remnant light grayed the faded white paint of the house. Crickets and cicadas sang their lazy chorus. Far overhead, the white exhaust stream from an airplane stretched across the sky. Nothing out of the ordinary except for that hideous noise coming from inside his house, confirming everything that he'd seen happen today at the church and in Pheasant Hill.

And as he watched, something from inside the house stepped in front of the window. Charlie cried against his fist, biting down hard. The shadowed head was enormous and perched awkwardly on narrow shoulders. It just stared outside, as if checking to see if anyone had pulled into the driveway.

Charlie crouched, hoping like crazy it didn't see him. What in god's name was that?

He had to get out of here. Now. He prayed his dad wasn't in the house. *Please don't be in there.*

The old truck was in the barn. The keys were in it, and he knew it would start. He'd just driven it a few days ago to pull the hay-trailer. No more thinking, just do. Do something. *You've got the devil's gifts son*, his father's words, *you're special. You always have been.* Get to the truck and drive out of here. Drive it like you do when you're working in the field. Drive it like your life depends on it.

The idea of levitating popped into his head again, just as it had when he thought about crossing the patch of woods between his house and the church. It may even be faster and quieter to do that very thing to reach the barn. But, for the same reason he hadn't tried flying on the way to the house, he wouldn't try now because he didn't actually know if he could. Floating a couple of feet in the air was one thing. But flying across a cornfield like Superman was completely different. Perhaps if he'd tried it before, that would be one thing, but he'd never done that. Not once. Fear of the unknown outweighed his courage. He'd stick with what he knew, and he knew how to run.

He had to wait until the thing looking out the window was gone. If he ran while that thing was watching, game over. He probably wouldn't make it a few feet before it caught him. Nothing but open grass, about a football field in length, stretched between him and the barn, which housed the old 1976 Ford.

He watched the window, waiting, wondering if the thing up there had seen him. He concluded it hadn't since it wasn't moving. It just stood there.

And then it turned and was gone. *Oh, thank god.* Charlie waited a second to make sure it didn't pop its ugly, deformed head back out. It didn't.

He broke into a sprint. The rough leaves of the corn stalks slapped at his face, and then he was in the clear, running across the open yard like a track-star toward the finish line. His open hands pumped up and down and his knees lifted to his chest in a fluid movement. He avoided every hole and rise in the yard; he knew this ground.

The yard stretched out in front of him, and for a horrible moment, the barn looked like it was getting farther away, like in those dreams where you can't seem to get moving! *Keep running!* Nothing but the thumps of his feet against the earth. His breath in and out. Almost there.

That was when his luck ran out. A roar split the air, followed by the breaking of wood, and then, out of the corner of his eye, he saw it jump from the window – a dark spot sailing through the air, landing on the ground, and charging after him.

His legs pumped harder. His eyes widened, there was no way he'd make it running like this. The barn loomed ahead, so close, yet so unreachable. His cries drifted on the humid air with not a single human being around to hear him. That thing would catch him and drive him down onto the grass, ripping and tearing, and killing him. He would die in his own yard, killed by something unexplainable.

If he kept running like this.

But he could do more than run.

The moments that followed were a blur. He'd always known he was different, that he could do things that others couldn't, but the days of levitating a few feet off the floor when he was home alone or moving small objects through the air were over. As he ran across his lawn, trying desperately to escape the certainty of death, the devil's gifts came alive.

He couldn't recall at what point his feet left the ground, but they did. For a second, a brief second in which he felt like he was trapped in a dream, he was flying; not just levitating, but soaring. The memory of crashing through the barn wall would always remain sketchy. Only a loud crack and the feeling of uneasiness, like the unsettling monster dip of a rollercoaster plummeting down that first gigantic drop. He plowed through the hay and dust, slamming his knee into an unyielding wooden beam. Another foot to the left and he would have smashed his head straight into the bumper of the truck.

Despite the horror chasing him and everything he'd seen on this wretched day, the first word that popped into his mind when he'd finally come to a stop was *awesome*.

He scrambled to his feet and staggered to the driver's side. He swung the door open and climbed clumsily behind the wheel. He'd just slammed the door shut when the side of the barn exploded into splintering wood as whatever was chasing him crashed through the wall. He yanked the key from beneath the sun visor and shoved it into the slot. A howl erupted and pierced his ears like an icepick. Charlie cried out, turned the key, and the truck roared to life. A wave of gratefulness swept through him – never had that running engine sounded so heavenly. He shifted to first gear and jammed on the gas. The truck lurched forward spewing gravel and dust in a huge cloud behind him.

He gripped the steering wheel, clamping onto it, as if it might fly out of his hand if he let it go, and shifted to second, maneuvering the shifter.

Something solid rammed the cab behind his head and the truck bounced. The aged springs squeaked and he thought for a second one of the tires had blown after hearing a *ka-pow* right outside the cab.

The old truck accelerated achingly slow. It ran well with the straight six-cylinder (*best engine Ford ever made*, his dad always said), but what he wouldn't give for a racecar right then. The truck roared down the gravel driveway and passed the house. Charlie cried out as he drove. The thing in the back smashed and tore, its claws screeching madness on the thin metal of the roof.

The back window fractured, then burst and Charlie ducked down, his mouth opening wider. He jammed on the breaks, locking the tires. The thing in the back crashed against the cab, and then he stomped the gas, downshifting at the same time to get a better jerk forward. It worked. The creature flopped over the side of the bed and landed in a rolling heap on the grass next to the driveway. Charlie watched in his mirror as it sprang to its feet and chased after him. *No, no, no...*

Furry and tall, at least eight-foot-tall, it resembled a dog, but ambled on two legs, with claws, and the enormous head was all mouth and packed with teeth.

He kept on the gas and shifted to third as the truck crossed from the driveway onto the road. The tires barked as they caught asphalt. He'd never driven like this and for one horror-stricken second, thought he'd fishtail straight into the ditch. The creature lumbered after him until it was out of sight, far behind him.

It occurred to him a few minutes later that his phone was still in the house. His dad demanded he leave it home while he helped Pastor Nead at the church.

His dad.

Both cars had been home, which meant that he had been home. Charlie slammed his palm against the steering wheel. "Stupid, stupid, *stupid!*"

Because he'd chickened out and ran.

Thirty minutes later, he drove in shock. *Dad was home, and you ran.* He cried hard in spurts, other times he just sat aimlessly as the world whizzed past in a blur of darkening cornfields. Earlier, he'd considered driving to the jailhouse to find Will Copper, the Constable of Pheasant Hill, but the jailhouse was in town, not far from the church. No way he was going back there.

He wished he had his phone. "*Wish in one hand and shit in the other and see which one fills up first.*" He could actually hear his dad's ghostly voice echoing those words.

Charlie was in Amish country now, and the rules changed out here. The roads turned to gravel when you crossed *the line* into their territory. The Amish didn't mind the locals from Pheasant Hill driving in to buy meat or furniture, but they frowned on folks just out joy-riding. Some of them didn't utilize cars, and most of them didn't even have electricity. Even though he'd been born and raised a mere twenty-five miles from their territory, his encounters with them were shockingly rare. His father was strict that he not venture there on his bike or in the truck when he was hauling hay. "*You got to respect them folks,*" his dad would say, "*they got their business, and we got ours. They don't bother us, and we don't bother them*".

A pang of guilt seeped in every time his mind replayed his dad speaking. *They'd have killed me too.* He knew it. Had he run into the house, he'd be dead too. Probably.

But he could do things others couldn't.

It'd be dark soon. He didn't want to be out here in the dark. Up ahead, a small cloud of dust caught his attention, and he rolled to stop. A line of horses and carriages dotted the road, coming toward him. The Amish. Where were they going? Maybe they'd heard about the calamity in Pheasant Hill and decided to get the heck out of dodge. He eased the truck forward.

As he neared the first carriage, he rolled down his window. The gravel crunched under his tires and the clop of horseshoes mixed with the stench of dust. The driver drew back on a set of reigns and his horse halted. Charlie stopped the truck and stared out the open window.

The Amish man's eyes, shadowed by the wide brim of his black hat, crawled dubiously over the truck and settled on Charlie.

"You okay, son?" The man asked. His dark beard hung like moss from his chin.

"I don't know." Charlie swiped at his eyes. "I think my dad's dead."

The man didn't seem interested, and Charlie didn't know what to think about that. The world had tumbled from its axis, and he needed someone to tell him what to do. As the Amish man leered at him, he felt abandoned, like a doomed vessel.

Finally, the man shot a thumb behind him and said, "Don't go down that way, son, there's something awful going on down there, just a ways back."

Charlie shifted his gaze to the road and beyond. The people in the carriages lined up behind this one gawked at Charlie, and it reminded him of those shows where people discover a lost tribe deep in some jungle, and the natives stare at the intruders as if they'd come from another planet.

The man asked, "Who killed your dad, son?"

"I don't know." Charlie glanced in his rearview mirror at the empty road behind him. "Some kind of animal, I think."

"In Pheasant Hill?"

"No. At our house about twenty-five miles after you cross *the line*. They're in Pheasant Hill too. I don't know what they are."

"What'd it look like?" The man asked.

Charlie thought about that and shrugged. "Big, and I mean huge. Reminded me of a dog, but it walked on two legs. I think there's a lot of them."

"This is the devil's work," the man settled back into his seat and plucked the large hat off his head. "There's something out here in these woods too. And there's something going on back at the empty house."

"The empty house?" That might be the place he was looking for.

The man nodded as his hat dangled from his fingers. "Just an old house nobody lives in."

"What's happening there?" Charlie asked.

The man looked up toward the sky. "We heard screaming, but not like people. Not sure what it was. We saw flashes of light, and something caught on fire down there, maybe the house. We fled because whatever it is, it's not about the likes of us."

Charlie wasn't sure what those last words meant, but didn't care and asked, "Where's the house?"

"'bout a mile or two down, but I'm tellin' ya, don't go down there. You're old enough to do as you're told."

Charlie stared straight ahead. What if Nathaniel was already at that house... *and what if the people I'm looking for are dead?* His guts twisted and he hated all of this.

"Don't go toward Pheasant Hill either," Charlie said. "I think the same thing might be happening there. I'd get somewhere and hide."

Hiding... that's what I should be doing.

But he couldn't. He wouldn't. He had to know if those people were there. Who were they? *What* were they?

"We'll decide what's best for us, son." The man shoved his hat back on his head and grasped the reigns lying loose on the carriage floor. "Heed my warning, there's nothing good the way you're goin'."

The man twitched the leather cord and said, "Get on." The horse trotted away, toting the man's carriage, and the progression of carriages followed in unison. The man never looked back.

Charlie shifted the truck into first gear and eased ahead. He avoided the incredulous gawks as the carriages flowed past until they were all gone. Then he got back on the gas, determined and terrified.

He fought the urge to flip around and high-tail it out of there. He could go all the way to Harrisburg and nestle safely there with the police. Maybe they'd throw him in jail for not having a license. Could they throw a fifteen-year-old in jail? He didn't think so but wasn't absolutely sure what sort of things they did in the city.

But he *had* to know if people like him were at that house; if they existed. It trumped everything, even common sense.

Finding that empty house shouldn't be *too* hard, not if all the stuff the Amish guy talked about was still going on.

CHAPTER 29

Collapse it!

Markus's projection blasted into Christopher, and he nearly toppled over. He clenched his teeth and grunted. Flashes reflected the sweat pouring down his face. If he fell, he would die here.

The deafening screams, bursting bodies, and the electric hum of the dome bore a horrific cacophony that drowned out everything.

Everything except for Markus's projection. That tough sonofabitch!

Charred body parts littered the barn floor, some still smoldering, and the pile continued to grow. The putrid stench infested his entire skull, coating his mouth and nose, and he retched with each swallow. They just kept charging to their deaths with tenacious enthusiasm that was, quite frankly, unbelievable.

He'd never collapsed a dome and didn't know anyone ever had. But it was genius, assuming he didn't hurt himself in the process. The rush of air into the vacuum would create a boom, a temporary hiatus, but only for a few seconds, maybe less. It would disorientate his attackers... *hopefully*. But what then? What Markus didn't know, had no way of understanding, was that the vampires were attacking him like a swarm of locusts. If he –

Re-engage with fire!

The bright light of his dome flickered like a snowy TV screen. The ferocity was slowing. Vampires were making it to the wall of the dome itself and charging headlong into it, at their own peril, but also evidence of the dome's waning strength.

The strategy was sound, but the energy to pull it off was another story.

If Markus could see, he would know. Christopher had made the wrong choice by engaging this Legion. Especially at night. How foolish. *I should have stayed tucked away in that hiding place until morning.* How could he know there were so many of them?

Custer's last stand.

Then run like hell!

This projection caught him as he glared out through the faint mist of his thinning wall. His eyes shot open, and his teeth gnashed in a painful clamp that shot agony through his jaw and neck. Precious seconds ticked by as he tried to put it all together.

Collapse the dome. Reengage with fire. Then run like hell.

The simplicity of it all triggered a flicker of hope. Collapsing the dome was the unknown variable; he didn't know what that would feel like, but if Markus said to do it, then he would. He could take the tunnel back to the house. Perhaps that's what he should have done to start with.

A sickening buzz, like one of those old bug-zappers, sizzled as another vampire charged directly into the side of the dome, melting away in a disgusting pool of burnt tissue. *Here goes nothing.*

Christopher mustered every ounce of power his weakening body could produce. The dome brightened and lanced against his eyes like tilting one's face toward the sun. The steady hum grew louder. His mouth fell open as something deep within his nose broke loose, and blood poured down into his mouth and dripped from his chin.

Oddly, an image of his grandmother materialized, conjured by precious memories, of her teaching him the old magic. The wrinkled skin of her face sagging as she'd spoken the Latin spells. How many years since he'd thought of her like this?

No one spoke the magic words anymore, but just as he reached that point where his entire head might explode, he wailed as loud as he could, "Ruina!"

The Dome's brilliant light shrank to the size of a pinhead. Immediately, the vacuum filled with a horrendous boom that rumbled the boards under his feet. Windows shattered and the entire barn wobbled precariously.

An ominous silence followed. Christopher caught his breath, and though he didn't yell the word, he thought it. *Ignis!* In his mind's eye, his grandmother's lips curled to the feather of a smile and her old eyes gleamed with pride.

The old magic.

Fire lashed out in a circle around him. Screams erupted in unison, and they charred like the beasts they were.

Dizziness swept over him, and he swayed, feeling the room grow smaller. *Not now! Do not pass out now!* One more thing to do. He whirled toward the small trap door a few feet away. He could see it, and amazingly, it wasn't covered with bodies. A few splayed legs and arms lay draped across the top.

He lunged toward it, his legs unable to carry his momentum, and flopped to his belly, then crawled to reach it. His mangled arm brushed against the hard wood, and he moaned. *Seconds*, he thought, *seconds is all you got right now. And they know you're out of gas, old man*. Out of gas.

Blood from his nose gushed onto the floor, and he crawled through it. The door was close enough to touch now. Could he still open it? He pushed with his mind, and the metal latch trembled. *C'mon, goddamn it! OPEN!*

The wooden door popped up like something startled from sleep, rising on its hinges and would have seemed perfectly natural if it had spoken and said, *Good evening, Christopher*. He plowed through the opening head first and crashed into the solid dirt floor below. Thank God, the floor was covered with hay, though a thin layer it was, but enough to cushion some of the fall. He grunted when he hit and lay there hoping he hadn't broken something. He wiggled his toes, his fingers, and sucked in a harsh breath.

He rolled to his back and stared at the trap-door he'd just fallen through. *Close, you motherfucker!*

It slammed shut.

Won't take them long to figure out where I went. He struggled to his feet, swayed a little, and lumbered to the back of the small space. He tore away the board propped over the tunnel entrance and ducked into the opening.

He shuffled along the dirt floor staying bent over to avoid whacking his head. It was dark in here, blacker than a coal miner's ass, but he didn't want to waste the energy to illuminate the cave with magic. He didn't need to; his intuition was strong, and he was moving at a good clip considering the shape he was in.

The sound of splintering lumber echoed in the darkness. Most likely, the trap door being ripped away. They'd found his hiding place. A few more seconds and they'd find this tunnel. *Time to get a move-on, old man*. Goddamnit, he was tired.

"Keep moving," he hissed, "just keep moving."

How far had he gone? How far did he still have to go? He debated whether he needed to go all the way to the house or reemerge someplace along the way. If he didn't go all the way to the house, then he would have to use magic again to break through the ground. Granted, it wasn't very thick, maybe five feet, but he wasn't sure he could light a damn match at this point.

The stench of damp earth filled his mouth as he sucked in air, gulping it, and tasted the blood still streaming from his nose and into his mouth. He swiped his arm across his face. The blood was both slippery and cold. The taste of ash from burnt bodies lingered on his tongue, and he thought soon, he might vomit.

Just a little farther.

If he burst through the ground (assuming he could), the vampires would certainly see him. However, they wouldn't expect him to pop up back in his burned-down house. At least not right away. He hoped. That would buy him a few seconds to run to the car that *should* still be parked in the driveway. If it wasn't there, he would try to make it to the woods and escape through the trees. His only shot at making that plan work was to avoid being seen. Good luck with *that*.

Almost there.

Voices echoed behind him. The chase was on; they'd found his escape route. Hearing them speak sent a chill through him. They were once human, all of them. An abomination, that's what they were.

At last, he reached the end of the tunnel, nearly smashing face-first into it. With his good arm, he reached up, felt the small round cover and pushed. It slid away easily, and he climbed out, grunting and huffing until he was on his belly lying in a pile of charred plaster. He rolled over. Stars splattered the sky, and his desk, which used to cover this opening, was gone. Piles of rubble lay in heaps all around him. *Keep moving, you old fuck.*

Through clenched teeth, he hoisted himself up, placed the cover back over the opening, and got shakily to his feet. He stood bent over, gasping, with his hands resting heavily on his knees and glanced toward the barn. Flames lapped high into the air chasing a column of dark smoke that blotted out a great swath of sky. He shivered.

Out in the driveway, the first refreshing thing since this infernal battle began gleamed in the infant starlight. The car! Long and black, it sparkled like an oasis of water to a man dying of thirst. The driver's side door was open, and a body lay beneath it.

Eric. *Goddamn it.*

The young man had given Markus a ride from the private airport to the ranch house. He'd been in awe, relishing the opportunity to meet Markus Blue. Around midnight, he had taken Markus and Phillip to the airport so they could get to Pittsburg. That was the last ride Eric ever gave.

Christopher broke into a lumber toward the car, nearly tripping over the debris scattered where the house had once stood, where the Society had once been. The car was close, but when your enemy had the strength of a gorilla *and* the ability to fly, it was more like ten miles. He reached the driveway, close enough to see Eric's dead, pale face when something crashed behind him. Likely, they were bursting from the tunnel. Christopher didn't turn to look, but pictured a snarling creature flying toward him, arms outstretched and teeth bared.

He dove through the open car-door, rolled back upright in the driver's seat, and tried to slam the door shut, but it stopped just short of closing. Eric's leg was still inside the car. The keys dangled wonderfully from the ignition, *can we all say thank you, Jesus.* He glanced at the house, saw the vampire screaming toward him, and started the car.

He shifted the lever into drive and jammed on the gas. The limousine shot forward just as the creature collided with the side of it, rocking the vehicle like a tiny boat on an angry ocean. By now, they would all be coming for him, swarming toward the car, more desperate than ever to stop him from escaping. The car thumped over Eric's body, and Christopher moaned at the loathsome feel of it.

He kept his foot on the gas. The engine whined as the car fishtailed off the driveway, into the grass, and then back out again as he fought to keep it going in the right direction. His door slammed shut, and he was finally barreling down the long driveway, outrunning the vampires as they chased him in a futile attempt to prevent another warlock from living.

• • •

He drove to Dayton, pulled up in front of the small hospital, and flopped out onto the pavement at the entrance to the emergency room. Someone burst out the door yelling. He remembered someone lifting him onto something that rolled, and they'd whisked him through the doors, into the building where fluorescent lights passed overhead, and doctors and nurses surrounded him. At some point, he passed out.

Two hours later, he groggily opened his eyes to the blurry sight of someone sitting in a chair next to him. An older man. *Markus?* Then he made out the face – brown eyes instead of blue and a gap in the front teeth. No one he knew. Christopher's nose felt squashed, and he realized it was a bandage pressed tight on his skin. His arm was bandaged and his chest hurt with every breath.

"Who are you?" Christopher asked and was shocked at the scratchiness in his own voice.

"You're waking up," the strange man said. "I'm Lieutenant Sorrenson, with the Dayton Police Department. How do you feel?"

"I've felt better." Christopher tried to move his bandaged arm and found it took considerable effort.

"You're pretty banged up," Lieutenant Sorrenson said.

"Yes."

"What happened?" The lieutenant spoke softly, nothing threatening.

"You wouldn't believe me if I told you." Christopher placed his hand to his head. His vision was starting to clear, and he glanced around the room. "What time is it?"

"Almost ten." The lieutenant glanced at his watch as if to confirm what he'd just said. "I have a lot of questions for you, starting with who did this to you."

Almost ten! Two hours! He heard Lieutenant Sorenson ask him something else, but he didn't care. He needed to get out of here... and fast.

CHAPTER 30

"If they attack us, they'll come all at once," Alexis said. She stepped carefully down the wooden steps and kept one arm hooked around Liam's elbow. She felt better, but not great, not by a long shot. That goddamned Michael. She hoped to meet that sonofabitch again, and soon. A dull pain, just above her navel, still lingered. Not an ache, but more of a pull, which bothered her. Something could still be wrong in there.

She glanced at Markus. "Indeed they will," he said scanning the tree line. Both of his hands rested on the top of his cane.

Just as she and Liam left the last step, she heard the car. Thank god.

She gripped Liam's arm tighter. She liked him, liked him a lot, but she hated that he was here. If anything happened to him, that guilt would be hers and hers alone, and she didn't need that shit in her life. Not now. Not ever. They'd need to drop him somewhere and get him out of all this, despite his objections, or anyone else's for that matter.

Still, she guiltily loved the feel of his arm, of his muscle beneath the shirt, and most lovely was how he regarded her. He'd bravely stand between her and danger, she knew he would because that's the kind of guy he was. Were there men still like that in the world? Men who would sacrifice for things greater than themselves?

Her eyes crawled back to Markus. Yes, she thought that there were.

Headlights splashed across the trees lining the driveway. It would be full dark soon. They had to keep moving. She and Liam hustled out to the edge of a short sidewalk.

"They're not coming yet," Markus said. The clunk of his wooden cane against the boards of the porch told her he was coming down behind them. "They're waiting."

"Waiting for what?" Liam looked over his shoulder at Markus.

"Nathaniel would be my guess," Markus said. "I assumed he was pursuing Christopher, but there's no other reason why the wolves would wait."

"Great. That guy again."

Markus said, "Not sure I'd call him a guy."

"Won't they..." Alexis coughed hard and covered her mouth with her fist. She anticipated the ensuing pain inside her and braced for its wrath. But it never came. *Thank God for that!* "Won't they attack once they see we're leaving?"

"Oh yes," Markus stated as if everyone should know. "They'll try to stop us, at least."

"How the hell did they find us?" Liam asked.

"Don't know," Markus said.

The car shot out from behind the shed and barreled down the driveway, slinging gravel and throwing up a cloud of dust. Strange, but she sensed something in Markus, a hesitancy. His eyes never drifted from the woodline as the car stopped abruptly next to them.

"What's wrong?" she asked him.

Markus's eyebrows shot up, and he cast a sideways glance at her. "You won't like it."

"There's a lot I don't like," she said the words confidently enough, at least she thought she did, but in the back of her mind she wasn't sure she wanted his answer.

Markus shifted his gaze back to the trees. "I don't think we should run. They're waiting, which means Nathaniel is not here yet."

Was he thinking of fighting them? *Of course, he is.*

This is what Markus does.

Liam popped open the door and swung it open to an empty backseat.

"Be careful with her, Liam!" Phillip was twisted around with one hand on the steering wheel and was looking at her. *Oh, Phillip.*

Liam said, "Just be ready to haul ass out of here."

Just then, a screeching howl followed by a deep-throated grumble drifted from the trees. It was too dark to see clearly as everything took on varying shades of gray. She'd heard that noise before and knew it all too well. Goosebumps broke out on her arms.

"Let's go." Markus opened the front door and climbed in with a grunt, apparently deciding not to stay and fight it out. She was just fine with that.

She ducked down and slid delicately across the seat. Liam shuffled in behind her and slammed the door shut.

Phillip jammed the accelerator, and the rear tires spun in the loose gravel, the car inched forward, catching traction with painful slowness. She dug her fingers into the leather seat and cinched her arm tight around Liam's. Liam uttered, "Oh, holy shit."

She followed his gaze out the window. Huge creatures, their heads low to the ground, charged from the trees across the field. Even in the dim light, she could see the open mouths, the wide eyes, and the thin frames reminding her of giant Hyenas.

God how she hated them.

The car crept along, still seeking traction, spewing gravel in a shower behind them. "Here they come!" Alexis gripped the seat in front of her.

Markus said, "Stop the car, Phillip. We're not going to make it."

"What!" Phillip gripped the steering wheel so tight his knuckles turned white. "Are you fucking crazy? Why in..."

The car stopped abruptly and the engine shut off. Alexis felt Markus's magic seeping out of him and taking control of everything. He rested his wrinkled hand on the dashboard. "I think it's about time we show them what we can do." Markus calmly opened his door and got out. Just before he closed it, he ducked his head back in and said, "Stay in the car."

The door banged shut, and he was gone.

Phillip yelled something about getting out of here with Markus's name peppered in here and there. Liam muttered, "Oh Jesus... Oh, Jesus Christ..." while staring out the window with eyes wide and one hand pressed on the glass.

She thought, *Goddamn it, Markus.*

She clenched her hand tight on her belly and slid across the seat. It didn't hurt as bad now.

She opened her door. "You guys do *not* get out of this car," she said.

She didn't wait for their response.

She got out and shut them safely inside.

·　·　·　·　·

He had a hunch she'd join him.

She braced herself against the back fender and breathed heavily, almost gasping. Markus glanced at her. "Try to calm down," he said.

The wolves bore down, a few hundred yards away and closing in. Their maddened growls drifted across the field.

"It's not the wolves that worry me, Alexis," he said turning back to face the onslaught.

"I know."

"If Nathaniel has already arrived and brought his Legions, this may not be a long fight."

The wolves were within one hundred yards.

"I don't think he's here yet," she said. "They're coming after us because we're leaving."

He nodded. He agreed.

Fifty yards.

She reached out and gripped his long coat. Markus was fine with that.

"We're surrounded." Markus gripped her shoulder and pulled her to him. "Keep your aim true."

Twenty yards.

She tensed.

Markus let go of her. He needed both hands free for this.

Through clenched teeth, he said, "Show them no mercy."

• • • • •

Markus thrust his arms forward as if pushing a drunk out of his face, and Alexis felt the air shudder, followed by a large *crack*. A thin ribbon of blue light shot out in a circle and fanned out like the concussion ring of an explosion. Behind them, the car rocked in squeaky protest and the rocks of the driveway peeled up in the wake.

The wolves didn't make it another inch. The ring of light collided with them, shearing them in half, slicing chunks of flesh from their grotesque bodies. The entire first wave blew apart and showered those behind them with blood and bone.

She turned toward the house. Hordes of wolves assailed from that direction. As Markus's deadly light streamed toward them, they fell flat on the ground and allowed the light to pass over, then scrambled back to their feet and continued the assault. She glanced over at Markus. His attention was focused on the ones coming from the woods.

She stepped to the back of the car and placed her hand on the cool metal of the trunk to steady herself. Markus's light ring hit the house, and it burst into flames and collapsed in a roar of crushing wood and bursting glass.

She lifted her hand, palm facing the wolves, and concentrated. The dull pain in her stomach throbbed. She clenched her teeth and squeezed her eyes shut.

Payback time.

The air danced in wavy mirages as the heat rose. It was all coming back and felt so good. She forced her energy forward like pushing a boulder.

Then the air ignited in a fury of flames that would have made Satan himself proud.

•　　•　　•　　•　　•

Markus watched her as she moved away from him. Her bout with Michael had rattled her confidence. Markus needed her back, and for a witch or wizard, that meant getting back into the heat of battle with both guns blazing.

Now, don't let her hurt herself, you old buzzard.

He also knew this was no ordinary enemy for her. It was the wolves, and her loathing ran deep for them.

To his front, the wolves advanced, though this time far more cautiously. They reared tall on their back legs, circling in anticipation, inching their way closer.

And so far, no Nathaniel.

Not yet. This fight needed to end before he arrived.

There was a good chance Christopher escaped, much to Markus's delight, the little bald guy had survived so far. If Alexis had another day or two for recovery, they'd be a force to be reckoned with.

Time to wrap this shit up.

Markus raised his arm and brought it down in front of him, splaying his fingers as if he had just passed a football. The wolves leapt at him, but it was too late. The sparkling ball of blue light shot into them like a comet.

The wolves in the front disintegrated, their wide eyes taking in the surety of their deaths a split second before they melted into a cloud of ash. The ones further back dove away, but their efforts proved just as futile.

He turned to Alexis as she collapsed against the side of the car. Wolves plunged through her weakening fire. The creatures charged, their fur singed and smoking, their teeth bearing a triumphant snarl.

Alexis screamed, but Markus sensed fury in that sound, not fear.

He stepped up next to her and placed a comforting hand on her shoulder (at least he hoped it was comforting) – it was her hatred that was exhausting her, not the fire. He leaned close to her ear and said, "It's magic, Alexis, and it comes from within you."

He stretched out his hand toward the wolves. "Sometimes it helps to say the words out loud." He slipped his other arm around her, pulling her closer and bearing her weight. As the wolves descended, he said, "Fulmen!"

Lightning erupted from his fingers and split as if striking a prism, and each spear sought a target with deadly precision. His skin thrummed as the energy surged through him. The small hairs of his arm and neck stirred and danced.

What *didn't* feel natural at all was his ka-thudding heart. Not something he'd experienced before and he wasn't exactly sure what to think of it.

He heard scuffling in the gravel behind him. He spun and faced a wolf leaping at him, soaring into the air across the car's top. He threw up a wall of fire, like a thick ribbon twisting and turning in a fanciful dance to unheard music. The wolf struck it and fell back onto its side, writhing in the gravel and clutching its face.

The remaining wolf-pack stopped at the edge of the yard, their comrade dead in the driveway. Markus's ribbon of fire elongated and stretched high into the air where it lingered like an apparition, and then descended rapidly onto the pack. The flames spread out like a blanket, swallowing everything that moved, even as the desperate creatures tried to escape back into the trees.

Just as quickly as it had started, the attack was over. The stream of lightning sputtered out and the fire dissipated and faded to nothing. Smoldering bodies littered the ground; fanned out in a massive circle around them. Markus stared at the severed head of a wolf, one glassy eye opened wide and the other shut.

For the first time in his life, a wave of dizziness swept over him. *Wooah... what the fuck was that?* His heart slammed against his ribs, and he could feel the blood throbbing in his neck and fingertips. He stood still, not sure what else to do. His body regained composure, but it imprinted a feeling on him that he'd never forget.

Markus glared back toward the woods. In the darkness, he could see their deformed frames, ghostly illuminated by the rising moon, and none of them moved any closer. They stared at him, some shifting uncomfortably from foot to foot.

"Come Alexis." Markus reached down to help her.

She took his hand.

"We've got to go. Nathaniel may be on his way here and we're best not to fight him in pitch black." Markus grimaced as Alexis used his hand to pull herself up.

"How fast can he travel?" She reached the back door of the car.

"Fast enough," Markus said. He actually didn't know for sure.

Alexis glanced at him, her soft green eyes open wide and perfect and Markus, for just a second, found himself lost in them. His wrinkled skin might as well have been silk, and the cancer killing him was forgotten. For that brief moment, Markus Blue was as good as he had ever been. A smile, one that appeared both forced and genuine, touched her lips.

Markus's eyes stung, and he blinked away tears that threatened to spill down his cheeks. *Get a hold of yourself.* Everyone dies, even warlocks. It seemed cruel that God allowed vampires the gift of immortality.

He didn't want to die.

He no longer accepted the inevitable truth as just another page in the book of time. His magic struck fear in the souls of those who opposed him. But despite everything he could do, there was nothing, not a damn thing, to stop the rot in his own body.

He smiled back at her, hoping she couldn't detect the hurt behind the effort. "I'm glad to see you've still got it."

She touched his arm and then climbed carefully into the car. Markus shut the door behind her and took one last look at the wolves. He debated pursuing them and finishing the job but decided he and his small band would be better served getting out of here. The wolves, at least *these* wolves, were no longer a threat.

He opened his door and climbed in, plopping down in his seat. "Are we ready to get out of here, gentlemen?"

Phillip didn't move at first, as if in a trance, and then shifted the car into drive and began to roll forward. Finally, he spoke. "I've never seen anything like that."

Markus looked back at Liam who stared at him with eyes big enough to lay a half-dollar coin on the eyeball and never touch his eyelid.

"Are you okay?" Markus asked.

Liam nodded but didn't speak. The car picked up speed, but Markus noticed the slight tremble in Phillip's hand as well as the thin bead of sweat that gleamed on his forehead. He'd settle down soon enough.

"Where we goin' now?" Phillip asked.

"We need to get to a small town in Nebraska called Rice's Crossing," Markus said.

"Nebraska?" Phillip's lip curled.

"Yes. It's another hiding place." Markus coughed into his fist. "Let's hope it's a little more hidden than the last one." The house in Rice's Crossing was owned by Christopher alone and, to Markus's knowledge, it was only he and Christopher that knew about it.

"Nebraska?" Phillip shook his head. "How are we supposed to get there?"

Markus leaned back in his seat and eased his eyes closed. He didn't feel well. "Just drive, Phillip. Do not stop driving."

"Is that the closest one we've got, there are no hiding places closer?"

"Of course there are, Phillip, but we're going to that one." Markus didn't have the energy to explain further. He just wanted to rest.

The car suddenly stopped, and Markus popped his eyes open. *Jesus Christ...* now what?

Markus squinted out the windshield and peered through the clearing dust. He saw an old Ford pickup truck parked in the road. Someone stood in front of it, staring back at them. This was goddamned strange.

Markus never shifted his gaze from the shadowy figure and said, ""Be ready to go and no one get out of this car."

Then he opened his door and got out.

CHAPTER 31

Charlie raised his hand to shadow the glare of the headlights. Dust swirled in and out of the beams.

Should I say something? Or walk up to it?

He didn't know.

But he felt... *something.* A connection of some sort, inarticulate, but still there, like looking across a crowded room at your best friend and knowing what they're thinking.

The passenger car door opened and Charlie squinted as an old man, leaning heavily on a cane, emerged. He hobbled out to the front of the car.

After a short pause, the old man said, "Get in the car, son."

What? This was so weird. But it felt so right. "Where are we going?"

"Anywhere but here."

Charlie crossed his arms over his chest and cupped his elbows in his hands. Was he seriously considering this? He wondered how kids felt just before entering a car or taking a short walk to their deaths at the hands of some crazy (his mother used to say the crazies... *stay away from people you don't know,* she'd say, *they may be one of the crazies*).

"My name's Markus," the old man said. "We have to leave now, young man. Now or never."

Recognition tingled as Nathaniel's words echoed, *Christopher and Markus, I will find you.*

Markus.

Charlie stepped forward. "What about my truck?"

"Leave it, son," Markus said.

Leave his dad's truck? He nearly said, *I can't.* The words danced on his lips. He pictured it parked along this gravel road, abandoned forever, and something about that image hurt.

But he *could* leave it. He would. It's just an old truck. Even his dad had said that many times. *It's just an old truck, son; they make more of 'em.*

He stepped toward Markus.

Past Markus, some ways behind him, Charlie noticed a red glow cast by the embers of a dying fire. Probably the chaos that the Amish guy mentioned when he'd said, *"it's not about the likes of us."*

His eyes caught movement a few hundred yards out into the bean field. At first, he thought it might be smoke drifting lazily across the ground, but then he realized that it was something else. Beady eyes reflected what little light the night contained and their bodies loomed tall like nightmarish silhouettes against the blackness of the woods behind them. A scream climbed from the pit of his chest, rising in his throat.

A hand gripped his shoulder.

"Let's go." Markus led him to the open car door, and he climbed inside, his heart banging so hard he felt it in his ears.

The door shut and Markus waved his hand, the signal *go.* Charlie pulled his knees up to his chest and wrapped his arms around them, holding them tight. He watched out the window as they drove past the truck, leaving it behind, and a strange emptiness engulfed him. He leaned his head down.

Something in this car stunk like they'd all been camping for a few days.

Were the people in the car staring at *him?*

"Can someone map us out of here?" the driver said. "I don't have a clue where we're at or how to get out of here."

Markus turned to Charlie. "Do you know how to get to the highway?"

Charlie heard the words but didn't know how to answer. Despite growing up here, he didn't know how to get many places when it came right down to it. And, it was awkward speaking with people he didn't know, even though being here felt overwhelmingly *right.* He wondered if everyone in this car was aware of what happened in Pheasant Hill. Did they know that a man named Nathaniel was looking for them or even who that was?

Finally, he said, muffled but audible, "Keep going straight. We have to get out of Amish country, I know that."

The guy in the back seat said, "I'll map us to Pittsburg, but my battery's close to dead. We need a car charger."

"We can stop once we're a ways from here," Markus said, "My phone's dead too."

Charlie thought, *mine's still at my house.* He couldn't remember if it was in his room or if he'd left it in the dining room on the counter next to where his dad hung his keys. He wished he had it.

He also didn't know why the words tumbled out of his mouth, "Everyone in my town is dead. All of them, I think."

The old man placed a hand on his shoulder, and it felt good.

Silence filled the space, and only the sound of the engine and gravel tinkling lightly off the undercarriage gave any indication that they were moving. He wondered what everyone was thinking and if they were staring at him.

"Just out of curiosity, when did you discover you had powers?" Markus asked.

Charlie's head shot up, startled. He didn't expect that question. He looked into the eyes of Markus, and though the darkness in the car hid the color, Charlie found himself lost in them. Recognition. Familiarity. *Someone who knew.*

Charlie's tears burst forth, and he leaned against Markus, laying his head on the old man's shoulder and bawling into the sleeve of his rough coat.

Markus sat silently while he cried.

They all did.

CHAPTER 32

Only a few minutes outside of Pheasant Hill, the cops pulled them over. The cops identified themselves as FBI (there were two of them), but Markus could give a shit what the difference was. After a tense couple of minutes where Phillip did all the talking, the cops let them go, which seemed odd given everything that happened there, but Markus didn't question it. He assumed Phillip intervened with a little mind-melding and left it at that. As long as they were moving.

Within an hour, they reached Interstate 80, just outside of a little town called Brookville. Liam slumped against his door; out cold. His mouth hung open, and his neck was bent in the shape of an L. *He's going to wake up hurting*, Markus thought.

They all needed rest. He considered that they should alternate drivers and stay on the road, but after a few hours, he wanted out of the car, if only for a short bit. His goddamned knees hurt so bad.

Just after midnight, before crossing into Ohio, they pulled into a deserted rest stop where he walked out the cramp in his knee. He tried smoking another cigarette, but like last time, it tasted like shit, and he flipped it into the damp grass. Why in the hell did he keep trying that? After some ample unfurling of the joints, it was time to go.

Phillip and Liam switched places, so Liam could drive for a while. At close to 2:30 AM, as they drove a desolate stretch of I-80, Markus looked over at Liam and said, "We should pull over the next chance we get and try to catch some sleep."

"That works." Liam glanced in the rearview mirror.

Markus shook his head. "I think Phillip is quite harmless back there and Alexis is safe. He's sound asleep." A smile curled the corners of his mouth, and he gazed out his window at the passing night.

Liam said, "Yeah, well…" his words faded off, and Markus let the silence linger.

After a few minutes, Liam kept his voice low. "Phillip told that FBI-guy that we're going to Michigan. I don't think the other guy bought it. I'm pretty surprised they let us go,"

"That's what Phillip does." Markus shrugged. "He *persuades* people. He persuaded that guy to let us go."

Markus's hand crept up to his side, and he gently massaged his ribs, more prominent than they'd ever been. He tried to recall the last time he'd eaten and couldn't remember a single thing since arriving at Christopher's ranch the day before. Had he eaten there? The fact that he still wasn't hungry after so much time was unsettling.

Then there was that dizzy feeling today. Did cancer cause that? It must. He'd never had that before, and the feeling lingered, and he couldn't quit thinking about it. Strange too that it happened when it did. He'd felt good, strong as ever, no coughing or anything. Then all the sudden, dizzy.

He also hoped Liam would keep talking. He rather enjoyed the conversation and found himself more and more fascinated by him. Looking back on his life, which he'd done a lot lately, he didn't understand why he hadn't spoken to more people; gotten to know them.

It seemed cancer prompted a whole host of shit he'd never done.

•   •   •   •   •

Liam checked the rearview mirror again. Phillip was sound asleep, and Alexis was sitting up, leaned against her door. Liam couldn't tell if she was asleep or just sitting with her eyes closed. He hated that Phillip was back there with her. He couldn't help wondering if Phillip had ever read *his* thoughts. How would he know? Would he feel it, maybe like a radio channel picking up two signals and sounding garbled? Silently, he questioned whether he could beat Phillip in a fist fight if it ever came to that. Liam had never been in an actual fight, but knowing Phillip was in love with Alexis made him think about it.

He needed to get his mind off all that.

Markus seemed willing to talk tonight, which Liam decided he'd take advantage of. He imagined what it would be like to write about a man like Markus. Can you imagine? After watching him back at that old house, the world had changed. Alexis too. It confirmed for him that *she* was the one who started that fire in Pittsburg. Christ on his throne, what had he stumbled into?

Liam looked over and noticed the deep lines in the old man's face and the sunken eyes. For a second, Markus resembled a corpse. Charlie slept between them; his head leaned back on the seat and tilted to one side. Liam wished he could sleep like that.

He spoke to Markus barely above a whisper. "What do you think Nathaniel is up to?" He checked his rearview mirror to see if Alexis moved. She didn't.

"Chasing us would be my guess," Markus said. "Hopefully we've thrown him off our trail for a little bit, enough time for us to recuperate."

"Can I ask you something?" He felt awkward.

"Sure," Markus said.

"It just seems like the Society is so unprepared. There's no one else but us?" Liam snorted and added, "No one else but you three, I should say."

"It does seem that way." Markus coughed into his hand, wet and hoarse, and then regained control.

"But you're the only warlock left," Liam said, "Doesn't the Society have more people than that?"

Markus sat back in his seat. He seemed to be in physical pain. "Jobe would have been a warlock. He wasn't a natural, though. Christopher was teaching him. At the end of the day, Jobe was a very powerful wizard. The Society has not found a natural warlock in decades. I suppose Christopher was the last."

"Christopher was younger than you?"

"About ten years younger, yes."

"Why weren't you the leader of the Society?"

"That's a long story." Markus smiled but didn't elaborate.

"So, counting Jason, William, Christopher, Jobe, Alexis, and you... the Society only had six people."

"Seven if you count Jonathan."

"That seems pretty slim."

"It is slim. Typically, we'd have a few more, but over the last hundred years, finding wizards and witches is much harder. Stories of gifted people used to be recognizable, but today, with all of the tabloids and crap, it's tough to distinguish between potentials and bullshit."

"Things like the The Unexplained Truth probably don't make it any easier," Liam said.

Markus coughed and then glanced down at Charlie, who was sleeping. "I suppose the Society is somewhat to blame as well. We got lazy. We weren't planning for war."

"I suppose not," Liam said. Deep in his own thoughts, he began to feel the first inklings of writing this story. He could start his *own* tabloid with all the shit he'd seen over the past two days. *Now I have a story that no one can beat, and to think that I saw it on Mulberry Street.*

Markus shifted in his seat and cast his gaze out the window. "I don't think anyone saw this coming. I'd guess that Nathaniel Smith was thinking the same thing, probably why he chose now to act."

"Great timing," Liam looked at him and said, "Right before they elect a new Pope."

Markus glanced back at him, a sense of alarm etched on his face. "That is *damned* odd."

"What, you think there's something to that?"

Markus turned back to the window. "Damned odd indeed."

They rode in silence listening to the sound of the car humming down the deserted interstate. In the distance, he could see lights from a town approaching, like spotting a small batch of distant stars. He hoped like hell there was a motel in that town. He decided he'd also call his editor, Jeremy, first thing in the morning and fill him in on what was going on without disclosing where they were. They also needed a phone charger something fierce. Everyone's phone was dead.

Markus didn't say another word and stayed awake. Liam had not seen the old guy so much as doze since he'd met him.

Did he ever sleep?

CHAPTER 33

Christopher crossed the border of Texas and entered Kansas on Highway 131 at 4 AM. He'd just popped three painkillers hoping to relieve the constant throb in his right arm. He wanted to stop and sleep somewhere but hated the idea of taking the time to do it. Nebraska was five hours away.

Markus had not contacted him since the barn. They couldn't project because Nathaniel may hear it. He'd tried calling everyone's phone but not one of them answered. Didn't anyone know how to charge a goddamned phone?

Christopher *had* to arrive before them. If he fell asleep now, he may not wake up for hours. If he kept driving, he'd arrive several hours before the others, which was ample time to warn them.

He tried calling every fifteen minutes, hoping like hell someone would eventually pick up. Dear god, what if they were all dead? He wouldn't entertain that thought. Plus, it seemed unlikely since he found out they were heading to Nebraska. The Chasers had told him that based on an intercepted message from one of Nathaniel's' main spooks, Sydney. The worst part was that it didn't sound like Markus was aware that Nathaniel knew.

That goddamned Phillip!

Christopher decided to call the Vatican for updates. It would also help him stay awake. The Camerlengo, fill-in for the Pope until a new Pope is elected, took the call himself and the concern in his voice told the story – the Society, the Chasers, and even those within the Vatican had become the hunted. Nathaniel Smith was now in charge.

By what little background noise Christopher could pick up through the phone, it sounded like utter chaos at Vatican City. Christopher heard sirens, muffled discussions, and even thought he heard someone crying at one point.

"What's happening there?" Christopher asked. The cell phone lay on his leg, emitting the noise through speaker-phone.

"We are being moved," the Camerlengo said. His voice sounded distant, and Christopher thought he heard an echo, as if the man were in a tunnel, "We are all in danger."

"Where to?"

"I don't know. The Swiss Army will not even tell us. But it is happening quickly."

"It's for the better," Christopher said, "You must stay safe. Nathaniel is going after you to remove any political leadership."

"We are being escorted by the Swiss Army, which is all I know." The Camerlengo's voice trembled.

"Is Nathaniel there?" Christopher asked.

"We don't know. I don't think so. We think he is in pursuit of Markus Blue."

Christopher crinkled his eyebrows. "I think so too. One of the people with Markus is a mole, and I believe it's Phillip Sawyer. Someone tipped Nathaniel off where Markus is going, and I don't think Markus knows."

"My prayers are with him. Can you not call him?"

"No one's answering." Christopher shook his head in the darkness of the car, frustrated. Damn cell phones. "Listen, sir, follow the Swiss, they'll keep you safe. We desperately need you to stay safe. I'm on my way to intercept Markus right now."

"We are counting on you, Christopher. And Markus. God's hand be over you. I have to go." The Camerlengo hung up.

Thank god the Camerlengo was safe for now.

He dialed Markus's number again and held the phone to his ear. It rang once, twice, and a third time before the voicemail picked up. The greeting on the voicemail was still the generic greeting by some computer-generated voice that came with the phone – Markus had never changed it, which wasn't a surprise. Christopher listened patiently. "... if you'd like to leave a message, please press one or just wait for the tone. To page this person, please press...."

Christopher waited. Piss on it. He hadn't wanted to leave all this detail on a voicemail, but he needed to use all means possible. Finally, the beep came.

"Markus," Christopher spoke fast. "Nathaniel knows you're going to Nebraska – I think Phillip might've told him somehow. I also think

Nathaniel's plan may be off since he failed to kill you or me." Christopher ran through the past week's events, reciting them into the phone, and found the breaking point – that point where Nathaniel's plan had failed on execution. "Here's the whole puzzle.

"Nathaniel killed the high council governance of vampires in Germany. The Chasers were sent to investigate – the Chasers who went there disappeared, and we assume they walked into an ambush. I sent Jonathan to New York to investigate an alleged Legion ceremony. Jonathan was found in Florida, decapitated in a swamp." Christopher took a breath, cleared his throat, and continued.

"An old priest in Pittsburg reported to his hierarchy that he'd witnessed the sighting of a vampire, Michael, and a Legion. I sent Jobe and Alexis to investigate. Another ambush, but not a slaughter. Somehow, Nathaniel found out you were alive, my old friend! I believe he thought you were dead. He had to come up with a hasty plan to deal with you. So, instead of killing Alexis, Nathaniel visited a Lutheran minister, ostensibly to beg for forgiveness, but the reality is... Nathaniel had counted on the Lutheran pastor to report it to the police. It was all a set-up! When I heard that Nathaniel was in Pittsburg, we assumed the worst, and you left immediately. Exactly as Nathaniel had wanted. Nathaniel then had me alone, and you were virtually unreachable while flying in an airplane. The trap was set to kill the two living warlocks – Nathaniel would kill me and then go to Pittsburg and kill you. Divide and conquer. But it didn't quite work that way. He didn't expect the job of killing me to be as difficult as it was – it took too long. He didn't make it back to Pittsburg before you found Alexis and freed her.

"Now Nathaniel has everything in place to attack Vatican City, except he still has two warlocks running loose. Well... one he knows for sure is out there, which is you. And I'm sure he knows by now that I escaped the compound."

Christopher thought for a moment. "He also found out you're heading to Nebraska. Watch out for Phillip, I believe he might be betraying us." Christopher crinkled his eyebrows. He hated the thought of that, but all signs were pointing that direction. The goddamn question was *why*. "I hope to see you soon, old friend."

He ended the call and let the phone rest on his leg. He breathed a sigh of relief and once again found himself coveting the vampire's ability to fly.

He wanted to be in Nebraska, *needed* to be there. Too bad the private jet was sitting somewhere in Pittsburg! Still, amidst the calamity and chaos, Christopher was feeling better about things, especially after Markus's last projection. He felt they had a chance to regroup and possibly come up with a plan to win.

Christopher yearned to see Markus and to discover a way to regain the upper hand.

PART III

MARKUS BLUE

CHAPTER 34

Markus rested his hand on the metal railing of the balcony outside his third-floor motel room. It was cool to the touch and slippery with morning dew. He gazed across the landscape of this little Ohio town. The sun was about to crest the horizon, and it cast a majestic display of soft red and orange reflections on the underside of the clouds. An old water tower jutted above the treetops with rusty streaks running through the faded, blue paint of its surface.

He stood there, alone. His pack of KOOLs was almost empty as he fished them from his coat pocket and shook one out, then lit it. He exhaled the smoke in a steady stream and then coughed, grimacing at the fluid rumbling deep in his chest. Just like before, the stale cigarette flavor clung to the inside of his mouth and tasted like shit. He flipped the entire cigarette out into the dirty parking lot below not sure why he'd had an urge to light it in the first place. Jesus Christ, you'd think lung cancer would kill any desire to smoke a goddamned cigarette.

Alexis, Liam, Charlie, and Phillip were asleep. Markus wished they were out here with him to see this. He pictured Alexis standing next to him, not talking, just relishing this moment in time, as if this were the last one. A man's pride made him stupid, and even warlocks were not exempt from that. He'd never thought he needed anyone.

Now as an old man, he was nothing but a dying fool.

He coughed another strong spasm that left him bent over and clutching his knees. When it passed, he eased up and placed his hand on his chest, listening to the hoarse, raspy air moving in and out of his body. His breathing was the reason he couldn't sleep anymore. He was afraid of never waking up. In his mind's eye, he saw Liam and Alexis shaking his lifeless body, trying to wake him, and then leaving him there lying in a messy bed in a cheap motel room.

Nothingness. *Except,* he thought, *that old water-tower will go right on standing, and the sun will go right on rising and setting.* Strange thinking about the world going on without him.

These death-thoughts widened a growing void. He didn't know what it was that made up the void; emptiness, sadness maybe? It wasn't the physical act of dying that scared him as much as wondering how his little gang here would fare against Nathaniel without him if it came to that.

As if he were abandoning them.

• • • • •

Liam awoke to the sound of coughing outside his door and knew Markus was out there. Phillip's snoring echoed an annoying purr. Liam wondered if anyone would notice if he got up and snuck out with Alexis and just left Phillip laying here. Would anyone care? It was a nasty thought, but he thought it just the same.

Alexis slept with her back against him, lying on her side. He slid his arm over her shoulder and pressed his body against her, hoping like hell she wouldn't elbow him in the face. She was warm and perfect against him.

She rolled onto her back and peered up at him, her deep green eyes sparkling and vibrant, and her presence engulfed him. The very essence of her seeped into him, *through* him, and his greatest fulfillment was her existence. A harbored tension he hadn't known was there relaxed and his muscles softened. Her brown hair was strewn across her face, and she looked absolutely mesmerizing.

"Hey," she said.

"Hey." He kept his voice low.

"What time did we stop last night?"

He yawned and said, "About two-thirty, I think." Much of the color had returned to her face, and she didn't seem to be in any pain.

"Where's everyone else?" She put her arms above her head and stretched. She winced, but nothing major. He also noticed the hem of her shirt exposing her navel.

"Phillip's asleep in the bed next to us. Charlie's in the other room." He gently pushed some stray hairs out of her face and added, "I think Markus is outside on the balcony. I heard him coughing a minute ago."

She smiled. It was so good to see her smile.

Her smile faded to a small crease. "I'm sorry," she said.

"For what?"

"For getting you into this."

"I think I got myself into it." It was the best thing he could think of right then. Technically, she *did* get him into it, but he didn't want to say that to her, not right now anyway. Plus, cracking a joke about something so serious might go over like a fart in church.

"Jobe told me to leave you alone, but I didn't listen."

"Hey," he looked into her eyes, lost in them. "I *want* to be here. With you."

"*Sure* you do." She chuckled.

He smiled and kissed her cheek. "Well, I can't start fires or anything, but I'm still glad."

A loud pounding on the door caused both of them to jump.

Markus's voice, "Time to get moving."

"Okay," Liam yelled.

"Guess we need to get going." Alexis sat up.

"Guess so." Liam watched her and thought about all the little times in life when moments are perfect and how quickly they're gone and how, if we're not careful, we'll miss them.

"He's right, we need to go." Phillip's voice sounded like someone with laryngitis. "We were supposed to only be here for a few hours."

"How long you been awake?" Liam asked. *Has that fucker been lying there listening to us, pretending to be asleep?*

"Markus banging on the door woke me up," Phillip said.

"Guess we're not taking showers." Alexis leaned against the bed frame. She definitely looked ten times better than she had last night.

"Here." Liam reached out and took her hand. She gripped it willingly. As they strode toward the door, Liam could feel Phillip's disgusted stare searing into the back of his head.

      •   •   •

Driving across Ohio was boring. They bought three car-chargers. After about thirty minutes, Markus's phone chirped to life. He checked his voicemail while everyone discussed where they wanted to eat lunch. He listened to Christopher's voicemail and clenched his jaw tight enough to feel the ache deep in his teeth. *Shit.*

His initial reaction was to order Phillip to stop the goddamned car, inform everyone their plan had been compromised, then deal with Phillip right there on the spot. *Goddamn it, Phillip.*

There was also the chance that Christopher might be wrong about the betrayal. At the very least, he wanted to understand why before he took any action. He would need to speak to Alexis soon about this. He'd also need to call Christopher as soon as they were at a place where he could be alone.

So much for a secret regrouping in Nebraska.

They all agreed on Burger King. While Phillip pulled through the drive-thru, everyone else ran inside to use the restroom and then gave Phillip his chance to go when they all returned to the car. Markus stole the opportunity to step off by himself and call Christopher. It went straight to voicemail. "It's Markus, got your message. Call me when you can."

He hobbled back to the car and rustled into the backseat. Alexis asked, "Everything okay?"

"I'm not sure," he said and left it at that.

No one said anything, which was fine with him for right now. He needed to think. As they pulled back out onto the highway, the one thing that clung to his thoughts was Christopher's statement about Nathaniel's plan (which was sounding far more brilliant, and global, than he'd ever anticipated) and hitting a wrinkle due to his (Markus's) existence and Nathaniel's failure to kill him and Christopher.

Which meant that going to Nebraska was not part of Nathaniel's master plan either. If there was an upper hand to be gotten, it may not get better than that. Time was a factor also. They couldn't just keep running. Staying the course may work better by –

"They don't have a Burger King in Pheasant Hill," Charlie said. Everyone stared at him, shocked that he'd spoken.

Markus had never been a fan of fast-food, but as they'd ordered and then handed out the bags of burgers and fries, his stomach growled. As he unwrapped the burger and watched it resting on his lap, he couldn't eat it. He swore he was hungry, but the thought of eating was almost nauseating. That had been happening more and more lately.

The burger rested on his knees for several minutes before he wrapped it up and dropped it back in the bag. He said, "We should be close to Chicago. That'll put us about five hours from Nebraska."

"You never really told me why we're going to Nebraska," Liam said from the front seat. Markus and Alexis sat in the back with Charlie between them. Liam was stuck up front with Phillip. Markus had no idea how *that* had happened.

"You never really asked," Markus said. Could Liam be a snitch for Nathaniel? Markus didn't think so, but no one really knew Liam at all and he'd come into their presence rather oddly. But Alexis seemed to like him, which if he was a rat, she'd have sniffed him out long ago. She may be young but certainly didn't lack intuition.

"You said it was best to get as far from Nathaniel as possible." Liam twisted in his seat, chewing vigorously, and caught Markus's gaze. "So *why* are we going to Nebraska, exactly?"

"To kill Nathaniel," Markus said, then thought, *Oh Christ, now he'll ask more questions.*

"You couldn't kill him back there in Pennsylvania?"

"Perhaps. But perhaps not. Alexis needs more time to heal. I need her. And I need Christopher."

Phillip looked at Markus in the rearview mirror. "Christopher?"

"Yes, Phillip," Markus said, "Christopher will be joining us there."

Phillip slapped his hand against the steering wheel, all smiles. "I had no idea."

"He certainly didn't have an easy day yesterday, but he is alive and on his way to Nebraska as we speak," Markus wondered if Phillip having that information could hurt them. Of course, it could. *Shut up, old man.*

"Why didn't you say anything?" Phillip asked.

Markus said, "I wanted to make sure we were clear of Nathaniel. I didn't want him to find out Christopher was alive, or where he was, or where we were going... right now, we have the element of surprise." He watched Phillip closely and caught the slight downcast of his eyes.

Christopher was right.

"How would Nathaniel find out?" Liam asked glancing first at Phillip then back at Markus.

"There are many ways, I suppose," Markus said, then added, "Phillip, do you care to elaborate?"

Phillip's startled face reflected back at him in the rearview mirror as if someone just slapped his ass. He stumbled over the words, "I don't know."

Alexis cleared her throat and pushed her hair back behind her ears.

"How do you know Nathaniel thinks Christopher's dead?" She asked. Even though she kept her excitement of Christopher joining them at bay, it still rested just below the surface where Markus sensed her exuberance.

"I don't know for sure," Markus said. "But we can hope."

"Who *is* Nathaniel?" Charlie asked wolfing down the last of his sandwich.

"Nathaniel," Markus said, "is a vampire."

Markus, Phillip, and Alexis explained the entire scenario with Markus doing most of the talking, except for the part about what happened at the hotel in Pittsburg... Alexis told most of that. The recitation sparked good conversation, which never hurt a damn thing in long car rides. Just as they were about to cross from Illinois into Iowa on Interstate 80, as Markus was gazing out his window, Charlie said, "I saw Nathaniel back in my town. I hid from him and listened to them."

An awkward silence filled the car, and Markus wondered why this had not come up earlier. "Them?" he asked.

Charlie nodded. "There were two of them. One was ridiculous tall and wore this weird robe-thing like a Jedi Knight or something, and the other one wore like an old Army uniform."

Michael.

"The one in the uniform is named Michael," Alexis said, "What did they say?"

"Mainly, they just talked about you guys. Oh, and the tall one was always praying. Isn't that weird? And he limped and looked like he'd been burned on one side."

Nothing at all wrong with that, Markus thought and wanted to elaborate on it later, but first, he wanted to know if Charlie experienced the Projection of Vagaries. "Did you ever have any weird visions or feel cold?"

Charlie scrunched his eyebrows, seriously considering this, and then said, "No, I don't think so." Before anyone else could say anything, Charlie asked, "What is so hard about killing Nathaniel?"

Phillip glanced in the rearview mirror. "He's only the most powerful vampire in history. And the oldest." Phillip said this as if it explained everything.

"Yeah, but you're a warlock." Charlie shifted his gaze to Markus.

A faint smile crossed Markus's face as he debated on how to answer.

"A fair question," He wondered if Alexis had any inclination as to what made Nathaniel the threat that he was. "Care to answer, Alexis?"

Alexis looked caught off guard like she'd been thinking about whether the moon was made out of cheese or rock. "I don't know as much as Markus. I've never actually met Nathaniel, but I met Michael a few days ago. I hope to meet him again. Soon."

"But you can create fire," Charlie turned toward her.

"I can, but I'm only one person." She looked up at Markus as if seeking approval. He nodded, and she continued. "I have my limitations. Remember what I said happened at the hotel in Pittsburg?"

Charlie nodded.

"There were too many of them. The only other option would have been to destroy the hotel entirely." She clasped her hands together on her lap. "That would have killed dozens, maybe hundreds of innocent people, including me. It's hard to fight in places where there are lots of people."

Liam snapped his fingers. "*That's* why we're going to Nebraska," he said with a beam of understanding.

"Yes." Markus gave a quick nod. "That's one of the reasons. And to regroup with Christopher in a place Nathaniel doesn't know about." His eyes trailed to Phillip to gauge his reaction. Nothing out of the ordinary, but if a snitch was among them, a little misinformation wouldn't hurt a damn thing.

Charlie shuddered and asked, "Is Nathaniel a warlock?"

Ah, now *this* was the question. Markus glanced toward the floorboard and not knowing how his next statement would resonate, said, "Not a warlock. But I believe he *is* a wizard. And he's at least a thousand years more experienced than me."

CHAPTER 35

The gravel along the edge of the blacktop crunched as Christopher stopped and gazed out the windshield. Acres of green cornfields lined both sides of the road. An old wooden sign jutted out of the grass a few yards in front of him with faded words in blue paint: Rice's Crossing.

He licked his lips and tapped the top of the steering wheel with his thumbs. A small flutter rippled through him, and he considered stepping out of the car to stand on this lonesome road in the middle of nowhere. Had it been twenty years? Or more? At least twenty since he and Markus were here. Hell, everything was twenty years ago nowadays.

He let off the brake and let the car ease forward. The decrepit sign slid slowly past, and soon after, the town itself came into view. First the rooftops, followed by sparse houses, a few mobile homes on the outskirts in yards dotted with junk, and finally the road that led into the quaint downtown where a lonesome flashing yellow light dangled above the street.

Just before entering, he stopped again and shifted the car into Park.

"Jesus," he whispered, "I didn't think there were this many people here." But surely there always had been. There were no new structures that he could see.

His phone, lying next to him on the seat, buzzed to life and the name *Markus* graced the screen. *Thank god!*

He reached down to grab it and then stopped when he saw the reflection in his rearview mirror. The cop was already striding up to his window. Christopher found it surprising how bright the blue, flashing lights were, even in the late afternoon sun.

Shit, he thought. *What a wreck I must look like.*

The officer made a little circular motion with his finger, the unspoken command for *roll down the window.*

Christopher obeyed, pushing the button on the inside of the door. The window hummed open.

"You aware this vehicle is stolen, sir?" The officer leaned down and peered inside.

"No, sir," Christopher said. "I rented this car night before last from Hertz in Dayton, Texas. I have the receipt right here." He plucked the Hertz envelope off the passenger seat. What the hell was going on? Who would have reported the car stolen? Who even knew he had it?

"Hmmm." The officer's eyes narrowed, and Christopher thought the man resembled a young Clint Eastwood. "Let me see the receipt."

"Yes, sir." Christopher handed him the envelope. "You can check it. No idea why the car would come up stolen."

"What happened to your arm?" The cop asked as he dug the folded paper out.

"Accident," Christopher said, then elaborated, "Car accident. Hence, why I rented a car."

"Accident, huh?" The man didn't look convinced.

"Yes, sir," Christopher patted his arm. "Car accident down in Texas a few days ago."

"I see." The officer flattened out the rental receipt and reviewed it. "I'll need your license too."

Most guilty people talk too much, Christopher thought, *just don't start talking like a blithering idiot and you'll be fine.* He handed over his driver's license.

The cop examined both items, glancing back and forth between them.

"Place still looks the same." Christopher shifted his gaze from the cop to the town.

"Been a lot of stuff going on around here the past couple of years," the cop said never taking his eyes off of the items in front of him. "We got a new bakery."

"It's been a few years for me," Christopher said and wondered what all the *stuff* was. He didn't see a damned thing new.

The cop handed him the receipt for the rental car and stood up straight. "Looks legit to me. Give me a second. Wait here."

Christopher watched in the side mirror as the cop walked back to his car, opened the door, and reached inside for his radio. The man stood with his elbow propped against the door frame looking confused and irritated at the same time.

How many people lived here now? Christopher would guess at least a few hundred by the looks of things, maybe more. Probably more. Goddamn it, he needed to speak to Markus about all this. He could assume that since Markus called him, that he'd received the voicemail, which meant they'd either decided to turn around and go somewhere else, or they were coming here anyway since Christopher was here. He could confirm that easily enough with a text.

He checked the side mirror to see if the cop had noticed anything. The officer still leaned against the door of his cruiser with his radio in his hand and glared out across a field as if waiting for an answer to something. *Who is that cop talking to*, he wondered. The state cops maybe? Or the FBI? Christopher had no idea how law enforcement out here worked. Probably nothing like Texas, which was a pain in the ass. Unpredictable.

Christopher tapped his thumbs on the top of the steering wheel, waiting. He could see his ultimate destination from where he was parked. An old farmhouse stood a few hundred yards away on the outskirts of town. He had no idea who the caretaker was anymore. He'd probably received a letter or maybe even a call about it at some point in the past, but couldn't recall. Most likely, Eric or one of his Messengers had handled that business. The only way he'd find out now was by strolling up and knocking on the front door. Meeting them face-to-face. Explaining the situation might get tricky. *Hi, my name's Christopher, and I own this house... there's a shit-load of vampires here somewhere. Can I come in?*

He smiled and wiped his hand across his mouth, which felt too dry.

"Sir," the officer said approaching his window again. "I need you to step out of the car."

Christopher had time to think, *now what the hell*, before he said, "Can I ask what the problem is?"

"Just step out of the car." The officer's hand moved toward his pistol, not drawing it, but holding it close to show he was serious.

Oh, for the love of Christ.

So much for the brilliant plan, if there had ever been one.

CHAPTER 36

"What's wrong?" Charlie asked. He sat on a picnic table, his butt on the eating surface with his feet resting on the long, wooden seat. They were stopped at a rest-stop just past Des Moines to use the restroom, unfurl the muscles, and relish the fact that this was most likely their last stop before reaching Rice's Crossing. The afternoon sun was already on its downward arc.

Markus raised his eyebrows, debating whether to get into this conversation and then decided what the hell. "I'm just concerned about where we're going." His voice was scratchy, and his throat felt like he'd eaten a bucket of dry sand. He gripped the top of his cane and leaned heavily on it.

"Nebraska, you mean?"

"Yep." Markus dug in his pocket for the pack of KOOLs and remembered he'd thrown the pack away at the previous rest-stop.

"Something else happen?"

Answering mundane questions at this point sounded as appealing as licking razor wire with his dry tongue. Sometimes he just wanted to be alone with his thoughts. *Selfish old man. What if you die before you get there?*

He looked over at Charlie who stared back with wide eyes. Liam, Phillip, and Alexis were all in the restroom. It was just the two of them out here basking in the late afternoon sunlight. One unknowingly held the future of the Society in his hands, and the other was on his way out. Life's nasty little dance.

"I told all of you about Christopher's voicemail," Markus said. "And how Nathaniel likely knows we're coming."

"Yeah."

"That's all I got. Just thinking about that." Markus considered mentioning that he was worried about Phillip but held back on that part.

He'd told Alexis earlier in the day about Christopher's suspicions, but no one else knew since they could still be wrong about him. She'd appeared stunned at first, then shook her head. *"No,"* she'd said, *"I don't think so. He's a pain in the ass and annoying, but not a traitor. Unless he doesn't know he's betraying us."*

"So we don't know anything." Charlie nodded in a gesture that said *that's all I needed to know, really.*

Markus smiled. He liked this boy.

A pause in the conversation hung in the air while the breeze ruffled their hair and the traffic on Interstate 80 whizzed past. And then Charlie asked, "Are you going to teach me how to fight?"

Markus cast a sideways glance at Charlie with smirk curling the corner of his mouth. "Why would I want to do a fool thing like that?"

Charlie peered over at him, and Markus read that expression clear as a bell. *Are you shitting me?* that look said.

"Yes," Markus said and chuckled, "baptism by fire, I'm afraid." He clapped a hand lightly on Charlie's shoulder. "You'll be fine, I should think."

He glanced toward the small, brick building containing the restrooms and noticed Liam and Alexis striding down the sidewalk, past the trash cans, coming toward them, lost in a conversation between themselves. He wondered if Phillip was still in the restroom or out sulking in the car. Phillip's attitude had grown steadily worse during this drive, and he seemed to be hiding something, which sparked even more uneasiness. He'd considered confronting Phillip, just to see what type of reaction he'd get. But, if Phillip was aiding Nathaniel with information, it was best he didn't know that Markus knew.

Charlie looked at him and said, "What if I can't... you know... do it?"

"Then I suppose our meeting outside of Pheasant Hill, a monumental coincidence in and of itself, was nothing but a point of two strangers coming together for nothing. No plan, no order, no nothing."

Charlie rested his chin on his hands.

Markus said, "You'll learn, Charlie, that the world is not actually chaos. There *is* a higher power, be that God or whomever you choose, and that power deals in checks and balances. I suppose if I had to sum it all up, I'd say it's nothing more than energy. There's good energy and bad energy, and they're constantly playing each other for the upper hand. For centuries, the good energy has ruled and maintained order. But right now, the bad is attempting to upset the apple cart and reclaim the rule. That's the war we're fighting, and that's the war we must win."

"I think it's God." Charlie stared down at the ground.

"Perhaps," Markus shrugged. "Not my revelation or brilliance. Not to bore the shit out of you, but these are teachings of a warlock named Nostradamus, whom some believed could see the future. A long damn time ago, centuries ago, he defeated the vampires and planned to annihilate them, but was stopped by The Vatican for fear that the war would never end. He actually predicted the vampires would never settle for peace and would return with a vengeance."

"What's the Vatican?"

Mundane questions. "I'm not in the mood to give more history lessons, but for now, think of the Vatican as a very powerful church the size of a small city."

"How come The Vatican runs everything? Why not the government or something?" Charlie ran his hands through his hair.

"Hell if I know. They just always have. Christopher will be better than I at explaining all these things."

Charlie nodded.

A tickle pestered Markus's throat, and he coughed into his hand. Red speckles dotted his palm, and he winced. *Fuck.* "Let's be getting on the road, shall we? The sun will be down soon, and we're almost there."

He moved toward the car, coughing and limping feebly on his cane.

CHAPTER 37

"You must alert me if you see anyone suspicious." That is what the dark man told Betty Haddock just before promising to bring her husband back to life.

Getting around this old house wasn't getting any easier, but she needed to look out the window. She heard a damn noise out there, like a cop siren, and needed to see what it was. She hobbled to the living room and pushed the laced, semi-transparent curtain back and gazed outside, noticing Everett Hendrick's police car, less than quarter a mile away, parked along the road with the flashing lights on. In front of him was a car she didn't recognize. She'd known Everett since he was in grade school and she'd been watching out this window since before he was born.

"I need to get my glasses," she murmured and let the curtain fall back over the large picture window that faced town.

Her hips had started going bad around 2007, just before her husband, Harry, passed away from his third stroke, God rest his soul, and nowadays, just walking from one point in the house to the other was becoming a struggle without her cane. *Goddamn it, Betty*, Harry would say while sitting in his recliner (he sat in his recliner a lot toward the end, and she'd left the chair in the very spot it had been when he was alive), *you're going to fall and break something if you keep forgetting your cane.* He was right about falling; she'd fallen over half a dozen times in the past few years. Luckily, she had yet to break anything, thank Jesus. Harry had always looked out for her, and she missed him terribly. Many folks thought he was gruff, maybe even rude, but those were the people who didn't know his heart.

As she reached the kitchen, she spotted her cane propped against the end of the dining room table. She grabbed it up and leaned on it, feeling instant relief in her hip. "Now where're my glasses?"

She heard the women in the other room, most of them packing up to leave for wherever it was they came from, laughing and talking about what a great time they'd had. She loved the weekends when the women came for scrapbooking, and the house was full. Several years ago, just after Harry passed away, she was told by a few of the older women in town (some of whom had lost their husbands as well) that she needed to do something to occupy herself, keep herself busy. She had no children and no nieces or nephews, and she was just sixty-five years old when Harry passed away.

The idea to rent out the upstairs bedrooms had dropped into her lap, quite literally, by accident one morning when a woman stopped by to try and sell her Mary Kay make-up. Betty remembered thinking, *Jesus, Mary, and Joseph, woman, you must be hard up to try to sell that stuff to me.* Betty hadn't bought any make-up, like she needed that stuff anyway (Harry would roll in his grave if she started painting herself up), but just before they parted ways, the woman said, *you should make this into a little country cottage thing... an old house like this, people would love to stay here for the weekends, like one of those bed-and-breakfasts.*

A few days after that, she drove into Hastings to buy materials for her scrap-booking (she was putting together a scrapbook of Harry's life and needed special paper and materials – he'd had such a full life). The woman running the store mentioned a crop she was planning to have in the store that weekend, which is a scrapbooking term meaning a get together for a group of people, usually women, to scrapbook together. She wondered if Betty would be interested in coming.

I live in Rice's Crossing, Betty said, *don't know that I'd want to drive all the way out here at my age.* Normally, crops lasted until midnight – Harry had never liked her to be out past dark. It was just like him to worry about her every minute of the day.

Well, the woman smiled. *Give me a call if you'd be interested.*

Maybe we could have it in Rice's Crossing, at my house, Betty was joking, at least that's what she'd told herself anyway, but she absolutely loved scrapbooking and loved crops and had always wanted to host one.

Within a year, using Betty's house for the monthly crop was a common occurrence. One night, during a particularly long crop, at close to two in the morning, a young woman asked to spend the night. *I don't want to drive all the way to Omaha this late,* she'd said, and Betty had obliged and made up one of the four spare bedrooms.

Five years ago she'd named the place *Betty's Hideaway,* and within half a decade, she had all four upstairs bedrooms (with three beds in each room) filled on nearly every weekend charging each woman $150 for their entire stay – normally three days and two nights: Friday through Sunday. In fact, the place had turned into a prestigious spot with a waiting list. Most of the women came from Omaha or Lincoln, but there were a few who drove all the way from North Platte or even Des Moines, and she knew of one lady who drove from Denver once a year. She sometimes wondered what Harry would think of all this. Likely, he'd have said he didn't agree with it, but then massaged her shoulders and told her how hard she worked and that he was proud of her for it. He was always doing little things like that. But, he didn't like strange people staying in their house either.

Mainly because the house wasn't theirs. Truth be known, Betty didn't actually know *who* owned it, except that Harry was hired to be the caretaker decades ago. Harry had taken care of all the logistics in that deal, Betty knew nothing about it except that he'd made the decision and that was that.

A check for $5,000 came in the mail every month, still made out to Harry. Even in death, he still took care of her in his own way. Though nothing would replace his warm body lying next to her, snoring in bed. Or his crooked smile when she did something silly. She'd done okay the past several years, but nothing could replace him.

Not until the dark man appeared last night and promised to bring Harry back to life.

•   •   •   •   •

"There they are." Betty spotted her glasses next to the sink and shuffled over to the kitchen counter. She wanted to see who Everett had pulled over out there on the road, not that she'd know them, but so she could tell the dark man if it turned out to be someone strange inquiring about the house.

She made her way back to the window. She heard women out in the foyer burst out laughing, but Betty ignored them as she usually did unless they needed something. She pulled the curtain back to resume her stare at Everett and the strange car. They were still parked in the same place, but Everett was now standing back by his squad car with the door open. Betty watched Law & Order, and she knew that Everett was probably calling in the license plate.

Anything at all, the dark man had said. His name was Sydney. *Most likely it will be someone claiming to own this house.*

The dark man, tall and dressed in a long coat, had stood politely in the walkway until Betty asked him to come in and sit down. He moved gracefully, almost as if his feet were not touching the floor – more of a gliding effort to reach the faded couch of the living room.

DAVID ODLE 165

Three things seared into her memory forever: his eyes, his words, and how darn cold it had gotten.

The eyes, distant and glassy, reminded her of something familiar, though she wasn't sure what. Perhaps, it was the neatly combed hair, slicked back with what looked like a gallon of Vitalis hair gel. Harry had always used Vitalis, and the aroma followed him like a wet fart, she hated it but adored it at the same time. Maybe those things distracted her ability to place the eyes and what they reminded her of.

And the words. Sydney explained in painstaking detail about what Betty should do if anyone arrived at the house and claimed to be part of a Society or if they claimed to own the house and needed to use it.

"I don't know who owns this house, Mr. Sydney," Betty said, her eyes big and round under her wavy, gray hair, "how would I know if they're telling me the truth. Harry took care of all that kind of stuff."

"Because, this is my house," Sydney's mouth curled slightly at the corners. Those eyes... she desired to touch them, lick them... they were the eyes of –

"And," Sydney continued, "you and your late husband have done a splendid job of taking care of it."

Betty heard the words as if they'd been spoken in another room, distant and dreamy. She inhaled the aroma as if it were the last free air on earth, opening her mouth to take more in, gobbling it. Harry's scent. That's what it was. Harry was in *this* room, standing just out of sight, and he was young. Even though she couldn't see him, she knew he was there.

She shivered. Her teeth began to chatter.

And where did she know those eyes from? And as she stared into them, lost in Harry's wonderful scent, she felt a tingle deep inside her where she'd felt nothing for decades. *You're feeling it old girl, sure as Harry's bones are resting in the Rice's Crossing Cemetery.*

Sydney leaned toward her and said, "I can bring Harry back to you."

She placed a hand to her mouth and trembled as she said, "oh...ohhhhh." Tears spilled down her cheeks. Betty wasn't easily fooled, but she believed this man. This strange, dark man named Sydney. Sydney, who she thought might well be an angel, thank Jesus, could bring Harry back to her and she knew it because Harry's scent was thick in the house and she could *feel* him, no matter how weird that sounded to her, she really could feel him.

"Just do as I ask," Sydney said, "you must tell me if you see anything suspicious."

And she agreed to do just that.

She didn't know if the man Everett had pulled over out on the road was the stranger Sydney was talking about, but she watched closely out the window. Everett was walking back to the strange car now, and he looked to have his hand near his gun!

Anything at all.

"Mrs. Haddock," a soft voice startled her.

"Yes, dear?" Betty whirled toward the pretty, young woman.

"A group of us would like to stay until Wednesday. Is that okay?" The woman, damned if Betty could remember her name, smiled nervously.

"That's fine sweetheart. Wednesday's fine. You can come down later, and we can get it all worked out." Betty forced a smile. *Now get the hell out of here, I'm busy.*

"Thank you so much," the woman said, "some of us have a few extra days to spend and don't have children to go home to... yet. It just seemed like fun to stay an extra few days."

"That's fine dear." Betty waved a hand at her, and focused back toward the window, staring out, chomping at the bit to call Sydney.

Excitement surged through her hands like tingly sparkles. *...anyone suspicious*, Sydney had said.

She thought this qualified. She'd call Everett later and see what type of information she could get about the guy. But she'd call Sydney now.

She shuffled toward the phone a few feet from the window. Her fingers trembled as she dialed. The thought that Harry could be sitting in his recliner, smiling at her, in the next few days swamped everything.

CHAPTER 38

No one spoke as they neared Rice's Crossing.

Charlie tried to focus on what Markus and Alexis told him about Nathaniel Smith, but his thoughts kept creeping back to home and the events that occurred there. The weird thing was, he kept picturing his iPhone sitting alone on the counter and how there were no messages on the screen since there was no one left to contact him. Of all things, he's thinking about his dumb iPhone. Stupid.

The death of his father, the death of his friends. He supposed there could be more survivors than what he thought; people hiding in closets, under beds, in old buildings, hunkered down and out of sight while the mayhem ensued around them. But not his dad. *Maybe if I'd left the church earlier, gotten home before the wolf entered my house.* Maybe, maybe not. If anyone did survive, there's no way they could contact him since his phone was sitting on the counter at home with no one around to see it.

Back to the iPhone.

But something was different with Markus next to him. The old man kept the pain at bay. For the first time in his life, Charlie felt safe, and he felt *found.* A place he belonged. No longer an outcast. With Markus and these people, he was treated just like everyone else, as if the things he could do were an everyday occurrence. He supposed for them, they were.

His mind, and even his body, felt dreamlike as if he might wake up at any moment to the sound of his dad saying, *time to rise and shine, son, we need to get the calves fed.* His dad always called them calves, whether they were full grown cows and bulls didn't matter, always a calf. That thought made him realize that no one would feed the calves today, or tomorrow, or the next day. He pictured them—

"Slow down." Markus glared straight out the windshield.

Charlie didn't have a clue of where they were, only that they were in Nebraska and had driven through Omaha an hour or so ago and it was almost dark. After the last stop, the seating arrangement returned to what it was when they'd left Pennsylvania: Phillip driving, Markus in the passenger seat, and Charlie in the middle. Liam and Alexis rode in the back.

"I saw the sign," Phillip said. "It said Rice's Crossing."

Markus shifted forward in his seat. "I thought I saw something run across the road, ahead of us there."

Silence in the car.

A scowl spread across Markus's face.

"Keep going?" Phillip asked and slowed.

Charlie's muscles tensed and goosebumps broke out along his arms. They were the only ones on this road, not another car in sight, and the sun was nearly down.

"Yes," Markus said, "Maybe I'm just getting jumpy."

Markus smiled, but to Charlie, it looked forced, almost as if the old man were trying to convince himself of something he knew to be wrong.

Charlie didn't like it at all.

CHAPTER 39

Stuck in jail. Christopher massaged his injured arm, thankful the ache had abated, but reminded of it every time he moved and felt the tight stitches pull.

He leaned back against the stone wall and licked his lips. How in the world would Markus contact him, except through projection, which they were avoiding? In this age of technology, to find one's self in this spot was astounding. He wondered, and not for the first time if he was making the right decision by remaining patient. He had no idea he'd be here this long after that damn cop had brought him in. *Small town Barney Fife*, Christopher chuckled. *Ole' Barney.*

The officer's actual name was Everett. Christopher had read it on his uniform. But Barney sounded better. Barney was a name he could get behind.

Finally, after what seemed an eternity, the metallic clink of keys jingled, and his cell door opened. Barney stepped in and said, "Come with me, please."

Barney led him to a small waiting area, and he sat there for at least another thirty minutes. Thank heavens they didn't cuff him this time. He expected Barney, or someone, to return at any moment and tell him everything was okay and he'd be on his way. But oh hell no. Barney came strolling out, shaking his head, and said to Christopher, "I'm sorry, but Texas State Patrol says we need to detain you."

"For what?" This shit was getting ridiculous. Nathaniel had someone trying to make life difficult, no doubt about that. Christopher would likely never find out who or how.

"Didn't say. Just said to detain you until they can contact the Dayton police." Everett shrugged his shoulders. "I don't think it'll take long."

Depending on who Nathaniel had on the inside and how much influence they had, Christopher had his doubts about that. Hell, he'd already been here... he checked the clock on the wall... almost six hours!

Barney asked, "Do you need anything for your arm? Painkillers or medication?"

"Yes," Christopher said. "I need my goddamn pain medication." *Keep it cool, this isn't Barney's fault. He's just doing his job.*

Barney disappeared again, then returned with the small bottle the doc in Dayton had given him full of 800 milligram ibuprofen tablets. "Sorry, sir, but I need to put you back in the cell until this all gets sorted out. Seems like bullshit, if you ask me."

"Can I make a phone call, at least?" he asked. "People are expecting me here."

Barney shrugged. "I don't see an issue with it." He handed Christopher his iPhone while standing outside the main door to the jail-cell room.

He dialed Markus's number – no answer. He dialed Alexis's – no answer. "You've got to be shitting me," he said. *What the hell? Were they all ignoring him?* He shook his head. He considered dialing Phillip but thought better of it.

"Can I try again in about thirty minutes?" he asked handing his phone back to Barney.

"Yeah," Barney took it. "Should be fine."

"Wait." Christopher held out his hand for his phone and Barney handed it to him. He pulled up the text screen, found Markus's number, and typed. *I'm in Jail in Rice's Crossing. Call when you get here. I'll call you back in a bit.* He handed the phone back to Barney again and said, "Thanks."

Barney locked the cell door and left, promising to be back shortly with some news. Christopher watched the minutes tick by. His anxiety grew. *This is just great.*

A half an hour later, noticing the day's light waning through the small window above the rickety cot in his cell, he walked to the bars, gripped one of them, then leaned his forehead against the cool metal. *Where the hell are you, Barney?* He had to assume Nathaniel was likely here already, waiting on them like St. Peter at the pearly gates, and here he stood not doing a goddamn thing.

The thought festered and he contemplated getting out of here right then. He'd blow the walls apart if he had to. Markus also knew that Nathaniel may very well be here and Christopher knew exactly why his old friend would come here anyway. Markus was sick, very sick, and when the shit hit the fan, Christopher had no intention of sitting in this cell listening to it.

Piss on it. He'd had enough. He'd give these small-town shit-asses one more chance to do things nicely.

"Hey, uh, Bar..." Christopher almost yelled Barney. "Hey, Officer Everett! We need to talk."

No answer. He waited, growing more irritated.

"*Officer?*" He yelled. "We need to talk. *NOW!*"

Nothing. No jingling of keys. No squeaky steps on buffed floors. Nothing.

He let go of the bars and stepped back to the middle of his cell. The silence swelled, and a wicked chill enveloped him. Goosebumps broke out on his arms and his breath fogged the air in a misty cloud.

Oh shit.

CHAPTER 40

Alexis wouldn't argue that she'd under-estimated the vampires in Pittsburg. Woefully under-estimated. Pittsburg was her burden to carry. She could still see Jobe walking beside her along the sidewalk. And now Jobe was dead.

But there was one thing she would never be questioned about. One thing she'd never get wrong.

The stench of the wolves.

"They're here." Alexis sat up. The scent caught her attention as they entered town nearing a flashing yellow streetlight.

Markus nodded as if he were about to say the same thing. Alexis fought nausea building in her stomach. The stench was strong. Real strong. *They're waiting for us.*

"Wolves." Markus rubbed his chin. "Pretty sure that's what I saw run across the road earlier."

"They're definitely here." She gripped the seat rest behind his head as Liam's sweaty hand unclasped from hers. "A lot closer than they were in Pennsylvania... I couldn't smell them when we got to that place."

She stared past Markus down the empty road in front of them, lined by streetlamps casting a gloomy glow on the deserted pavement. There was no movement, no sign of life; it could have been a photograph had they not been driving. Markus followed her gaze. He coughed and then wheezed as if expecting another fit to pass over him. Alexis placed her hand on his shoulder. Under her palm, she felt the frailty of his shoulder, the bone pressing through the padding on his jacket. The bone.

Markus's eyes squeezed shut, and for a terrifying moment she thought he might be passing out, but then he opened them and inhaled a gargled breath.

"Let's get to the house," Markus said.

"Is Christopher there?" Phillip asked.

"Not sure. Tried calling him, but the cell signal is shit in this town. Goes straight to voicemail." Markus drew a labored breath. "I was hoping to get a look at the house since it's right up there." Markus patted her hand resting on his shoulder, and she understood the gesture perfectly... *I'm fine*, it said, *please take your hand off me.*

Liam's eyes widened. Most of the color had drained from his face. He looked like a ghost. "Am I the only dumbass who doesn't know why in the fuck we're still here?"

She sat back in her seat and looked at him, debating on the best answer that wouldn't give away that she and Markus knew anything about someone feeding information to Nathaniel. "We're here to get Christopher," she said. She reached out for his hand, but he withdrew it.

"Just doesn't make any damn sense." He rubbed his palms on his jeans. "We ran from the other place because wolves were there. Why aren't we running from here?"

Markus's head cocked, listening. She watched Phillip's grip tighten on the steering wheel. *He will betray you.*

Oh, Phillip. When Markus had first told her his suspicion, she'd denied the possibility of any such thing. She knew him. Knew his heart. As time had gone on, and it became clearer that Nathaniel had gotten to Phillip, she expected dark hatred to swallow her. But it didn't. A strange sort of pity formed in its place.

As selfish as it sounds, and though she'd never say it openly, she was thankful it wasn't Liam who sold them out. If it had to be anyone, thank goodness it wasn't him.

"We're doing the best we can." She forced a smile.

His rigid expression softened. "Seems like everything keeps getting weirder and weirder." He didn't move closer or take her hand, and that was fine. This was enough for now.

They turned onto another blacktop-road, passed two more floodlights, and then they were in darkness again, appearing to drive back into the lonely abyss of the Nebraska country. Up ahead, she could see a lone floodlight shining like a beacon.

"Town's a little bigger than it used to be. Looks like several people at this house," Markus said, speaking to no one in particular.

They hadn't seen one single person as they'd driven through. Granted, it was almost ten o'clock, so maybe a lot of people were in bed, or watching some re-runs on the TV, but still, not one car, no one walking a dog, no kids outside riding their bikes in the early night air... it was summer vacation for the school kids, after all.

The gravel driveway wound up to an old garage where it expanded into a large parking lot lined by pine trees. Four cars were parked along the edge (none of which were Christopher's, that she could tell). She peered at the house. Several windows glowed from the lights inside, but she didn't see any movement, no shadows passing by curtains.

She trusted Markus, but fear crept up her spine like a spider. Phillip circled the car around, so they were facing the road and eased it to a stop.

"I'll go up to the door," Markus said. "There should be someone living here that's been taking care of the place. I'll wave you all in if everything's okay."

Markus tapped his hand on his thigh and stared at the house, waiting. Alexis had no idea what for. A part of her hoped he'd just say, *to hell with it, let's get out of here.*

"Have you ever been here?" Charlie asked. He hadn't spoken since they'd gotten off the highway.

"A long time ago." Markus shifted in his seat.

"Looks like someone's here." Charlie picked nervously at a pimple on his cheek.

"Yeah." Markus was looking in all directions: out the side windows, out the windshield, and then re-looking. "Like a goddamned party."

She was about to say, *I think we should get out of here*, when Markus opened his door and said, "Stay here until I say to come inside."

"I'll keep the car running," Phillip said.

She wasn't sure, but Alexis thought Phillip was sweating and there was something about that she didn't like at all. It sparked a frightening *something's-about-to-happen* feeling.

She gazed out Liam's window and watched Markus hobbling up to the house on that old cane of his.

CHAPTER 41

Halfway up the sidewalk, his phone buzzed in his pocket. He had to check it since it might be Christopher.

A text splashed the screen: *I'm in Jail in Rice's Crossing. Call when you get here. I'll call you back in a bit.*

Oh goddamnit all to hell. In jail… now what?

Hey, at least he's in town. Give him that much.

He wanted Christopher here, with him. He sure as hell didn't intend to stand here and try to type a text on that little bitty phone he could barely see. Whoever was inside had surely seen him by now.

The plan, if you could call it that, didn't change when they learned that Nathaniel likely knew about Rice's Crossing. Alexis agreed, especially after he told her that he felt his life slipping away, seeming to gain speed in the past few days as if the cancer knew he had shit to do and it was hell-bent to stop him. He even told her about the dizzy spell in Pennsylvania and most recently, the blood drops in his palm following the particularly cruel coughing fits.

We can't run anymore, Alexis. It's time to end this while I still can.

Standing in front of this house, dread knotted his stomach, and the fallacious quiet that surrounded him set him even more on edge. He'd known something was amiss, even before they'd turned off the highway to come here when he saw something run across the road in front of them. It had been watching and waiting in the darkness along the highway, crouched in the weed infested ditch, keeping a lookout for their arrival.

Maybe I should get my ass back to the car and go get Christopher. But he was only a few steps from the door. He'd knock since they'd already seen him. If shit hit the fan, he'd project to Christopher right then because who gave a shit if Nathaniel heard him at that point.

He slipped the phone back into his pocket and continued. A deep throb settled into his left hip and he didn't think it would go away anytime soon.

A short rise of steps loomed before him that led to an old wooden porch. He noticed a sign attached to the front of the house with fancy lettering. He couldn't read the smaller print but was able to read the words, Betty's Hideaway. *What does that mean?* He was positive he had the right place but didn't remember that. He made his way up the steps, his cane echoing off the wood with hollow thumps.

In his mind, he pictured himself knocking and someone greeting him with a kind smile. But with each closing step, his optimism faded. Maybe no one was here. Maybe everyone was. Maybe the caretaker was dead already. Maybe the whole town was dead.

Nathaniel was here.

The Legions.

The wolves.

Is this a mistake? He should get Christopher first. That's what he should do. What if, when this door opened, he was hit with everything Nathaniel had?

But nor was this Markus's first rodeo. If the door opened and the fight started, Markus would be ready. He had Alexis. He had Charlie. And Christopher was a projection away. His blue eyes narrowed and his jaw set as he stopped in front of the door.

His knuckles rapped on the wood of the doorframe.

This was a risk, a huge one, but Markus was still dying, and few opportunities lay before him. It was a risk that time, or his lack of it, demanded he take.

Steps inside thudded, coming toward the door. Up until that moment, Markus felt like he could've reacted to anything.

The car's motor revved, and Markus's first thought was, *now what in the hell is Phillip doing?* Then the car launched out of the driveway slinging dirt and dust as it fishtailed toward the road. The tires barked as the rubber left gravel and hit asphalt. For a second, Markus spotted Phillip driving, his hands clamped to the steering wheel, and his lips peeled back in a grimace.

And then Markus stood alone on the porch watching the taillights disappear toward Rice's Crossing. *You clever sonofabitch.*

That's when the door-lock slid open.

CHAPTER 42

Betty peered through the kitchen window at the car pulling into the driveway. Headlights splashed the wall, and that's when it dawned on her that someone was standing behind her.

She whirled and clapped a wrinkled hand to her chest.

Sydney was there. His eyes caught her gaze. Those eyes.

"Oh," she said. *When had he arrived?*

A smile creased Sydney's lips. "As promised."

"I called you as soon as I saw that man today."

"You did well." Sydney's smile widened.

That's when she noticed the teeth. They were too long. No one had teeth like that. And more people standing behind him, some standing in the living room, motionless like gravestones.

"I... I d-didn't know you would come so fast." That strange apperception in those eyes returned. She almost recognized it. Almost.

"You have served us well," Sydney said.

She backed away and drew her arms around her, cupping her elbows in her palms. She didn't like this. The room was freezing.

Sydney glanced up toward the ceiling at the sound of footsteps up there.

"Do you have guests?" he asked, his voice gentle, yet piercing.

"Yes... I have six guests. They're here through Wednesday." Something unsettling crept into her bones. A chill raced down her spine, and she envisioned Harry lying in his casket, deep in the ground, rotting to dust.

"How wonderful. We really must meet them."

"They're just women here on a getaway. They not hurting anyone." Her vision of Harry decaying in his casket grew more vivid. His eyes sunken deep into his skull, the lips pulled back by dry skin, and worst of all, she saw herself touching him, caressing his hands and face.

She squeezed her eyes shut through the sting of salty tears. When she opened them, Sydney had moved to the living room, close to the couch – the same spot he'd talked with her a few days earlier. She noticed Everett, the deputy, standing in there too. He was looking at her, but his face seemed distorted like it had grown longer.

She looked passed Sydney, out the front window, and noticed an old man ambling up to the house. He stopped and seemed to be staring at a phone.

"What's happening?" She felt as if she'd done something wrong. Just so wrong. "Please tell me what's happening."

"No longer your concern," Sydney said. He turned his attention to the window, and his expression shifted to an inquisitive glare. The old man lingered on the sidewalk a few more seconds, then peered through the window, as if staring in at them. Sydney clenched his fists and said quietly, "That's him."

The old man continued his slow trek to the door, moving past the window to the porch.

She didn't want to answer the door and wouldn't have if Sydney had not said, "Please answer the door."

The knock came shortly after and she waddled across the room as fast as her old legs would take her.

But then something strange happened. All of the sudden, the car outside took off, leaving the old man standing on the porch by himself. Sydney acted just as confused as she was and murmured, "What's he doing?" His hand shot up as if to stop her, but he was too late.

Betty had already opened the door.

CHAPTER 43

Phillip shocked everyone. When the car hit pavement, Liam fell back in his seat and clutched for the front headrest to right himself.

Charlie flopped against the passenger door.

"Phillip!" Alexis yelled and grasped Liam's leg. "Stop the car!"

Liam turned and stared back at the house through the rear window. The porch was shrouded in darkness; he couldn't see Markus at all. A sense of nakedness and vulnerability swept through him. Dread.

In his mind, Liam pictured himself jumping out of the speeding car and hoping to god he didn't break anything. He saw it so clearly that he shocked himself when he smacked Phillip in the back of the head and yelled, "Go back! Go back to the house!"

"I can't," Phillip growled through clenched teeth, as if in pain. "I can't stop doing this!"

Alexis said, "Oh my God," not in a surprised tone, but more one of horrified understanding. Liam had time to think, *she's been lying to me about something*. And then she reached over the seat and grasped Charlie's shoulder. "Charlie, stop the car!"

Charlie twisted around, gawked at her, and then said, "Okay."

The car slowed in jerky lurches as the engine screamed in protest. A second later, a metallic snap from somewhere below their feet rattled their seats, and something metal clanged on the pavement.

"I can't stop doing it," Phillip cried again. His foot jammed on the accelerator, but the vehicle didn't move. A burning stench engulfed them, and the engine began to sputter.

"We have to get out of here, now." Alexis opened her door. "Everyone out!".

Liam wasted no time. He clambered out onto the pavement, the outside air a welcome relief from the fumes of exhaust and hot friction. The engine finally stopped, popping to eventual death. Inside, Phillip clutched for Charlie. Through the window, Liam thought Phillip might have been holding something. A knife maybe.

"What the hell?" Liam yanked open Phillip's door, his actions more reflex than conscious movement. He wasn't planning a goddamned thing at this point.

Charlie yelled, kicked his feet and tried to open his own door. Alexis was there, pulling him with her hands hooked under the kid's armpits. She stumbled backward with Charlie and fell down on the street. Charlie rolled away. He hollered something.

Phillip turned toward Liam, his right hand clutching a blade that looked ancient and terrible. He jabbed forward, still sitting behind the steering wheel of the car. Liam jumped back, but not before the blade nipped his thigh, splitting his jeans and slitting a thin cut in his leg.

Asshole just cut me! Liam stumbled back, his mind reeling, and tripped over his own feet. His elbow cracked the pavement hard enough to rattle his teeth.

"You shitting bastard! She was mine," Phillip growled and climbed out of the car. He lumbered toward Liam with the knife raised, prepared to finish the job. "I should have killed you a long time ago!"

"Phillip!" Alexis stood bathed in the glow of headlights. "Phillip, stop this!" Phillip stopped and gawked at her, and in the pause, Liam scrambled to his feet.

"Imagine that." Phillip lifted his hands into the air and spoke like a drunk picking a fight. "A slut like you telling *me* what I need to do. I saved your ass!" Phillip laughed out loud, looking up into the sky and then back to Alexis. "When I'm through with him,"—he pointed the blade toward Liam, keeping his eyes on Alexis— "I'm going to come back and gut you."

Phillip focused back on Liam, and for the first time, Liam felt the invasion, as if he were standing outside of himself, looking in at someone rummaging through his mind. He shook his head, unable to stop it. Phillip was a messenger, he manipulated people's brains, and now he was in Liam's.

An eerie smile spread across Phillip's face, a shit-eating smile that said, *I found something.* Phillip opened his mouth to speak when suddenly he was thrown back toward the car, his body rebounding with a deep *thonk* like a rag-doll off the doorframe. He collapsed flat on his face and didn't move. The knife clanged onto the pavement and reflected the light from a street lamp above.

Liam clutched his leg. Blood soaked his pants where Phillip's blade had nicked him. Charlie stood at the back of the car, his hand outstretched, his chest heaving. He looked more like a child at that moment than Liam had ever seen him look.

"I didn't mean to kill him," Charlie said. "If I killed him, I didn't mean to."

They all three stood in the middle of the deserted street and stared at Phillip. Summer bugs chirped and a dog barked from somewhere close.

"Could someone tell me what the hell just happened?" Liam asked.

"Nathaniel Smith," Alexis said. "Nathaniel was controlling him."

Though Liam had never cared for Phillip, he'd come to think of him as one of their group, part of the team, one of the gang. *I can't believe he just tried to kill us.* "How can he do that?"

What if Nathaniel is controlling *me?* He remembered the elevator with Alexis at the Marriott, just three short nights ago, when he'd come face to face with a vampire, the blood oozing from the walls. He hadn't been able to stop that either. Even now, looking back, he had no idea how the thought got in his mind to start with, let alone, how to prevent it.

"It's not his fault," he heard Alexis say. "He might not have even known what was happening. *I* didn't know at first."

"How did you know?" Liam asked.

"When he said he wasn't doing it. Something about the way he said it."

Liam looked up at her and recalled that grimace on Phillip's face as if he'd been trying to fight it... whatever *it* was. "Could Nathaniel do that to any of us?"

The question hung in the air like an icepick debating on which eye to pierce. Alexis said, "I don't know. Markus feared that Phillip's loyalty may have shifted, but I don't think he was expecting this."

"Where was he taking us?" *Wait... when had Markus told Alexis that?* What the hell else were they not telling him?

Alexis said, "Let's get back to Markus."

Liam opened his mouth to say *what else have you and Markus been talking about* when a brilliant flash of light split the darkness back toward the house where they'd left Markus. The hairs on Liam's neck tingled, and his mouth grew instantly dry.

Charlie screamed and pointed down the street in the other direction. Liam turned.

Storming towards them, passing under the floodlights in vivid flashes, were the wolves. Hundreds of them.

"Oh, Jesus Christ." It was all Liam could say. His strength left his legs, and for a horrid moment, he thought he might fall.

They filled the street; their grotesque bodies hunched over and running on all fours.

"Get behind me!" Alexis yelled. "Now!"

Liam did.

CHAPTER 44

"Officer?" Christopher's voice echoed off the stone walls.

He crossed his arms and grazed his fingers along the rough stitches just above his elbow, amazed and a little sickened by how strange it felt. It reminded him of rubbing his finger along the teeth of a closed zipper. The pain had subsided to a dull throb, but that did nothing to ward off the invading cold.

He peered into the darkness beyond the long, gray bars. So far, he had not heard any commotion outside, but that silence wouldn't last long. *I'll hear something if things start going bad out there, surely I'll hear it.* What would he do if he did?

Perhaps being stuck in this jail cell sparked an illusion of helplessness, as if they had him locked away like an animal trapped in a cage. They'd learn quickly how untrue that was.

But only the eerie silence and bitter cold greeted him. He considered yelling for someone again but knew it was useless.

He needed to contact the Vatican, so they knew what was happening, and so they could brace themselves for what came next if he and Markus failed. Conclave was set to begin in just a few short days. Christopher imagined the Chasers guarding the ancient city, stationed along the walls and watching the darkness of Rome for any sign of Nathaniel's army. The Swiss Guard would be patrolling, working and coordinating with the Chasers, an alliance that had been in existence for over 500 years. Nathaniel would not attack the Vatican until the start of Conclave, when all of the Cardinals were present in the Sistine Chapel, voting on who would become the new Pope. Hence, the reason Nathaniel wanted to kill Markus, Christopher, and the rest of the Society now, prior to his move against the political and financial arm of the Catholic Church. If he –

The stench of smoke caught his attention first. He glanced into the adjacent cell, and saw nothing but the mattress lying on the bunk, stripped, with a folded sheet and blanket on top of it with a pillow at the head. Just an empty cell.

From the main hallway, where he'd last seen Barney Fife stride away, smoke roiled across the floor, flooding into the jail cells like fog. The building rumbled, causing the florescent lights hanging from the ceiling to sway back and forth.

From outside the small window of his cell, a white flash like a brief splat of lightning caught his eye. Distant cries drifted through the early night as something died a horrible and painful death. *It's starting*. Time to get out of there.

The orange glow from an enormous fire reflected faintly off the metal bars. *Alexis!* Just then, the ceiling caved, and huge chunks of concrete and wood rained down on him. He ducked and covered his head.

A rolling dust cloud engulfed him. His chest locked in mid-breath and panic rushed through him. The bars to his cell rattled and then bent as if the building were collapsing into itself.

Christopher coughed and pointed his hands toward the concrete wall, then muttered, "Dis." A blue-tinted bubble formed in the air then shot forward, like a giant index finger. The wall exploded in a spray of debris and mortar and left a gaping hole.

Christopher lumbered toward it holding his free hand in front of him to protect his face. The smoke blinded him. His feet dropped a few inches as he left the concrete floor. He nearly went sprawling on the lawn but somehow maintained his balance in an awkward stumble long enough to get clear of the building before falling clumsily onto the dew-covered grass.

"Kill him!" Someone yelled.

He rolled onto his back, and through the smoke, could see the outlines of the creatures descending on him, their white teeth bared.

CHAPTER 45

When the door opened, Markus tore his eyes from the receding taillights. Damned if he knew what was happening in that car, but knew it wasn't good. He even thought *I should've made Phillip shut the car off.* Goddamn it, very clever indeed.

A gray-haired, plump woman stood trembling in the doorway. She shivered as if she were standing in a freezer. Behind her, the inside lights shut off, shrouding her in darkness. If not for the outside floodlight, he wouldn't be able to see her at all.

"They've got women trapped upstairs," the woman said. She spoke as if she were at a funeral and didn't want to disturb the mourners.

Markus stared at her haggard eyes and defeated face.

"He told me he would bring Harry back." The old woman's face crumpled, and she cried.

"Who told you that?" Markus also wondered who Harry was.

The woman blubbered. "Sydney."

A male voice from behind her, deep and confident, drifted from the darkness, "Markus. I was told that you'd be arriving."

Markus said, "Ah yes, Sydney. I've heard things about you." He tried to look past the old woman, searching for any clue of how many were in there, but the entire room was blackness. The truth was, other than the name, he'd never heard a damn thing about Sydney, but the longer Sydney talked, the more Markus learned.

From upstairs, a woman's soft cry. The old lady, who Markus guessed was the caretaker, backed a few steps deeper into the house, into the murky dark. Markus stayed where he was. If Nathaniel was in there, he wanted to know it before doing anything.

"That doesn't surprise me." The arrogance on Sydney's voice was palpable, but so was the ignorance. A brief pause, then he asked, "I'd be curious to know what you've heard."

The charge built in Markus's hands, and in his mind, the lightning sparked from his fingers, ripping and searing everything in its path, killing anything that moved, and he saw himself stepping back, away from the house to avoid the collapsing wood.

That's what he saw happening in his mind.

But that would also mean killing innocent women. He needed to get Sydney out here, in the open, away from the house.

"As you can tell," the voice spoke from inside again, the voice of Sydney. "We're ready for you."

Markus said, "Did Nathaniel tell you what to say, Sydney? From what I've heard, your greatness is in your ability to follow orders."

"You know nothing, old man. My pride is not that fragile."

Markus doubted that and forced a smile hoping the gesticulation came through in his words. "Were those also Nathaniel's words, or yours? Maybe from a book somewhere?"

Silence from the house. From within, the stench of spoiled meat wafted out like a heavy blanket – the reek of a Legion.

"I get it," Markus said, "You've never actually spoken to Nathaniel yourself, have you?"

"Ha!" The comeback was immediate. But nothing followed.

In the distance, screeching tires stole his attention, and he listened to an engine screaming for its last breath of life. He could only assume it was Alexis and the others and had no idea what could possibly be happening.

It was time for action. For those caught in the cross-fire, he could only hope for the best. He'd do his damndest to spare them.

Sydney spoke again, but Markus ignored him.

Markus gripped the wooden frame of the doorway with one hand and maintained his grip on his cane with the other. Time to see what he was dealing with in there.

A lance of white light, like a flash of lightning, burst from his cane and lit up the inside of the house, sustaining for a few seconds, then dimming like the fade of an illumination grenade. In that few seconds, Markus saw everything he needed to see.

The ceiling was a writhing mass of vampires squirming and crawling over each other. Along the far wall, a well-dressed man sat on what looked like a long couch. Throughout the house, the faces of crouched vampires whirled toward him as the light exposed them.

Markus looked at the old woman and said, "You've got about ten seconds to find a room and hide."

He didn't wait to see if she understood. He stepped backward while maintaining his balance with his cane. He hobbled down the steps, across the sidewalk, and into the yard, stumbling twice, but stayed on his feet. A maddening cough lurched into his throat, but he swallowed it back and hoped it would stay down there for a while. He needed more room if he were to spare the old woman and the women upstairs (assuming there was anyone left up there to be saved).

The first wave swarmed from the door like giant bats clamoring for their chance at the kill. Markus raised his hand and a thin, murky wall appeared. The vampires plowed into it, piling on top of each other, wailing in anguish at their inability to penetrate the paper-thin surface.

He continued shuffling back, being careful not to fall on his ass where it may be difficult to get back up, or God forbid, he might break a hip. His thin wall of hazy blue light encircled him like a bubble as the creatures took to the air and attacked him from all sides. They covered him like a blanket – a mass of twisting bodies.

But within, Markus was calm. He watched their hate-filled faces, only a few feet from his own, biting and clawing at the surface of his sanctuary. Eventually, if he did nothing, they would penetrate it, but he had no intention of waiting that long.

He'd gone far enough. He had all of the space he needed. It was time for Markus to do what he did best.

To do what he was born to do.

CHAPTER 46

Liam and Charlie scrambled to get behind her as the wolves bore down. Alexis could see the whites of their disgusting eyes, gleaming reflections from the dull light of overhead streetlamps as they passed under them, getting closer, and closer.

Liam yelled from behind her, "Can I do *anything?* This is bullshit.*"

She glanced at him crouched down next to the car, his eyes wide. "Just stay down and out of the way!" She didn't wait to see his reaction.

The pavement rumbled, and she thought, *it's like a herd of buffalo.* But Jesus, there were so many of them. So many.

A silly song her dad used to sing... *Hickory said we could take 'em by surprise if we didn't fire muskets 'till we look 'em in the eye.* The smell of Brut aftershave drifted into her memory. The rough stubble of his beard against the skin of her cheek. How he'd screamed so horribly as they killed him. She would never forget that screaming.

God, how she hated them.

Look 'em in the eye, sweetheart.

And that, she did.

Fire rocketed from her hands like a missile and ripped through the air, cutting it like thick fabric. The wolves tried to dodge it, but they were too late. The inferno collided with the front line, incinerating them. Death howls erupted, and she relished every second of it. They began fanning out and surrounding her.

Flames spread out across the concrete, cascading like ripples in a pond. Wolves charged and hurled themselves into it, perhaps hoping to eventually wear her down. But it wasn't her power that they underestimated, it was her hatred and how long it could sustain her. She owed the wolves this death and pain. She owed them and intended to pay every dime.

She throttled back the intensity of the firewall so she could see through, like looking at someone across a campfire. They had stopped beyond her range and were pacing back and forth, most on all fours, staring intently into the blaze, waiting for their break, looking for an opportunity.

Waiting.

Adrenaline surged through her, and her confidence swelled with each passing second. She wanted to smile at them, to taunt them, but then thought better of it. She couldn't picture Markus doing that.

That's when the woman caught her attention. About a hundred yards away amongst the wolves. She stood with her hands on her hips with long brown hair that flowed down behind her shoulders. It was the eyes that bothered Alexis. The woman glared at her, her lips pressed to a thin smile. The eyes were deep red, and her skin was so pale, it practically glowed.

It was a vampire.

Alexis had never fought a vampire except in Pittsburg where she hadn't fared so well. She yelled to Liam and Charlie over her shoulder, "Get into the car!"

She heard shuffling behind her, then the car-door slammed shut. She hoped they'd done as she asked. She needed them clear while she dealt with this ugly-ass bitch.

Wait.

The vampires have split Markus and me up. Damn right they did. How did this happen? How did she *let* it happen?

We have to get back to Markus. Easier said than done. It wasn't like they could just turn tail and take off running. She would have to fight her way out of this; create the opportunity.

She blasted fire at the woman but knew she had missed as soon as the flames left her hand. The woman covered half the distance between them in a blur and then stopped. The vampire grinned and shook her head as if this were something she dealt with every day.

Patience. Control of the situation was slipping away, one slow second at a time. *Have patience, don't over-react.* But she wanted to. She wanted to send forth everything she had, cover the entire town with fire. But of course, she knew that she couldn't do that; she wasn't *that* powerful, and worse, she would exhaust herself trying. The wolves could not get to her (at the moment, at least) and that was good, but she didn't know what the vampire could do. Could it run through fire?

The woman sauntered toward her, a lurid smile stretched across a mouthful of teeth.

"Alexis Jade," the woman yelled over the dull roar of the flames, never breaking stride, "The famous witch." Behind her, the wolves paced, their hellish eyes reflecting the fire between them and their prize.

She's taunting you. Christopher's main lesson since she was young - stay aware of your surroundings, do not be distracted.

The woman, now a few yards away and no longer having to yell, said, "I'm surprised Michael let you go in Pittsburg. I hear he was quite fond of you."

Let me go? Alexis almost laughed out loud at that and then cursed herself for listening. *Stay aware, damn it!* The wolves remained at bay, and Alexis considered directing all of her flames at this woman, to scorch her right on the street. But the wolves would attack as soon she did; hell, that was probably their plan. Plus, she wasn't confident that she could kill this woman like that. So much she didn't know.

The woman drew closer.

"He'll be here shortly, you know," the woman said, Alexis assumed referring to Michael. "I'm sure he's excited to see you again. Assuming I don't kill you first." The woman shrugged. "I'm surprised you don't know me. I would have thought you knew all of us."

Alexis kept her hands at the ready, listening, but not listening. She needed to keep this woman, this *creature*, in front of her. She heard the words, maintained direct eye contact, but peripherally sought every advantage. She glimpsed at the streetlights, at Phillip lying on the ground, at the wolves gathered beyond the fire barrier, grasping nothing she could use to her advantage.

"Christine." The woman gleamed with arrogance as if hearing herself say her own name was somehow divine. "That's my name. Have you heard of me?"

The name didn't sound familiar.

Christine shot forward, her hair streaming behind her, and her arms outstretched to grasp whatever part of Alexis's body she could get a hold of. The vampire moved, unlike anything she'd ever seen, like a spirit.

Alexis fired a short, intense burst and the creature swooped away and disappeared. *Goddamn it!* She lost sight of her.

Just then, the ground rumbled, reverberating from what felt like an enormous bomb detonating from somewhere close by. Her fire died down to a small roar, enough to keep the wolves where they were, but did nothing about the vampire.

She had to get out of here, off of this street, and back to Markus. Perhaps maybe they *should* run. Options were getting slim. She couldn't stop the fire completely due to the wolves. She still felt strong, thank god, but how long could she keep this up? She had no idea where Christine was, nor did she know if there were more of them. What if the Legions were out there, or worse yet, Nathaniel himself?

The car door opened and Liam climbed out.

Goddamn it, Liam. "I said stay in the car!"

"I can't just sit in there and do nothing!"

She glanced at him. He held a metal pipe of some sort, she didn't stare long enough to know what it was. Damned if she knew where he got it. "Did you see where she went?"

"I saw her go up, but lost her after that." He scanned the area, and she did the same. Her eyes darting from place to place, finding nothing.

"Just stay out of the way," she said to him, "I don't want to burn you." Then she asked, "Where's Charlie?"

"I don't know," Liam said, "He took off a second ago."

Well now, wasn't that just great. He'd likely gotten scared and ran to God knew where. How did he run past the fire?

A second later, the charred body of Christine crashed onto the roof of the car. Both she and Liam ducked and shuffled a few steps away. The creature's eyes were open and sightless, the dead face slack. Smoke drifted from Christine's hair and clothes. Alexis had a second to think, *thank goodness Liam got out of that car.* She stared in shock, concentrating to ensure her fire ring didn't fail and let the wolves in.

Charlie levitated above the car, his young face beaming. He smiled down at her.

Liam yelled, "Holy shit!"

Alexis said, "Jesus, Charlie." She'd never met a wizard who could fly. They were the subject of stories and legends, even amongst the Warlocks.

"I just... just knew I could kill it." Charlie descended down to the road and stood next to her, both of them staring at the dead vampire. "Somehow I just knew."

She wanted to ask him how he'd done it and to hear all of the gory details, but they needed to move, and they may not get a better chance. The story would have to wait.

"We need to get back to Markus," she said.

"What do you want me to do?"

She thought about that and asked the only question she could think of, "What *can* you do?"

Liam just stood there, his jaw nearly hanging down to the road.

A confident smile spread across Charlie's face. He looked at her and said, "I think almost anything."

She didn't like his statement, though she didn't know why. Something about the look on his face when he said it. *I remember thinking like that,* she thought, *over-confident maybe, perhaps naïve.* No matter, that too was a subject they'd need to address later. She simply said, "Don't get cocky." Then added, "We need to get back to Markus. I think I can cover us from the back, but we must move quickly. Charlie, I guess your job is to make sure nothing kills us before we get there."

He smiled bigger.

"You guys ready?" She considered asking about Phillip, then didn't.

They nodded. Liam still held the pipe, and she considered telling him she didn't think it would do any good, but then thought better of it. Strange, but she liked seeing him with it, prepared to beat the shit out of something. Not a coward.

"Let's go, stay together. Don't run yet, but move with a purpose." She maintained the fire-circle surrounding them, protecting them.

She watched Charlie's thin body striding ahead of her, in awe of him. Liam followed closely behind, close enough to her that she swore she could smell his sweat.

She didn't know how far they needed to go but knew they could reach Markus if things stayed like this for just a few minutes.

CHAPTER 47

A split second before the creature smashed into him, Christopher forced a shield around himself; a murky bubble. Two vampires slammed into the glassy surface, and Christopher almost cried out as their faces squashed and their bodies flopped sideways onto the grass. His breath came in gulps as he got shakily to his feet.

He recognized Michael standing defiantly a few yards away, his pale skin almost blue against the backdrop of the burning jailhouse. Other vampires stood motionless throughout the lawn, like ancient statues, watching and waiting. Some drifted in the air, hovering like hawks. Christopher decided he would kill the flying ones first, when it came to that, which it would very soon.

Michael glanced down at the ground, then his eyes crawled back to Christopher.

Christopher said, "It was Phillip, wasn't it?"

The vampire's shadowed face was stoic as he shifted his gaze to the sky.

Flashes split the night off to his left and Christopher knew that it must be either Alexis or Markus in battle; maybe both. He needed to get there right now.

Christopher summoned his magic and was about to attack when Michael blurted out, "Phillip was *my* idea." He spat the words and clapped a hand on his chest. "Nathaniel said it wouldn't work, but I knew that it would. I've invaded the minds of the messengers before."

Such emotion. Anger. Something was amiss here, and though it may be foolish to delay killing Michael, Christopher wanted to know what it was. He couldn't help sparing a thought of Phillip. A pang of hurt wedged itself in his heart. Perhaps even more than he'd admit, he'd hoped they'd been wrong about Phillip.

"How?"

Michael stepped forward, locking eyes with Christopher, and for the first time, Christopher detected something beyond the grotesque teeth and pale skin. Behind Michael's glare, he sensed their common humanity, something he never thought existed in a vampire. Maybe it was unique to Michael.

"Phillip's heart is blackened by love," Michael said, "his vulnerability is in his blindness to see the hatred of himself; do you think that makes me a shit for exploiting it?"

I'm pushing my luck here, but goddamn it, he thought Michael might genuinely be seeking an answer as if trying to better himself in some strange and twisted way. Christopher's curiosity burned as he mulled Michael's words.

"Of course it does," Christopher said. "Love can be destructive."

Michael's expression grew distant as if he were thinking of something far, far away. "That it is." His voice trailed off as he said, "And she is so beautiful... so, so beautiful."

Wait... who are we talking about here? "Do you love Alexis, Michael?"

"How could one *not* love her, Mr. Gray?" Michael's face became taught. "It would be the same as asking me if I love blood, then denying it to me."

And for the first time, Christopher saw what he wanted to see; a crack in the foundation of loyalty. Michael's speech stammered, ever so slightly, when he spoke. "Mark my words, Mr. Gray, I..." Again, Michael slapped a hand against his chest. "*I* will have her before this night is over. Your petty magic tricks will not steal her from me again."

And here is where the rubber hits the road. "And Nathaniel?"

"Fuck Nathaniel," Michael growled. "As long as he gets his victory, he cares not who I spend my time with."

Men and their primitive bullshit, their over-arching weakness. It always came down to the same thing, and it seemed even vampires were not immune to it. Throughout history, the topplers of legendary men, the ruination of empires, or the fight in the boys' restroom after school...

All for a pretty girl.

By not having that particular temptation, Christopher had always felt he had the upper hand on the emotional front. This was Michael's weakness, thus something to cloud the creature's judgement. Christopher could use that.

"Perhaps I could help you," Christopher said. "She listens to me. But I must reach her."

Michael glared at him, then said, "I'm not a fool, old man. Killing you is a must. On that, Nathaniel and I agree."

Christopher considered pursuing this path; if he could convince Michael that he could somehow help with Alexis, that would make Michael his ally, albeit for only a short time. He wasn't even sure Michael would ever go for it.

And Markus needed him now.

"That's a shame," Christopher said. "The most poignant of lost opportunities – love unspoken."

Michael's gaze softened, and he glanced at the ground as if deeply considering those words. Christopher didn't wait to see what would happen next. Michael missed his chance. *I'm on my way, Markus.*

Christopher's shield melted away; replaced by a round, transparent sphere that materialized over his head, roughly the size of a basketball. Inside, blue and red sparks swirled from side to side. As suddenly as the sphere had formed, it began firing streams of lightning, flashing across the sky, and striking half a dozen vampires simultaneously, blowing them out of the air with deadly accuracy.

The lightning stopped. Michael and his army scrambled for cover. The sphere then shot out four fingers of lightning, but rather than flashing, it hovered like a large hand, awaiting its targets to reveal their faces.

"We have to swarm it!" Michael yelled. "If we swarm it, we can drown it. I want all of you..."

Michael's words faded as Christopher slipped away, hopefully not yet noticed by the vampires mounting a plan to attack the sphere (which wouldn't last long if he got too far away). Once out of sight, he broke into a clumsy run. His feet clobbered the damp grass as he lumbered across the backside of the lawn. His shoes slipped in the dew. Something ripped, his pants maybe, then he was stumbling on his feet, fighting for balance, and heaving for air.

You fat fuck, he thought, *I'm getting too goddamned old for this.*

CHAPTER 48

One second. That's all the time Markus would have, maybe less. Vampires swarmed him, furious and determined to break through his shield. It was time to kill them and to do that, he would need to dissolve his protective bubble. Within a second, they would be on him tearing, biting, and destroying.

But one second was a lifetime for Markus Blue.

He dropped to one knee, grasped his cane to keep from toppling over, and placed his free hand out in front of him, palm down. The bubble surface of his shield faded, dissipating to nothingness. The eyes of the vampires grew wild.

He thought, *rigescunt indutae*. Amazing how the words remained locked in memory, never fading. The magic words.

An earsplitting *CRACK!* startled everything to stillness. Even the vampires halted as if wondering what the hell just happened. From below his hand, streaming from his palm, a flash of light shot straight to the ground.

One second was up.

The earth rumbled. Blue sparkling light rippled away from him, spreading out like a smoke ring. The vampires stiffened as the light passed through them, their flesh faded to a stony shade of gray, and their mouths hung open, frozen in agony.

A second blue wave thundered out in a perfect circle, but this one hummed as if made of charged fabric, dancing with static flashes and floating across the ground like a deadly shock-wave. All of them, stiff and helpless, blew apart in clouds of dust and charred bone, their remains raining down like volcanic ash, giving the deranged appearance of snow.

Splintering wood and bursting glass split the air as the old house, Betty's Hideaway, tore reluctantly from its foundation and collapsed to its side. The old boards surrendered easily followed by a huge plume of dust and debris.

Goddamn it. Those women. Markus cursed under his breath. Why hadn't he told her to get out? He didn't expect the house to collapse, not by a long shot. There was not a damn thing he could do to stop it either.

Paper, fabric, and God knew what else plumed into the air. He watched, rising back up to his feet, as the entire structure crashed down. *Sonofabitch.* Behind the house, an old barn rocked unsteadily but didn't fall. Just as quickly as the wave had come, it stopped. It was eerily like the end of an earthquake – the creepy stillness.

He stood alone in the middle of the lawn. Every tree and structure within a hundred feet of him was charred and destroyed. The house rested in a heap of busted wood and shattered glass.

I'm so sorry, ladies. And he really was.

All around him, disintegrated bodies lay scattered… a finger here, a foot there… but nothing was whole.

Markus thought maybe that was it. He hoped it was. But the guest of honor had yet to be seen. Nathaniel was still out there, somewhere.

He needed to get to Alexis and Charlie. God knew what they'd encountered, he just hoped he wasn't too late. He took one step and then stopped when he saw the distant shadows shooting up into the sky, silhouetted by the moonlight, coming from the darkness of the cornfields that surrounded this little town. The dark figures drifted high and circled like hawks.

From off to his right, the voice of a thousand dead souls thundered in his ears, "Death comes for you, old man."

The hooded figure loomed tall against the pale light of the full moon. Nathaniel.

He stood at least half a football field away, maybe more. Markus peered into the blackness of the robed face, seeing nothing.

He could kill Nathaniel from here. Probably, he could, but he wanted closer to be sure. A near miss wasn't good enough in this fight. Not by a long shot. Markus forced a smile at the corners of his wrinkled lips, and said, "I was wondering when you'd show up."

Nathaniel stepped closer. "I would not have missed the fall of the Society and the defeat of the great Markus Blue."

"Shall you fight now, or will you send more of your minions to their deaths?" His heart raced, and he breathed deep to calm himself. He couldn't risk another dizzy spell or light-headedness. Not at all.

"To die for my cause is true divinity for my Legions." Nathaniel strode closer.

Come to me. A few more steps and there'd be no doubts. Markus gripped his cane.

"You cannot comprehend victory as I've known it, old man, through centuries of defeating people like you." Nathaniel's words grew bitter; laced with sharp hatred.

"Victory like that in Pennsylvania?" Markus scoffed and shocked himself when he chuckled. *This* was how you picked a fight. A sudden urge to rub his aching side seized him, but he kept his hand where it was; where it needed to be for what would happen next.

"Your lack of respect will be your undoing!" Nathaniel roared.

"And your arrogance will be yours." Markus raised his cane and fired a bolt of lightning that tore through the air like a bullet.

Nathaniel's hand shot up, and he caught it, like snagging an arrow. He snatched the damn thing right of the air.

Whoa. Markus stepped back. This was a first.

Nathaniel tossed the blazing bolt to the side where it impacted like a mortar. "Such a foolish old man! You will know my wrath!"

The Legions in the air swooped down in unison; descending with claws out and teeth bared. Markus raised his cane again; preparing to light up the sky, but was shocked to see that he didn't have to. From behind him, flames rocketed over his head and spread into the flying hordes, incinerating them. He ducked to avoid being burned.

He turned to see Alexis a few feet behind, her hair swept back and her face set in grim determination as columns of fire spewed from her hands. *Beautiful, girl.* The vampires that weren't destroyed in the initial waves of fire stopped and retreated back in the direction they had come. They flew several hundred yards away and then landed in a nearby field, keeping a safe distance from the flame-throwing witch.

Her flames subsided as she neared.

Markus snapped his attention back to Nathaniel, but he was gone. *Damn it to hell, where is the son of a bitch?*

Charlie ran up to Markus, out of breath.

"I killed one," he said, his face beaming. "I killed it in the air."

"Well done, my boy." Markus clapped a hand on Charlie's shoulder. "Now stay ready, we're not alone out here."

"I know. The wolves are chasing us."

Great.

Markus shuffled back to Alexis. Her eyes were focused on the distant fields where the Legions had gone.

"Nathaniel is out here," he said to her. "Somewhere."

"What do you want me to do?" she asked.

Next to her, Liam held a pipe, but his eyes were distant as if seeing something that none of the rest of them could see. The Projection of Vagaries. The lurid visions would affect him if Nathaniel was close.

Markus asked, "What do you see?"

Liam's gaze caught his face and held it. "Blood," Liam stammered. "We're standing in it. There's stuff floating in it."

"It's not real," Markus said. "Remember that; it's not real. It's the vampire."

Liam nodded, glanced down at the ground, then looked back up as if unsure. He swallowed hard.

Markus shifted back to Alexis and Charlie. "Keep your eyes peeled. Where are the wolves?"

"They're out here, somewhere," Alexis said.

"Let's spread out," Markus pointed to a spot for Charlie. "Let's not face each other. Maintain focus. Kill anything that moves." He glanced at Liam. "Liam, you get in the middle of us. It'll help with the projections."

Liam darted into the center of their triangle.

Markus held tightly to his cane and scanned the area. "Nathanial is tall and wearing a robe. Anyone sees him, leave him to me."

From the darkness, the heavy breathing of the wolves drifted out of the night. They were circling, keeping out of sight and ready to pounce as soon as either Markus or Alexis fell.

That was when the sky filled with the Legions, streaming toward them in a swarm, blotting out the moon.

"Here we go," Markus said and set his feet to meet them.

CHAPTER 49

He could have saved them.

His dad, maybe the entire town of Pheasant Hill. He could have saved them all.

But Charlie hadn't known that he could do this stuff. *I didn't know.*

He'd never kissed a girl, never had a real job (at fourteen, his income stemmed from mowing lawns and raking leaves for Pastor Nead), and he had no idea how the government worked. But as soon as he saw that vampire, Christine, take to the air and fly at Alexis, he knew that he could kill it.

Pheasant Hill, his dad; that was all before he'd met Markus Blue and Alexis Jade.

Charlie scrambled to the spot where Markus told him to go. His heart throbbed in his ears and blood rushed through his veins like cold water. He wished he knew more of the words for the magic he possessed. The words helped keep order; like a catalogue of tricks where you could pick the one that best suited your needs. Focus.

Vampires, hundreds of them, maybe thousands, filled the sky reminding him of a flock of those black birds that he sometimes saw moving like a dark cloud over the fields. He heard Markus utter the words, "Here we go."

Alexis threw out a wall of fire as the hordes descended. Markus blasted a white flash from his cane so bright that darkness no longer existed. The light showed everything. To his right, dozens of vampires crept from the surrounding fields. They stopped when the light exposed them, then disintegrated to dust. Most were able to get an arm up in front of their face before they melted away, others didn't have time.

The flash sustained for a few seconds. Something exploded behind him, but he couldn't see what it was. He gagged as dust filled his mouth. Ashes. *Someone tell me what to do!* Markus told him to stand right here. Did that mean he shouldn't fly up like he did before?

Markus rocketed lightning into the onslaught. But there were so many of them. With all of the firepower Alexis and Markus threw at them, they still kept coming, and they were getting closer.

Just do something, I know I need to do something.

"*What can you do?*" Alexis had asked him.

What can I do?

Directly in front of him, swimming out of the blackness, masses of vampires converged. Charlie extended his hand and thought of the lightning bolts that Markus was delivering. Nothing happened. He pictured it, willed the magic to spring from his hands, and still, nothing happened. He'd killed Christine by breathing fire into her mouth. *I breathed out fire!* But now, he couldn't do anything. Not even a measly spark.

How do I do those things! He extended both hands and pushed. Nothing. Not a thing.

Stop trying to be like Markus. Calm down. *Be you.* Fly.

And then something streaked past him. A blur, moving fast. It slammed into him, and suddenly he was lying on his back. He blinked through fuzzy vision. He couldn't breathe! *Markus!*

His eyes found Markus several feet away, engaged in battle. The old man delivered deadly streaks of charged light from his hands, alternating and turning his body like a gunfighter. Magnificent.

Can't breathe, he wanted to scream.

Whatever had hit him would be back to finish the job, god knew why it hadn't already. Whatever *it* was. He had to get up. Whatever had clobbered him, had whacked him good. He rolled to his side and onto his knees, gasping. He saw Alexis still throwing flames into the air. Liam knelt next to her, his eyes closed tight, gripping that same piece of pipe.

"Liam," Charlie croaked.

Liam didn't hear him; there was too much noise. He sucked in a full breath and yelled, "Liam!"

Liam's eyes snapped open and found him.

"Help me up!".

Liam shuffled over and gripped his arm. He yelled, "What happened to you?"

"Something hit me. Like it flew into me." Charlie got to his feet. Wooziness swept over him, but it cleared quickly.

The vampires were gaining ground despite the massive deaths Markus and Alexis were inflicting. The numbers were too great. Alexis was slinging fire within a few feet in front of her. Her teeth bared and her hair lay matted from sweat.

Something rushed past him again, only this time, whatever it was, hit Alexis square in the back. Her head whiplashed back, and she fell hard onto her stomach. Charlie glimpsed the creature swooping back up into the air to join its comrades. Another dive-bomb nearly hit Markus, but he killed it with fire from his cane. The creature plowed into the ground like a crazed kamikaze, and then rolled over dead a few feet away.

Alexis hoisted herself to one knee and resumed her fight. The creatures were almost close enough to touch her. Charlie wasn't for sure, but he thought she may have been screaming as she fought.

Markus backed toward her until he was touching her. He swung one arm in front of him, his fingers splayed out as if he were about to catch a tennis ball, and cast a strange glow of deep green light across the yard. He wrapped Alexis in his arms and fell on top of her, forcing her to the ground.

He yelled to Charlie and Liam as he fell, "Get down! Get down, Now!"

Charlie and Liam both fell flat, both of them covering their heads with their hands. Charlie clenched his eyes shut. His hair stirred as if charged with electricity, and his skin tingled and then burned. But it was the smell that shook him: sulfuric and damp. He had the feeling that if he tried to inhale, his lungs would fry.

And then it was done, like clicking off a television, just silence.

A second passed. Then two. He opened his eyes to a deserted lawn, and a strange silence hung ominously in the air.

He staggered up, staying cautious, and noticed Liam doing the same. Markus rolled off of Alexis, got shakily to his feet, and stumbled before regaining his balance. He leaned heavily onto his cane. He looked exhausted, defeated, and old. Charlie watched as the old man examined the yard. Markus's skin was pale white, and the lines of his face seemed to have darkened. His old cheeks bubbled out, and he started to cough. Not just any cough, but a wet, hoarse cough that seemed to be coming from the deepest part of him.

Charlie hustled over and placed a hand on his shoulder. Alexis was on her feet gripping Markus's arm. Charlie swore he saw tears in her eyes – something about the look on her face frightened him more than anything. He and Alexis held onto Markus as he slumped over, his body still being racked with the relentless coughing.

"Markus!" Alexis yelled.

He didn't answer.

"Say something!"

He fell to his knees. He gasped, "Nathaniel... out here... somewhere."

Charlie glanced around. Still no vampires. Markus had killed them all.

From behind them, Nathaniel's voice thundered, "Step away from him, Alexis."

Charlie whirled to see the robed figure with its arms outstretched. He knew what lived beneath that robe. He'd seen it already; he'd watched it kill the people in Pastor Nead's church. He'd watched it pray.

Next to Nathaniel stood the other man in the Army uniform; Michael.

"I won't." Alexis stretched her hand in front of her. Charlie noticed it trembling.

"You will," Nathaniel said. "Michael has some unfinished business with you."

Michael's eyes settled on Alexis, pleading. "Will you please come with me?"

Alexis ignored him and asked, "Your Legions are gone, you have no army. You're through."

"Ah," Nathaniel clasped his hands in front of him. His shadowed face was still too dark to see. "How little you can comprehend, young one."

Charlie shifted his weight from foot to foot. Hatred roiled within him. He wanted to kill this man.

"Now," Nathaniel said, "Step away from Markus."

"Never." Alexis moved in front of the slumping old man.

"So be it."

Charlie's rage peaked and he couldn't wait any longer.

His feet left the ground, and he was twenty feet above them in seconds. Alexis yelled from below him, "No, Charlie!" But he didn't care, he wasn't listening.

Michael soared into the air to meet him. Charlie saw him coming and prepared to breathe the fire, but just as Michael was close enough for Charlie to act, he disappeared. A second later, a blow slammed into Charlie's back. He slung forward and caught a glimpse of Michael whipping through the air like a bullet. A fist impacted his chest, knocking the wind out of him. *He's too fast!*

Charlie's confidence slipped away as he realized he was going to die here. He had no idea what to do; he couldn't think of things quick enough. He squeezed his eyes shut. The pain in his chest throbbed and his bruised back might have something broken. Tears stung his eyes. Had he been given these gifts for nothing, so that he could die at some farmhouse in Nebraska?

You have the devil's gift, son.

No, Charlie thought, *I have God's gift.* A gift from God to maintain balance.

God's gift.

The tingle started in his legs and surged through his body, spreading like a shockwave. Instantly, a thin wall appeared in the air in front of him, drifting like a mirage. He had a second to admire it before Michael slammed into its surface.

Something cracked, he thought it might have been a bone, and then Michael fell. He hit the ground like a heap of dirty laundry and didn't move. That was enough for now. One more to go.

He spun to face Nathaniel, but not fast enough. Convulsions seized him, twisting him, and burned him from the inside. He tried to scream, but only a gargled muffle escaped. His helpless gaze found Nathaniel who stood with his arms raised, a beam of crooked light emanating from his hand. Blackness crept in. No more pain. No more monsters. A strange peace settled over him, and he relaxed.

The darkness got bigger, tighter, and wrapped him in a cold embrace.

CHAPTER 50

Christopher lumbered onto the street and saw the boy falling.

A quarter mile away, maybe less. *He's one of ours.* Christopher knew it, intuitively, and decided he'd live with the consequences if he were wrong.

He stopped, uttered "Rete" under his breath and cast a glob of light from his hands. It streaked across the ground and spread out like a web. The light-net flew under the boy and caught him. It then folded and floated to the ground, out of Christopher's sight.

That was good.

But what he saw as the light soared was unsettling.

Movement, between here and there, like rats scurrying from the beam of a flashlight. Except these weren't rats – they were wolves. Wolves didn't scare Christopher nearly as much as vampires, but fighting them would cost precious time.

"Let's get it over with." Christopher forced a bitter grin and said, "I've got shit to do."

One of the wolves stepped close and said, "Relax, old man." The voice rattled as if spoken through phlegm.

What the hell? Christopher stutter-stepped back, and he was pretty sure his mouth hung open. *They talk.*

"Our suicide was never part of his deal." The wolf cocked its head.

Still in utter disbelief, Christopher stammered, "W... Who?"

"Nathaniel." The wolf sneered. "He guaranteed victory. But the warlock has destroyed his entire army. Still Nathaniel fights. He expects us to die with him."

The warlock... Markus. Christopher swallowed hard. The wolves were abandoning the fight.

"Pass on, old man," the wolf waved a clawed hand, "no one here will touch you."

The wolves parted. Christopher thought of attacking them anyway. Wolves were like rats - if he let them go, they would become his problem a different day.

But he needed to reach Markus. Now. The wolves were giving up, but that still didn't mean Nathaniel had lost the fight.

Especially after seeing that kid fall out of the sky.

Christopher nodded and stepped off. It was one of the strangest and most unnerving walks he had ever taken. He picked up the pace. The wolves lumbered off into the grass and weeds. He knew that if he turned and looked now, he wouldn't see anything behind him except for the dead town of Rice's Crossing.

·   ·   ·   ·   ·

A small cornfield was all that separated them. A heap of crushed lumber jutted above the edge of the field. He heard voices but had no idea what anyone was saying.

He jaunted off the smooth pavement of the road and shuffled down the short driveway toward the house, breathing heavy. Twenty years ago, he could have made this run in about a quarter of the time. But in his sixties, it reminded of him of how old and out of shape he was.

A jet of fire exploded in the sky and shrouded him in an orange glow. He could hear something that sounded like electricity crackling. Someone was screaming.

"Alexis! Markus!" He was so close.

His legs felt like rubber, and his lungs burned as he rounded the corner of the field, and faced a war zone - trees flattened, buildings ruined, bodies piled.

Alexis fought alone.

Markus's crumpled body lay next to her. She was on one knee with her hands outstretched and delivering a stream of fire that even the best flamethrower on earth could not have matched.

The last stand.

He glimpsed someone else crawling away from her, carrying what looked like a pipe, edging closer to the smashed house, trying to escape.

And in front of Alexis, stood Nathaniel. The ancient creature still wore his robe and had both hands splayed in front of him, producing a murky wall that Alexis's fire was unable to penetrate.

Oh, Jesus Christ.

Christopher gulped and sprinted toward her, one hand rising up, pointing toward Nathaniel.

CHAPTER 51

Liam crawled away from Alexis's fire. The grotesque visions intensified. The blood-covered ground squirmed with maggots - they squished between his fingers.

It's not real, Markus had said.

It's in my mind... it's all in my mind...

He glanced back. Alexis crouched next to Markus who was flat on his face.

I think he's dead.

Her face was turned away from the massive firestorm streaming from her hand. He didn't know how it wasn't burning her. Hell, maybe it was.

Was this it? The end of everything for him? For her? The thought of her gone prickled his heart. The very idea of her simply no longer existing prompted sorrow and the cruelty that the sun would rise the next day without her in it angered him. Her sweet breath, her green eyes, her strong heartbeat... her *aliveness*.

And he couldn't do one thing to help her.

The pipe rolled from his hand as he crawled toward the crumpled and splintered lumber of the farmhouse. If she died, then he would soon follow.

His novel popped into his head, the one he would never finish, stored on his computer that was still in his room at the Marriott hotel in Pittsburg. What had they done with his stuff?

His dad would likely think *I knew he would end up getting mixed up with the wrong crowd*. No kids, no wife, no life. The failure who graduated from NYU, landed a job as a journalist (journalist used sparingly when referring to tabloids such as The Unexplained Truth), and finally *got mixed up with the wrong crowd*.

An ear-splitting crack scared the shit out of him, and he cried out. He lurched forward and flipped onto his back; then he watched in silent amazement. Someone else now stood next to Alexis, someone Liam had never seen.

Christopher?

From the man's hand, a thick bolt of lightning rocketed toward Nathaniel, creating a temporary flash that, for a second, turned everything white, even Alexis's fire. The scene was nothing short of spectacular. Nathaniel somehow held the fire and lightning at bay – all of it wrapped around him in a half circle.

The hood of Nathaniel's robe fell back and revealed a horrid, ancient face that was pale white with hair braided tight to the skull. The lips were stretched into a grimace. The sight of Nathaniel induced dread as he imagined that face coming at him out of the murky depths of black water.

For a hopeful moment, it looked like Nathaniel might collapse under the strain of holding both the fire and the lightning, but then in a blur, he disappeared. Alexis's inferno filled the void, and the lightning blasted through with a dull *smacking* sound.

Christopher's gaze followed what looked like a distorted bubble across the ground, moving at a ridiculous speed – it reminded Liam of a reflection. Christopher's lightning still blazed from his hand and chased the distortion until it disappeared into the sky. The lightning stopped, and so did Alexis's flames.

"Where is he?" Alexis scanned above her.

"He's here," Christopher said. "Keep your eyes peeled, he'll be hard to see."

Hot smoke drifted into Liam's nose and dying flames crackled around him. Surely this isn't the way things were supposed to go. Vampires, werewolves, and wizards were not real. They were the focus of stories and fairy-tales. He thought this as he gazed at Alexis.

I love her.

Any moment, he would wake up, drenched in sweat, panting heavily in his bed and remembering the most vivid nightmare he'd ever had. Any moment. He would swing his legs over the edge of his mattress and sit up as it all faded the way dreams do. Maybe he'd jot it down before it all disappeared. Eventually, he'd drift off to sleep again, thinking about writing it. He'd need to remember the character names... this would be the story of the century. Take that, Stephen King... there's a new boss in town, and his name is Liam Balsing.

But he didn't want that. He wanted *her*. From that magical moment when she'd helped him pick up the scattered paper from the hotel floor, he'd known it was far more than just meeting a pretty girl. It was so much more than that. Things like this didn't happen to people without a purpose.

Her scream pierced the night and Alexis fell hard onto the ground. She rolled to her side, tried to get up, then collapsed. She wasn't moving.

Liam called out, "Alexis?"

Nathaniel shot over him like a bullet, and either hadn't seen him or didn't care.

Alexis still didn't move.

"Alexis!"

Christopher's piercing eyes darted from place to place, frantic, searching. He was the only one standing.

Liam scrambled to his knees, his eyes set on Alexis lying helpless in the charred grass. *My girl.* To hide and live was a coward's life. To go another second without her was absurd. But what could he do?

To Liam's amazement, Markus caught his attention. The old man was trying to push himself up.

Alexis stirred. Nathaniel would kill her on his next pass, maybe Christopher too.

"Alexis!" Christopher yelled at her and watched the sky at the same time. "Alexis! Get out of here!"

But she couldn't. Her feet scraped uselessly on the ground, her hands clenching the grass. *Go to her!*

Yes, he could get her out of there, just like he did in that warehouse.

From the corner of his eye, the mirage sailed across the ground, heading directly toward her. The distortion was going to pass right over the top of Liam once again. His first impulse was to fall flat on his belly, burrow into the debris of the house, squeeze his eyes shut, and lie perfectly still so that Nathaniel wouldn't see him.

I will not watch her die!

He gripped a jagged piece of lumber from the ground and lurched up into Nathaniel's path. He braced the board in the crook of his arm. God knew what would happen next.

I love you, Alexis.

Nathaniel plowed straight into him. Liam's feet left the ground. Something cracked and broke in his shoulder. He saw the sky for a split-second as he flipped into the air. His ankle snapped when he slammed into the earth.

He didn't have a chance to acknowledge the pain.

Liam was out cold as soon as his body hit the ground.

CHAPTER 52

First, a squeal, followed by the calamity of smashing wood and something hitting the ground. It crashed into a pile of broken lumber and rolled in a cloud of dust like a giant birdshot out of the sky. Nathaniel sprang to his feet, but his eyes drifted down and glared at the large timber protruding from his chest.

Markus plunged one end of his cane into the ground and hoisted himself up. He fought a sudden urge to vomit and his stomach cramped.

Stay on your feet, old man!

Christopher, kneeling by Alexis, fired a blast of green light that hit Nathaniel square in the stomach. The vampire's gaze froze with his arms drooping at his sides.

Markus raised his cane and fired a streak of lightning into Nathaniel's body. The creature flew backward and landed flat on his back, the timber in his chest pointing up into the air like an absurd exclamation point.

Markus wobbled and coughed. He decided he'd just stand still for a bit and hope like hell he didn't fall down. He kept his gaze trained on Nathaniel, ready to act if the sonofabitch so much as twitched.

Several long seconds passed. Markus's head cleared and he felt stronger, more stable. Nathaniel never moved, but Markus wasn't taking any chances; he was going to make sure the bastard was dead.

He raised his cane.

From behind him, Christopher yelled, "Wait, Markus!"

Oh, you've got to be shitting me. He shuffled around to face Christopher who was still knelt and holding Alexis's hand as she rolled up to one elbow. Goddamnit, it was good to see him. "Wait for what?"

"Don't you want to know why?" Christopher asked.

Markus shrugged. He supposed he did. But he certainly didn't want to risk Nathaniel getting away again. Escape seemed damned unlikely; not with that massive board sticking out of him.

His eyes settled on Alexis as she pushed herself up, gripping Christopher's good arm for leverage. She glanced at Nathaniel lying motionless on the ground.

"Is he dead?" she asked, then winced. Markus recalled her condition from a few days earlier, leaving Pittsburg. The pain she'd been in. Tough girl, this one.

Christopher said, "I don't think so, but I hit him with a pretty good stun spell. I don't think he's hosting any more parties." He stood up and then helped Alexis to her feet.

She glanced around, still keeping a tight grip on Christopher's arm. "Where's Liam?"

"I saw him stab Nathaniel with that board," Markus said. "Brave sonofabitch jumped up right in front of him."

"Liam did?" Alexis let go of Christopher. Her eyes still searched, but bodies and debris lay strewn everywhere. Markus wondered about Charlie as well. He wasn't sure if the kid ran off. He hoped like hell he was okay.

"Find Liam and Charlie," Markus said, "I'll handle Nathaniel." He stepped past Alexis and Christopher and hobbled toward Nathaniel who lay still on the ground. Christopher walked next to him, and he was glad for that. Alexis veered toward the rubble of the house, yelling for Liam.

"You always were most curious, Christopher," Markus said, "Why the longing to know the answer to everything?"

"Don't you wonder?" Christopher asked.

Markus *did* wonder.

He let Christopher's question hang in the air, unanswered. The lightning Markus had delivered left a large, dark burn on Nathaniel's chest. With his eyes open, gleaming up toward the sky and his mouth hanging ajar, he looked like a dead animal.

Markus stared down at Nathaniel's face. The vampire's skin appeared aged and worn. His eyes reflected knowledge and understanding that was creepy. Trepidation seeped into Markus's frail bones as he thought about all of the things those eyes had seen. He tore his gaze away and peered at the fatal wound in Nathaniel's chest.

Christopher waved his hand and emitted a sparkling green cloud that seeped down and settled on Nathaniel's arms, face, and neck. Markus gripped his cane tight, ready for anything. They were playing with fire here;

a dangerous fire. Nathaniel blinked and looked curiously at Christopher and Markus.

"Who did this to me?" Nathaniel asked, his deep voice choked with blood.

"You'll be disappointed," Markus said.

"It wasn't you, old man. Of that, I'm sure." Nathaniel's hands crept to the wooden stake buried deep in his chest. "I deserve to know who it was."

Markus wasn't sure he *deserved* anything but obliged. "He's just a regular man."

The corners of Nathaniel's mouth curled to a ghostly smile. Markus couldn't tell if he was upset or simply relieved. Amid the destruction, Nathaniel looked small lying so helpless in the grass, his robe spread loosely around him. Strange seeing something so ancient come to its end, like the sadness of a fallen Redwood Tree. So much knowledge; so much we could learn.

Markus braced his cane out ahead of him and settled down onto the grass, keeping one leg straight to avoid cramping his hip and curled the other beneath him. Nathaniel's eyes settled on him.

"We are both at the end of our paths, it seems." Nathaniel heaved himself up on his elbows then laboriously scooted backward until he came to rest against a tree a few feet away. His breathing came in gulps, and he looked at Markus with his mouth hanging open and his arms limp at his sides.

"Why?" Markus asked, "Why did you do this?"

Nathaniel glared at him as if debating on whether to speak, then said, "You cannot comprehend the irrelevance of time to me." Nathaniel heaved in a deep breath and coughed out a thick black liquid that spilled over his chin and down his front. Markus guessed it was blood, or at least, once had been.

"What I cannot comprehend are the actions you've taken," Markus said.

"Do you dare display the audacity to understand me, feeble man?"

"Feeble, I agree with." Markus forced a smile.

"At least you are aware of your limitations."

"And now I am aware of yours." Markus saw anger flicker in those archaic eyes, but it dissipated and yielded quickly.

"Your ignorance... such a perfect picture of... humanity's defiance." Nathaniel inhaled another wheezing breath and coughed. More black stuff spewed across his front. "You're nothing to me, old man. Why should I tell you anything?"

Markus considered this, not totally sure what it meant, then said, "Your desire to kill me brought you here, so I must mean something. Perhaps your final reconciliation?"

Nathaniel regarded him with cruel sorrow, and Markus swore the creature's eyes bore fear; an understanding of death's approaching embrace. He said through gurgling breaths, "There was a time when I thought like you, Markus."

Markus raised his eyebrows, surprised. "Oh?"

"When it first happens, you understand what you are. Your thirst for the blood, but comprehension of immortality is beyond human understanding."

Nathaniel clenched his hands into fists and grimaced. Pain. *He's dying.* A few seconds later, he found his breath again and uttered, "To touch the edge is not everlasting or a significant claim to know the truth. Blood seeks not innocence nor guilt, it simply exists."

Markus had no idea what the hell *that* meant.

"It is not until those in your birth-life die-off that you understand the power you have." Nathaniel glanced up at the sky and then back down at the stake in his chest as if he'd forgotten it was there. "I witnessed the rise of Vatican City over the grave of Saint Peter, fought against their secret armies of wizards and witches, and only stopped when the vampires bowed in superfluous fear of Nostradamus and agreed to the truce."

Markus nodded. He knew the story from old books.

"It was not until the mid-1800s that I realized my true calling, and I understood that God had called me to perform His bidding." Nathaniel sucked in another painful breath. "I begged the vampires for their allegiance. But they refused fearing another war." Nathaniel's voice was becoming raspy, and his eyes were losing focus. Markus had to lean closer to understand him well. "And they informed the Vatican of my rhetoric."

All of this occurred before I was ever born, Markus thought, *nearly a hundred years before.* Unbelievable.

"The Vatican sent their Chasers and killed anyone who sympathized with me. Even my beloved wife." Nathaniel spat those words and his anger flared. "Them and their arrogance that they alone should be touched or called by God. I had no army and no means to battle against the mighty Chasers, and by this time, the Society had formed in the New World."

New World.

"By the turn of the century, I began to secretly build my army. I found Michael on the battlefield outside of Ramstein, in Germania. He became my *New World* leader and built his Legions here. It was my destiny, Markus, to defeat The Vatican and claim my place at the right hand of God, to rule in the Holy City from the chamber of the Pope."

Nathaniel strained to stay upright; to continue his outpouring to Markus.

His confession.

"I needed to strike when the cardinals were all gathered at The Vatican for conclave. I saw my opportunity when the Society allowed its numbers to drop in the late 1900s. And the Chasers had no warlocks. Our armies were ready and our time had come. We decided, almost five years ago, that upon the next death of a Pope, we would attack. We used your messengers as our conduits and gathered our plans."

Phillip.

The vampire rasped. "Warlocks are... not..."

Nathaniel fell over onto the grass, one hand lolling against the stake in his chest, the other bent awkwardly underneath him. He was dead.

A vampire, killer of innocence, who believed himself redeemed and ordained by God, who after centuries of existence, determined his destiny was to take over the Catholic Church by attacking Vatican City.

My beloved wife. Perhaps the catalyst for war was no different than it had ever been – all for the love of a girl.

"Guess he got his last confession in," Markus said.

"So it seems." Christopher wiped a dirty hand across his mouth. "The Legions at the Vatican will disband now. They'll need to be hunted down, but they are collective mind based on the creator. Now that Nathaniel is dead, they'll not be hard to find and destroy."

"And the wolves?" Markus asked.

"They abandoned the fight before it ended. They've already fled." Christopher chuckled. "Remind me later to tell you what happened with them."

Markus still couldn't look away from Nathaniel's dead face. It was as if even in death, some sort of conscious still lingered.

Christopher placed a hand on Markus's shoulder. "You okay, old friend?"

"I suppose I am."

"Alexis found your other two guys. Both are banged up, but alive."

"Charlie and Liam," Markus said. "I want you to meet Charlie. He's going to need you."

Markus tore his eyes away to see Charlie stumble up next to Christopher, breathing heavy and looking from Nathaniel to the others. The kid's hair was matted on one side, and his eyes were brimmed red. Markus was glad to see him and proud of him.

"Is he dead?" Charlie asked and crossed his arms.

"Quite." Markus glanced at Nathaniel and then back at Charlie. "Good to see you up and about. Meet Christopher Gray."

"Charlie." Christopher smiled and held out his left hand, "It must have been you I saved a short bit ago." Charlie shrugged, and Christopher said, "Great to meet you."

Markus looked at Christopher who looked back at him.

"Help an old friend to his feet?" Markus asked.

"Figures, you would ask for the only good hand I have."

"At least you can joke about it," Markus gripped Christopher's hand.

Once on his feet, Markus got his cane under him and felt steadier. Across the yard, Alexis was on her knees, next to Liam. The house was a pile of broken lumber. The grass was burnt to a crisp and the trees were either blackened or still burning.

Along the edge of what used to be the yard and the cornfield, Markus caught the outline of the old woman, Betty, standing in the darkness. Even from here, Markus could see her wide eyes staring at him. Next to her, he could see the outline of three other women huddled together.

Holy shit, the old lady had gotten them out. Good things *did* still happen.

Markus, Christopher, and Charlie made their way to where Alexis held the hand of the unconscious young man who had killed Nathaniel Smith. His shoulder looked painfully wrenched behind him and his foot was twisted like a corkscrew. Goddamn, that would *not* feel good when he woke up. One side of his face was bruised and blood had dried on his mouth. Alexis knelt next to him, gently stroking his hair, and saying his name, trying to wake him up.

A regular man had killed Nathaniel Smith: killer of William, Jonathan, Jason, Jobe, and Phillip. The most powerful vampire in history.

Perhaps miracles did happen. Warmth spread through his chest and tears welled in his old eyes.

Markus Blue thanked God that he wasn't alone.

THE LAST CHAPTER

Three weeks later, Markus slipped into a coma.

"I can't believe it happened so fast." Liam eased himself down in the porch swing next to Alexis. She held out her hand and placed it in his.

"I know. I miss him already," Alexis said and stared down at the wooden patio floor.

Charlie leaned against a large, white pillar with his arms crossed over his chest.

"We'll all miss him," Christopher said standing against the battered, outside wall of the Taylor County Home. "Michael was never found. I can't imagine he'd show up here, but we should be vigilant."

They all sat silent, deep in their own thoughts.

Charlie stepped away, his feet echoing off the wooden planks with hollow thuds. The others stayed where they were as he walked out into the yard, loving the solitude and serenity of this place. It reminded him a lot of where he'd lived in Pennsylvania. He shoved his hands into the pockets of his dress pants.

It seemed so strange that they were all just waiting for Markus to die. It could happen at any moment.

Later that afternoon, he sat next to Markus's bed, holding the skeletal hand of the great warlock, and wishing it was someone else who was there instead of him to watch Markus pass away. The room smelled like mildewed sheets mixed with the unmistakable stench of death. Markus's skin clung to his skull like old leather, stretched tight and his eyes were closed. The old hand trembled as Charlie held it, he wished like crazy that Christopher and Alexis were there too.

Suddenly, Markus's eyes flew open. His wild eyes searched the room and found Charlie.

"It's the darkness," Markus's voice was choked and barely audible. Charlie leaned closer. "It killed my brother." Markus gripped his arm and clenched his teeth, speaking almost in a hiss. "Promise me you'll stop it!"

"Stop what?" Charlie said as a cold fear settled into his chest. He fought the urge to yank his hand away and run to find Christopher.

Markus gasped. "It's here."

ACKNOWLEDGEMENTS

First off, thanks to you, reader, for reading my story. I hope we get to know each other quite well over the next few years. You can find me at DavidOdle.com.

I wrote *Markus* while traveling weekly to Dallas, Texas as an IT consultant. I'd write while alone in my hotel room and over lunch in the tunnels below the city. Originally, I envisioned a short story about a mysterious old man living in a retirement home, but as events unfolded and more characters decided to show up, it evolved into an interesting premise and ultimately, a fun story to tell. I do hope you enjoyed it. The Taylor County Nursing Home is a fictional account of a real place in Indiana that has since been torn down.

When I was in grade school, a blind man gave puppet shows to children while we'd all sit on the front porch and I recall wondering if he had magic powers. I still think he might have.

So many people make writing and publishing a book possible. It starts with those who believe in you, even in the darkest hours. It ends with that person who says, *I want to publish this; I believe in it.* That's not easy to get, folks. Just ask any writer.

I'll undoubtedly miss someone and for that, I sincerely apologize. I didn't mean to. But this group of people carried me, some for many years, and stoked the flames of this story.

Mike Maher – my first reader and devoted believer. I can't thank you enough, my friend.

Dave and Dani Johnson – Dani's opinion of the early draft shaped what the world sees on these pages and Dave never fails to ask me what I'm writing now.

Ken Meinen – That first writers' conference in Austin started it all for us.

My editor for this novel, Nadine Brandes, my coach and savior of this book. Nadine is no longer a freelance editor, but she's a great writer. You can find her work at nadinebrandes.com.

Black Rose Writing – Thanks for taking this on, Reagan, and publishing my book. And especially for answering all of my questions, even the difficult ones.

Other first readers and believers who influenced me are my Aunt Jane Snyder, Mike Herzog, Christian Brennan, and Kirsten Nuehaus.

Of course, Tammy, my wife, my love, and best friend. You are in every story I've ever told.

For any writer, there is that person who believed in you from the beginning. The encourager, the one who loved everything you ever wrote, even the terrible stuff (especially the terrible stuff). *The one you write for*. My Aunt Joy Beckett, this one is for you.

NOTE FROM THE AUTHOR

Word-of-mouth is crucial for any author to succeed. If you enjoyed the book, please leave a review online—anywhere you are able. Even if it's just a sentence or two. It would make all the difference and would be very much appreciated.

Thanks!
David

ABOUT THE AUTHOR

David Odle discovered his love for writing at the age of thirteen while growing up in Warren County, Indiana. After seven years in the military and over twelve years as an IT consultant living in Austin, Texas, he now resides right back in Indiana with his wife and five children where he is currently finalizing his next novel.

Thank you so much for reading one of our **Paranormal Fantasy** novels.

If you enjoyed our book, please check out our recommended title for your next great read!

The Graveyard Girl and the Boneyard Boy by Martin Matthews

"... a compelling and eminently likable cast of characters."

–Authors Reading

View other Black Rose Writing titles at
www.blackrosewriting.com/books and use promo code
PRINT to receive a **20% discount** when purchasing.